THE
ACCIDENTAL
ASSASSIN

THE ACCIDENTAL ASSASSIN

An Island
A Poodle
A Body...

JAN TOMS

The
History
Press

First published 2011

The History Press
The Mill, Brimscombe Port
Stroud, Gloucestershire, GL5 2QG
www.thehistorypress.co.uk

British Library Cataloguing in Publication Data.
A catalogue record for this book is available from the British Library.

ISBN 978 0 7524 6270 7

Typesetting and origination by The History Press
Printed in Great Britain
Manufacturing managed by Jellyfish Print Solutions Ltd

ONE

Victor Green had long come to the conclusion that the sun only shone on weekdays. From Monday to Friday he caught the number 2 bus to Newport, where for seven hours he stared from the window of the tax office, a caged creature locked away from the summer glory. The view from his office was tantalising, looking as it did across Church Litten, the old Elizabethan burial ground where once plague victims had been hurriedly disposed of because the churchyard was full. Now most of the tombstones had gone, the area was landscaped and mature, and beautiful trees provided summer shade. Victor loved to sit there during his lunch hour. One of the remaining gravestones was dedicated to John Hamilton Reynolds, who had been John Keats's best friend. Like Keats, Reynolds had been a poet, and Victor liked to think that the two men would appreciate his own modest verses. Sometimes he had imaginary chats with them, sitting under the weeping birch tree.

The view from the office also served to remind him of what he was missing at home – his sweetpeas, his hanging baskets, blue tits nesting in the bird box on his wall and the occasional glimpse of a fox. When he finally surfaced full of hope on Saturday mornings, the first thing he usually heard was the patter of rain.

Today, however, was different. It was one of those fresh, glistening mornings that promised a balmy day ahead. Suddenly alert he flung back the duvet, visited the bathroom, boiled an egg with toast, cleaned his teeth, stripped off his pyjamas and put on his gardening clothes. Two weeks ago a letter had arrived from the council, telling him to get his lime tree trimmed back or they would take matters into their own hands. Victor lived in fear of upsetting the authorities and for two weeks the letter had lain heavily on his conscience, but between them, work and the weather had prevented him from obeying the law.

Hurriedly he washed up, dried the dishes and put them away, fed the birds on the table outside the kitchen window then repaired to the garden shed, where a ladder, saw and various other paraphernalia were lined up in readiness. Victor was not very keen on heights. Indeed, two rungs up the ladder and his hands became clammy. In its own way, this was an act of heroism, overcoming the fatal flaw that was his vertigo. He had already studied the overhanging tree at some length and knew which branches must be amputated. To his mind it was an act of vandalism, but the law must be obeyed. The tree was a lovely tree-like shape, smooth straight trunk with lemony foliage fanning out to all points of the compass. He knew that by the time he finished it would look butchered – a word that conjured up images of mindless violence.

Victor liked words, not only their meanings but their shape and sound. He had once had a verse published in the village magazine, stirred by the memory of the pond that had formerly graced the grounds of the local manor house. Now the house was a hotel and it was up to the council to keep the pond according to its former glory but, sadly, the busy visitations of ducks and the addition of an old fridge and battered mattress meant that it now had a neglected air. Silently he recited some of his poem: *Trembling weed amid the rushing foam* – he thrilled to the metre of the line.

As he walked down the drive he had already made up his mind that if there happened to be a bird nesting in the tree then he would refuse to act and face whatever penalty the council might impose rather than have it disturbed. He saw the headlines in the *Clarion*: '*Local man faces gaol to protect blackbirds from council slaughter.*' Like butcher, slaughter was one of those words red in tooth and claw. He shook off the lurking thoughts of death and destruction.

Victor was not much of a handyman but he had read up on ladders and safety, and knew about how to secure the steps, ensuring that they stood on level ground, stabilised with a wedge so that they would not slip away and leave him stranded in the tree. *Local man spends night among the branches . . .* From the garden shed he fetched two warning road signs that he had purchased in Halfords. Twice a year he had to trim the front hedge and, there being no pavement, he was careful to ensure that a distracted driver did not come round the bend too fast and plough into him. Accidents were always high on Victor's list of preoccupations.

Having placed the signs and looked up the road several times to ascertain whether a lost juggernaut was about to attempt to negotiate the lane, he grasped the saw and ascended the ladder. Don't look down, that was the advice that had come from somewhere, a film perhaps, some cliffhanger that had made him grip the arms of the cinema seat and look away.

As he braced his knees against the rung of the ladder he felt them begin to tremble. Steady on, get on with it, get it over and done with. Later he would have the satisfaction of a job well done.

Tying the top of the ladder to a branch, he leaned across and, with a deep intake of breath, began to saw. The angle was difficult and his arms quickly began to ache but he ploughed on. After an eternity he heard a cracking noise, the branch suddenly succumbed and fell away. Victor followed its flight with his eyes, grabbing the trunk for support. Don't look down!

He breathed out long and hard, and gathered himself to tackle the next branch, a bigger and longer one reaching out across the lane. When he had cut it down he would have to descend and move it to the side of the road. Going down was worse than coming up. He had the same trouble in castle towers, spiral staircases, lofts. It was always the coming down that worried him.

He began to saw with intensity. The branch was made of sterner stuff than its neighbour. Perhaps it had witnessed his attack and was ready to fight back. Victor felt sweat running between his shoulder blades and stopped for a second to wipe the back of his hand across his forehead. Afterwards he couldn't remember exactly what happened next, except that a wood pigeon preparing to crash-land onto the absent branch had realised too late that it was no longer there. With a squawk it veered off, struggling for the safety of the electricity cable above, but the sudden fluttering in his face caused Victor to jerk back and his worst nightmare became reality. Somehow his boot slipped on the rung of the ladder and he took flight, a short, sharp descent to the road below.

At the same moment, he heard a shout and the alarmed yapping of a small dog. He hit something soft but solid, and as his head cleared he realised that he was lying on the ground, only not the ground but something cushioning his fall. Groggily he struggled up to find a large man spreadeagled beneath him.

'I'm so sorry. Are you alright?' He leaned over ready to help the man to his feet but the man did not move. Victor blinked and looked closer. On the gravel of the path he noticed a trickle of blood slowly seeping into the dust. Like the millstream in his poem, it seemed to be gaining momentum.

'I say,' he touched the man's shoulder but he did not respond. Across the lane the little dog, a white poodle, had taken refuge on the bank and was barking spasmodically in a high-pitched key.

'Sir?' Gradually Victor metamorphosed from a man who had fallen from a tree into a first-aider at work. Check for vital signs. Do not move – or should that be put into the recovery position? Uncertainly, he placed his fingers on the man's neck, hoping for the gentle throbbing of a pulse, but there didn't seem to be anything. Oh god, surely he hadn't killed him? Would this be murder? Of course he hadn't meant this to happen. Was it the equivalent of driving without due care and attention? No one had warned him that an absent-minded pigeon might barge into him. At the very least it must be manslaughter. His legs buckled beneath him and he grabbed the foot of the ladder for support. It felt totally secure. At least he had done something right.

He looked helplessly up and down the lane hoping that someone would come along, but the road was empty. From the houses opposite, no one emerged to see what was going on.

Somehow Victor stumbled his way up his drive and into the house, grasped the phone and dialled 999.

><

They soon arrived; the police, an ambulance and the neighbours attracted by the flashing lights and the wailing sirens. By now, Victor was sitting on the bank under the assaulted tree, struggling with black waves that whooshed in and out of his head. On the ground the other man, now well and truly dead, formed a motionless obstacle at the side of the road. The ambulance had to pull in further up, and on the other side, to avoid hitting him.

'Can you tell us what happened, Sir?'

Victor's tongue seemed to have lost contact with his mouth. Disconnected words escaped in a jumble. 'Tree . . . pigeon . . . man.' The policemen looked around at the growing audience. 'Did anyone see what happened?' No one had.

At any other time, Victor would have enjoyed the spectacle. He only knew about crime scenes and accidents from television dramas. Now real policemen and surgeons and photographers were plying their trade, right on his doorstep.

The ambulance men had examined the man on the ground, shaking their heads and brushing the gravel off their trousers. They turned their attention to Victor.

'Are you hurt anywhere?'

He didn't know. He didn't think so as he had managed to negotiate the drive and the telephone, but he certainly felt strange.

They took his pulse, looked into his eyes, asked him if he had hit his head. Not that he remembered. Instead, he felt again the whoosh as his body landed on top of the man, who was even now being photographed as evidence. Someone had gone through the dead man's pockets in search of his identity. Across the road Mrs Randall, who lived in Princess Beatrice Cottage, had picked up the poodle, which was still whimpering.

'I'm afraid we'll have to ask you for a statement,' the policeman said. A big, solid man, he seemed very nice, understanding. He said, 'Let's get you indoors, shall we? I expect you'd like a cup of tea?'

Victor certainly would. He wanted to sit in his favourite armchair and close his eyes and wait for the darkness inside to go away. He wanted to wake up and find that it was all a silly dream.

The nice policeman sat himself opposite Victor at the kitchen table and took out a notebook and pencil. He seemed to spend ages simply arranging things before he asked, 'Right now, can you tell me your name and date of birth?'

'Victor Rudolph Green, March 21st 1963.'

'The year that President Kennedy was assassinated,' the policeman observed. For a terrible moment Victor wondered whether he was making some connection between the president's death and the unfortunate accident of the man outside. Something in his brain reminded him that he had the right to remain silent.

'And your address is?'

'Princess Alice Cottage, Queen Victoria Avenue, Shanklin.' He seemed to be running out of breath before he reached the end of a sentence and took a calming mouthful of tea.

'A nice royal neighbourhood,' the friendly policeman observed. Victor nodded. It *was* nice, much too respectable for murder.

Somehow he stumbled through the rest of the statement. He explained about the tree, showing the man the council letter as proof. The constable asked him about the man who had broken his fall. Did he know him? Had he ever seen him before? He didn't and he hadn't. He asked him about his job, who he lived with, if he had ever been involved with the police before? He answered all the questions as best he could, all the time wondering if the poor dead man had a wife waiting for him at home, and, what would become of his dog?

'Do you know who the man is?' he managed to ask.

'Not yet.' The policeman explained that there would have to be an inquest but that for the moment Victor's doctor was coming over to give him something to help him with the shock.

'It looks like an unfortunate accident,' the nice policeman said. 'Whatever happened, we'll get to the bottom of it but in the meantime, try not to worry.'

Clearly he didn't know Victor. He worried about everything; work, his garden, the world economy, whether there was a God... And now he had killed somebody – oh yes, there was plenty to worry about now.

TWO

Doctor Delaney signed Victor off work for a week. He had known him since he was a child and knew all about his nerves. In the distant past, Victor's mother used to bring him to the surgery for a variety of ailments that usually sprung from some fear engendered by school bullies. Victor's father had died when he was eleven, not early enough in Dr Delaney's opinion. He had bullied the boy, and made no attempt to hide the contempt he felt for this rather wan, willowy child who was more at home in the poetry class than on the rugby field.

Doctor Delaney recognised in the young man the boy he remembered. At thirty-seven, he was still wan and willowy, with a hesitant lisp and an inclination to stutter when he was nervous. 'Try not to worry,' he advised. 'It wasn't your fault. It was an unfortunate accident that might have happened to anyone.'

Silently Victor answered: Not to an intrepid tree climber who wouldn't flinch when a wood pigeon accidentally barged into him! He remembered once going to the America Woods and climbing a horse chestnut tree in pursuit of large conkers, which were hanging invitingly out of reach from a branch about twenty feet off the ground.

'Dare you!' Douglas 'Glossy' Glossop and James 'Jimbo' Gray had taunted him, classmates of the same age but twice the beef, boys always in search of amusement at someone else's expense. Victor had shaken his head, listened to the jibes, then, in a rare moment of defiance, scaled up the tree with remarkable agility for him. On a branch level with the conkers, he realised that they were still out of reach.

'I can't!' he shouted down. 'They're too far away.'

'No they aren't. Climb out on the branch. Go on!'

He tried but his nerve failed. He began to cry and they booed him, jeering, calling him cry-baby, sissy, namby-pamby. Once they calmed down he prepared to descend and face his humiliation, but something awful happened. His body seemed to seize up and he couldn't move.

'Come on! Come down!'

He couldn't. Finally bored and shrugging off any responsibility, Glossy and Jimbo left him there, still shouting insults until they were out of hearing. When he didn't arrive home for tea his mother went out to find him, defying his father's injunction to leave the boy alone, that he had to learn to stand up for himself, fight his own battles.

When his mother finally discovered him he was clinging to the branch as if his life depended upon it, which it did. It was she who summoned the fire brigade and, like a cat up a tree, he was hoisted down and told off for going up there in the first place.

He couldn't bear to remember his father's contempt, the endless, ongoing sneering.

'I will sign you off work for a week, so just take it quietly now.'

He realised that the doctor was speaking and with a gushing sense of relief he thanked him.

In the coming week, safely freed from the yoke of the tax office, Victor read about himself in the paper. In view of his condition he was excused attending the inquest, which was more or less a formality, the case being adjourned until more could be discovered about the man on the ground.

He was pleased to see himself described as a local poet, although they had got his name wrong, calling him Vincent Green instead of Victor Green. That aside, the strange thing was that nothing seemed to have been learned about his victim. No one had reported him missing. His photograph, taken with his white poodle, was featured in the press but nobody seemed to recognise him. Eventually, Mrs Harris from the Beau Rivage guesthouse down on the Esplanade had come forward to say that he had rented a room from her for a few days. He had paid in advance but on the second morning he had simply left. She had only just heard about the accident.

The police examined the room looking for clues but there was nothing to indicate who he might be. He had left no luggage and had signed in under the name of Smith. The only defining evidence as to his identity was the small white poodle that looked strangely incongruous alongside the bulk of the man.

Victor studied the man's face. It was large and pugnacious. He appeared to have suffered a broken nose and had cauliflower ears, although Victor couldn't imagine that *he* had inadvertently inflicted such damage. Remembering what a cushion Mr Smith had made, he thought that he might have been a bouncer or a bodybuilder. It was some tiny consolation that he didn't look like the sort of man who was kind and considerate and a valuable member of society, but then he chided himself for such unkind thoughts. Who was he to judge another man's worth?

The fate of the little dog kept him awake. If no one had claimed 'Mr Smith', then surely no one had claimed the poodle, who he had come to call 'Fluffy'. Poor Fluffy, where was he now? The next time the nice policeman popped round to report that there had been no progress, he asked him where the dog was.

'Dogs' Home. They're hanging on to him in case someone comes forward.'

'And if they don't?'

The policeman shrugged. 'Bit of an old dog, bit of a flea bag, I doubt if anyone else would want him.' The death penalty loomed for Fluffy. Victor, amazed at his temerity, said, 'I'd like to take him in. It is the least I can do.'

'Up to you Sir.'

The next afternoon, feeling guilty because he was off sick and therefore shouldn't be fit to go out, Victor caught the bus to the Dogs' Home at Godshill. Being summer, the village thronged with people meandering happily along the narrow road, filling the giftshops and overindulging in cream teas. This was the quintessential English rural village – thatched roofs, leaded windows, a stone church on a nearby hill giving rise to legends about it having been moved overnight to the crest of the slope by magical hands. The bus dropped Victor a little further on, at the corner, and, as he negotiated the narrow lane on foot, a cacophony of barking reached him long before the buildings came into sight. He had daydreamed about getting a dog before – ever since his mother had died in fact, and that was nearly three years ago – but then, being at work all day, it didn't seem fair. This was different though. It was either his house or the doggy heaven for Fluffy, no contest.

Somewhat hesitantly he explained who he was and what he wanted. The lady on the reception desk was less than forthcoming. Too late, he realised that the RSPCA didn't just hand dogs over to anyone who asked. They wanted to know more about him. He felt like an adoptive parent needing to prove his suitability. They asked if he had ever had a dog before – no. Was his garden properly fenced in – no. In any case, until it was established that no one, no 'next of kin', was going to come forward and agree to sign the dog over, 'Fluffy' was not up for adoption.

Victor felt the weight of disappointment but, just as he was about to turn away, the lady suggested, 'You can take him for a walk if you want to?' They were always short of dog walkers. One more would be useful.

She smiled, seeming to empathise with Victor's situation. 'You can see then if you suit each other and, if everything else works out, then you can apply to take him home.'

Victor readily agreed. He felt a thrill of expectation at the prospect of being a dog owner. For the moment this was the next best thing. The lady called for an officer who took him through a gate into the magic area of the kennels. The barking grew louder, an insistent demand for attention. They walked down a narrow alleyway, past cages occupied by a series of unsuitable-looking dogs – big, wild-eyed, frenetic, boisterous – and suddenly they stopped in front of what at first appeared to be an empty cage. There, cowering in the back, was Fluffy, all of a tremble and emitting the occasional pathetic yap.

The man got Fluffy out, fixed a lead to his collar and suggested that Victor took him down a path and into a wood at the bottom. 'Don't let him off the lead,' he warned.

Victor gave the lead a hesitant jerk, and in response Fluffy crouched down on the ground and refused to move. Victor tugged a little harder and Fluffy was dragged a few inches across the ground. All the time the officer was watching. Seeing Victor's dilemma, he said, 'You'd better carry him as far as the wood. He's scared of the other dogs.'

Victor realised that to reach the wood they would have to continue along the alley, running the gauntlet of an array of large, aggressive dogs throwing themselves against the bars. It dawned on him that they were the canine equivalent of Glossy and Jimbo and in that moment he fell in love. Scooping the poodle up, he shielded him from the threat and swept him along to the sanctuary of the trees.

Once in the peace and quiet of the wood, he put Fluffy on the ground and the dog instantly peed against a weed and then started along the path. He walked on tiptoe, a tiny, mincing bundle of white curls.

As they walked, Victor explained to him how sorry he was about what had happened to his former owner but not to worry because if no one else claimed him, he would take him home. After they seemed to have exhausted the wood, Victor took Fluffy back, carrying him again past the barking bullies. He felt guilty at leaving the dog behind. He looked so small and vulnerable, so in need of someone to love and protect him. Victor had found his goal in life.

He went again to the kennels the next day and the next. On the third day, Fluffy actually wagged his tail. It was now the weekend and Victor was due back to work on Monday – no more walking Fluffy in the afternoons. He wondered if Dr Delaney might sign him off for another week. Then he wondered if he might take some leave, but decided that he had better save it in case he could suddenly take the dog home. He'd need to settle him in, work out a way of leaving him while he was at the office.

Victor heartily wished that he could give up work. The tax office was only a slightly more civilised place than the school playground. People did not take kindly to being taxed. Angry, aggressive men came in to complain. Some of them reminded Victor of 'Mr Smith' – big and bulging and full of testosterone. Robbie Chambers, one of his colleagues, had been assaulted by a dissatisfied taxpayer. Assaulted sounded too vague. It could mean anything. In fact, he had been punched on the nose, resulting in a black eye. For a moment Victor wondered whether Mr Smith might be a tax officer who had been assaulted, thereby acquiring the bent nose and dodgy ears. It seemed unlikely.

If the public were a reason for unease, he did not find his colleagues much easier. He knew that behind his back they laughed at him and made up stories about his private life. Sometimes he wished that the stories were true, that he did live at home with a dowdy girlfriend, but those other stories about him lurking on the heath and exposing himself, giving sweets to little girls – and sometimes to little boys – were hurtful.

Victor had a favourite daydream where he worked as a librarian, not in the public library but in some reference place where he gave advice to interesting people wanting to research interesting things. Here he might meet a girl who would share his passion for words, someone he could take to concerts, go for hikes with on summer Sundays, make love to on Friday evenings. They were disturbing thoughts that roused his timid libido, and he only allowed himself to indulge them when he felt he deserved a little pampering.

The reality was that he had never really had a girlfriend, that he was not gay as some of his colleagues implied, and was not scared of girls but was rather shy, and that just because he had no interest in football or the pub, this did not make him a weirdo.

Thinking that he needed a little boost to prepare him for work the next day, he indulged himself in imagining the Friday night routine with the fantasy girlfriend he had long ago christened Elizabeth. Their lovemaking was invariably accompanied by a vast orchestra of violins and, when it was over, Elizabeth always said, 'I do love you Victor.' On this happy note, he fell asleep.

THREE

The events of the previous Saturday had unaccountably made Victor a hero at the office. When he arrived his colleagues crowded around, wanting to know all the details.

'Gosh, it must have been awful.' Pamela Yates, a rather dowdy woman of about his own age, stared at him with wide-eyed admiration. He had long ago schooled himself not to think of Pamela as a possible Elizabeth. Like him, she had worked in the tax office for a long time. Like him, she had lived, and in her case still lived, with her mother. She wore blouses with little frilly collars and skirts that reached just below the knees. Her shoes were sensible and her glasses were rounded, adding to the moon shape of her face. She had rather nice thick, brown hair, which she usually wore curled up at the nape of her neck. Once or twice she had let it loose and Victor had been entranced by its lustrous length. He would have liked to touch it but could just imagine the scandal if Pamela screamed sexual harassment! In any case, he knew that she had the hots for Robbie Chambers, and had been very anxious to mother him over the punched nose affair, but Robbie in turn had a wife at home and an easy way with women that Victor could not help but envy.

Anyway, the first day passed off quite enjoyably. For a while, at least, Victor was someone to be reckoned with. He embellished his role in trying to revive 'Mr Smith', and played down his non-existent injuries in a way that suggested they had actually been quite serious.

When he got home, he went through the routine of changing his clothes. For work he wore corduroy trousers and a tweed jacket, grey winceyette shirts in winter with a pullover, and pale blue cotton shirts in summer. Every day he wore the tie that his mother had given him for his last birthday before she died.

It had little starbursts on a blue background and he felt that it was understated but at the same time quite trendy. At home in his old jogging trousers and a red tartan shirt, he felt relaxed.

This was the point at which he prepared himself a sandwich (he had lunch every day at the tax office cafeteria) and allowed himself a glass of wine (always red as white was too acidic and inflamed his stomach). Coming up the path, he had been so aware of the now disfigured tree and of the drama that had taken place beneath it that he had forgotten to check if there was any mail. Putting on his slippers, he popped outside to the box fastened to the gate.

There were a couple of things inside, an offer of a free hearing aid, and a plain white envelope with his name and address typed on the front: V Green – not Mr or esquire, as he had been taught to address letters, although the latter was never used now at the tax office. Wandering into the kitchen, he took a sip of wine and sat at the table, carefully slicing the envelope open with a paperknife he kept on the shelf above the table.

A single sheet of A4 paper slithered out, folded in three. As he picked it up, another object slipped from the folds. He picked that up and turned it over. It was a cheque. For a while he stared at it, reading and re-reading the printed information. Pay V Green the sum of Twenty Thousand Pounds. There was no proper signature, only a scrawl and the printed name of a company, Solutions Inc. He read it through again – V Green, Twenty Thousand Pounds, Solutions Inc.

For a moment he assumed that it was one of those advertising ploys, telling you that you were in line for a fortune and that all you had to do was ring an expensive telephone number. Looking once more at the cheque, it appeared quite genuine and he saw with increasing disbelief that it came from the Banque Prive Suisse. Clearly there was some mistake here. For a moment he wondered if he had an unknown relative who might have passed away and made Victor his beneficiary, but he didn't know of anyone. Perhaps it really was one of those advertising gimmicks – *Congratulations, you have won a million pounds or a house in France or a trip to Barbados.* Perhaps he should simply tear it up? Although the cheque looked authentic, surely it was just a hoax? Ever cautious, he decided that first of all he should find out whether there was such a bank and, if it was real, return the cheque to whoever had sent it, explaining that there had been a mistake.

Remembering the sheet of paper, he unfolded it hoping for some enlightenment. Across the centre, five words were typed: *Be more discreet next time.*

What on earth did that mean? For a moment he wondered if he should hand it to the police. He had no idea how he might find the sender. There was no address on the cheque so all he could do was to look up the Banque Prive Suisse and try to post it back to them.

But £20,000; he felt a daydream coming on. A few more anonymous gifts like this and he might be able to give up work after all.

><

Shortly after Victor arrived home from work the following evening there was a knock at the door. Still in his office clothes, he opened it to find the nice policeman there. He had long since established that the officer's name was Alan Grimes, but he still thought of him as 'the nice policeman', as if he were the original village bobby like the ones in children's stories, Noddy, Trumpton, Camberwick Green, Postman Pat. In such communities the residents were always law-abiding. They only needed one arm of the law to keep everyone safe.

'Come in.' Victor was aware that his glass of wine was poured out on the table. He wondered if Constable Grimes, Alan, would take note and mark him down as a drinker. Perhaps he should offer him a glass, but then he remembered all those detective series – *Not while I'm on duty, Sir.*

Constable Grimes took his cap off and sat at the kitchen table. He wore a very crisp white shirt, the sleeves neatly rolled up to allow for the summer sun. He was what Victor's mother used to call 'well covered' and his trouser band strained against the bulk of his paunch. He didn't look like the sort of man who chased criminals and jumped over garden fences.

Victor would never have dared to wear rolled-up sleeves at the tax office, although some of the younger ones were very careless where a dress code was concerned. He supposed he was a bit old-fashioned, but there were standards.

'We've had a bit of a breakthrough,' said Alan. 'We've managed to identify our friend.' He paused for effect and Victor waited politely, his eyebrows raised to show that he was paying attention.

'You've actually done the community quite a service, Sir. Your landing pad turns out to be none other than Tommy Hewson.'

Not sure who that was, Victor waited for enlightenment. A little disappointed that his revelation has fallen on ignorant ears, Alan added, 'Gruesome Hewson? The Force has been after him for some time. He's part of the gangland Mafia, thinks nothing of slitting a throat or drowning someone in a toilet bowl.'

Victor shuddered, feeling profoundly grateful that Mr Hewson had not woken up and exacted a revenge for being fallen upon from a height.

'Anyway, that's it really. Just thought you would like to know.'

'I would – I do. Thank you very much.' Thinking of Fluffy, Victor asked, 'Is there a next of kin?'

'I shouldn't think so. Monsters like Gruesome don't have normal things like a family.'

Something about his words added to Victor's sense of having had a narrow escape. He was glad that a grieving relative wouldn't be coming after him to settle a score. At the same time, it crossed his mind that *he* had no obvious next of kin either. He and Gruesome had one thing in common, well perhaps two, assuming that for some inexplicable reason Gruesome had felt an affection for the little dog.

'Well, just thought I'd let you know.' Alan stood up, glancing at himself in the mirror as he stepped into the hall. He gave a rather soulful sigh followed by a slow exhalation of breath. 'Things aren't like they used to be around here,' he started. 'When I was a young constable, the worst that ever happened was riding your bicycle without lights. Now...'

Victor waited for some revelation, anticipating the pleasure of being let into a police secret. Alan obliged.

'The last two years has seen an upsurge in crime around here, serious crime.' He hesitated, as if wondering whether he should say anything, but then continued, 'Don't suppose you've heard of the Pretty Boys?

Victor shook his head.

'Or the Blues Brothers?' Ah, Victor had heard of them. They were in a film. Clearly the Pretty Boys must be another film. He felt a little disappointed that Alan only wanted to discuss the cinema.

'Well, they both started out in South London, but recently they've spread their theatre of activities as far as the Island.' He paused for effect, then, lowering his voice, added, 'Two worse gangs of villains you'd be hard put to find. There's the Hickman lot, they call themselves the Pretty Boys, and the Rodriguez clan – the Blues Brothers.' He shook his head at his private thoughts.

They weren't talking about films then. This really was about crime. Victor waited.

'I'm very much afraid that a turf war might be on the cards.' Alan lowered his voice even further. 'Just thought I'd mention it so that you can be on your guard.'

Victor began to feel alarmed. Was he in some way implicated? Alan gave him a paternal smile. 'Best not to say anything though, we don't want to alarm the public. Besides, it's bad for tourism.'

Victor nodded. He could see that.

They said their goodbyes, and Victor stood at the front door, trying to absorb what he had been told. Just as Alan reached the front gate, he remembered about the cheque. He should have asked his advice about what to do with it, where to send it, but Alan was already unlocking his car. He would leave it until the next time – assuming there was a next time.

FOUR

Barton Hickman, known to his friends as Barry, was at the strip club called The Earthly Delights. He had called in to collect the takings. He usually did so in the early afternoon, when the place was at its quietest and when it seemed less likely that anyone would try to jump him. There was always a considerable sum of money to take away with him.

The club stood incongruously in a parade of shops, many selling souvenirs of a happy holiday in Ryde. There had been a big hoo-ha when the Pretty Boys had applied for a licence, lots of hot air and righteous indignation. Barry's brothers knew how to get round that though, a generous hand-out here, a warning of what might happen there. Amid columns of outrage in the local paper, The Earthly Delights had opened its doors.

At this time of day the place seemed at its saddest, the piped music echoing round the stale auditorium and one or two old men sitting at tables ogling the girls who looked, frankly, bored, as if they could hardly be bothered to stir themselves. Barry didn't blame them. The club was a different place by midnight though, humming with laughter, very cheap (charged at a premium) champagne flowing, the hostesses animated and stashing back the dosh the punters tucked into their G-strings. He'd never really understood what they got out of it, these sad, inebriated old men. There was a policy that the girls didn't date the customers. Looking at the sea of sweating, bloated faces, it didn't look like much of a temptation.

In terms of appearance, Barry was a credit to a family generally known as the Pretty Boys. He had soft wavy hair, not quite brown, not exactly blond, and large blue baby eyes. If the women showed an interest in him it was because he roused a latent maternal instinct. Pretty he might be, but Barry did not have a girlfriend.

Today was different though, for he had just made a date. The girl was about seventeen with long brown wavy hair and legs that reached up to the heavens. He'd noticed her before when he came round to collect the takings. Too often the girls, for all they were paid to be nice to the customers, treated him with a sort of wry amusement, as if he wasn't someone to be taken seriously. As soon as he'd spotted the girl, though, he felt that she was different from the others, more innocent somehow, and easier to talk to. She was just coming off the stage wearing a couple of tassels on her boobies and a little powder puff thing on her rear. The rest of her was just about hidden under a G-string and she'd given him a smile as she walked by.

'Good afternoon, Mr Hickman.'

It was nice that, being recognised. Barry liked it too because she was polite, realised that he was one of the bosses.

'What you doing tonight?' he blurted out.

'Working, Mr Hickman.'

'And afterwards?'

She shrugged and smiled.

Amazed at himself, he said, 'Good. I'll pick you up then. What's your name?'

'Elaine.'

'You can call me Barry.'

He walked out of the club and onto Ryde's Union Street with a jaunty step, clutching the canvas bag in which the money was secreted. At the bottom of the hill, the glittering seascape of the Solent showed a startling cascade of sunlight on the water. As he made his way to the office he was jostled by holidaymakers. This was the busiest time of the year for the tourist trade – lobster pink parents, toddlers painted war-paint white to keep the sun at bay. These passing visitors were not the clients of the club, but they put money into the pockets of those who were.

It wasn't far to his destination and, cushioning the bag against his chest, Barry concentrated on the night ahead. It was the first time he had dared to proposition one of the girls. Quickly he fought

down any misgivings about how he might perform. Instead he
dwelt on the misfortune of being the youngest in his family.

More than ten years separated him from his brothers –
Harold (Harry) and Garfield (Gary) – an unfortunate interlude
when their old man, Lawrence, known as Larry, had been in
Parkhurst. Once Hickman Senior was released, there had been
some more trouble and he had fled to Spain, leaving the rest of
them to 'run' things while he orchestrated events from afar.

Barry missed his father. He had been his favourite son.
The other two had always seemed to be grown up, been
expected to look after themselves, but Barry had been the baby.
Unfortunately, his brothers still treated him as if he was a child,
even though he was twenty-one. It was two years since he had
seen Larry, his dad. He still missed him.

Never mind though, he'd actually asked that girl out. He
thought of the number of times he'd chickened out, gone over
the words in his mind but in the end never quite had the nerve
to say anything. Meanwhile, Harry and Gary seemed to work
their way through all the girls in the club. He was fed up with
being teased about being scared of women. This time he'd show
them. Elaine was going to be his.

Arriving at the office, it was Barry's job to count the money
and see if the figures added up. If they didn't, he was to tell Gary
and he would sort it out.

To look at the modest frontage of the Victorian terrace in
Prince Arthur Court, one would never think that it was the
headquarters of an international syndicate. The narrow front
door was flaked in green paint, the once cream stucco on
the walls was peeling and the downstairs windows were conveniently coated with years of grime. Juggling the bag, Barry
slipped the key into the lock and turned it, pushing the door
open and stepping into a neglected stairwell. Slamming the
door behind him, he took the stairs two at a time.

Upstairs it was a different matter, like stepping from a tene-
ment into a palace. On the first floor Barry had his own small
room. Like the three bears in the fairytale, the brothers had an

office each, but as the eldest Harry had the biggest, while Gary had the middle-sized one and it was left to Barry to make do with the smallest. He spent much of his time feeling affronted.

Quickly he sat down at his desk and went to work. As he counted piles of notes he felt an all-too-familiar sense of what he thought of as exam nerves, that feeling that came when he knew that later he would have to prove himself, be the man he wasn't sure he was.

A couple of hours later, just as he was getting ready to go over to the club and wait for Elaine, his brother Harry sent word that there was going to be a board meeting. Urgent.

'What, now?' he asked the messenger.

'That's what the Gov said.'

It annoyed Barry that Harry was always called the Gov, or sometimes Boss. Just because he was the eldest didn't automatically put him in charge. Anyway, the real boss was Dad; only he still couldn't come back to England because the Filth was after him. He'd heard that every port and airport in the country had a permanent notice up to look out for him. In a funny way it pleased him, for it showed that his Dad was really important.

Feeling fed up, he walked along to the boardroom. The corridor was lined with mock marble pillars and each room leading off had large sash windows and heavy curtains. From the window he could see the building opposite that housed a bank and a property development company. The developer had his eyes on the Hickman building, thinking to pull it down and renovate it. They had no idea what it was like inside, the expensive wallpaper, Persian carpets, chandeliers and genuine antiques. There were proper portraits in oils on the walls too, of old-fashioned, rich people. Nothing was said, but those admitted inside were left to conclude that they were Hickman ancestors, part of a dynasty. Barry couldn't suppress a sense of achievement. His dad had taste all right. Proper posh was that, it screamed money.

The boardroom was kitted out with a long, gleaming mahogany table, and twelve comfortable chairs ranged on each side.

Barry couldn't ever remember when there had been more than five people around the table, but it looked good.

An ornate silver inkstand thing with a rearing horse stood in the middle and each place setting had a leather pad in front of it with a leather-bound notebook and a pen, not a plastic one but made of silver. They had been expensive and Harry had moaned because someone had walked off with one of them. Crystal glasses and a heavy water jug stood on a tray on the side table, and a sideboard doubled as a drinks cabinet.

Barry was the first to arrive and he walked silently across the deeply carpeted floor to the window. In the street below, a Bentley was just pulling in at the kerbside. It bore the registration HH 1. His brother Harry knew how to look good. Barry was hoping to get something similar with BH 1 but unfortunately he had failed his driving test – eleven times. Barry had sulked and asked why they couldn't simply buy him a licence, but Harry insisted that he should pass his test legit and he was not to drive until he had done so. 'We've got to be kosher Bar, can't have you getting done for driving without a proper licence, can we? Besides, you can always have a chauffeur.'

Having a chauffeur was alright but it wasn't the same.

A few moments later, the boardroom door opened and Harry and Gary came in along with Sonia, a former dancer at The Earthly Delights and now Harry's secretary. She was also his mistress. Barry studied her and thought that she wasn't nearly as pretty as Elaine at the club.

'How long is this going to take?' he asked.

'As long as it takes.'

They took their places around the table, Harry of course at the head and Gary and Barry on either side. Barry noticed that his elder brother always sat on Harry's right – his right-hand man. It was like some Bible thing he remembered – about sitting on the right hand of God. Their mother had brought them up to go to church. 'You need to know the right way to live,' she had always said. 'A good grounding in religion and in table manners and you can go anywhere.'

'Right, the meeting is called to order.' Harry banged on the table with a gavel.

Why did he have to behave as if there were dozens of people present instead of just him and his brothers? Barry opened his notebook and wrote Eelayne on the first page, then he sketched a sort of hourglass girl with top-heavy tits. He was not very good at drawing.

'Right, item one.'

Sonia was seated below Harry and taking notes. He tried to catch her eye but she ignored him.

Harry was talking. 'As you all know, Reggie and Randy Rodriguez have both been locked up. This, as you will realise, is important. With business left in the hands of Roger Rodriguez – 'Dodge' – they are in a vulnerable state. This, gentlemen, is our chance.'

Barry drew another picture of Elaine, bending forward and waving her tassels at him. He felt warm and yet nervous at the prospect of meeting her. He wondered why Harry couldn't talk normally instead of putting on that public school accent he was so fond of using. Silly sod.

'What have you got in mind?' Gary asked.

'Simple. A take-over.'

'And how do we go about that?'

'We-ell,' Harry paused significantly and looked around at them. 'We,' he said, turning his attention to Gary, 'need to go and see Pop in Spain, urgently. Sonia's already booked the tickets so we are leaving tomorrow. That means…' He now settled his eyes on Barry, who was busy colouring in his portrait of Elaine, 'You will have to take charge of things. Do you think you are up to it?'

Barry was caught unawares. He couldn't stop the panic momentarily showing in his eyes before he managed to say, 'Of course I am.'

'That's alright then.'

Barry's mind was working overtime. There was a lot to oversee – the clubs, the drug runs, the money, everything.

His thoughts were interrupted as Harry said, 'We can't afford to wait. I want you to set things in motion.'

Having no idea what things Harry was referring to, Barry hoped for enlightenment. Fortunately it soon came.

'We've heard through certain sources that the Rodriguez boys are having trouble with a certain smuggling scam. They're planning to sort it out – permanently. They're going to send Gruesome Hewson to fix it.' Here he paused significantly and looked at Barry. 'You, my son, will arrange to fix Hewson.'

'How?' The question was out before he could stop it and he cursed himself. If he had waited, no doubt Harry would have told him the solution and he wouldn't have looked such an idiot.

Harry, however, showed no irritation. 'We need to keep our hands clean on this one. We need to get someone special in, someone who can be in and out before anyone even realises.'

Barry waited for his brother to give him more details, a name, a telephone number, but he merely said, 'Get Vincenzo Verdi.'

Who? Panic began to set in, for Barry had never heard of him. Gary was looking increasingly restless. Clearly, he wanted to get away. Harry tidied a pile of papers he had placed on the desk in front of him.

'Er, what about payment?' Barry asked, hoping for some clue, anything that might explain what he was supposed to do.

'Twenty grand should do it. Use the Swiss account. Right, any other business?'

Barry had plenty – like where in hell was he to find this Vincenzo Verdi, how did he get in touch with him and what was he to tell him to do? But before he could formulate any of his questions, Harry announced, 'That's it, the meeting is closed,' swept up his files and prepared to leave the room with Gary on his tail.

'Harry!' Barry called out. At the door his brother slowed down but looked impatient. 'Where do I find this Verdi?' he asked, feeling humiliated in front of Gary.

Harry shrugged. 'Rumour is that he's somewhere in the area – oh, and he might be using the name Vincent Green – you know, *verdi* is green in Italian.'

Barry didn't know. Already Harry was off down the corridor with his shadow Gary in pursuit. Barry was left alone with his thoughts.

He continued to sit at the table. In his notebook, beside the portraits of Elaine, he had written *Get Vinnie Verdi. £20k. Knock off Hewson.*

Easy-peasy.

The evening out with Elaine was not a success. It turned out that she was a student topping up her university fees and this was just a summer job. She was doing something called a D Fill, whatever that was, and her naturally educated voice made Barry feel nervous.

The firm's odd-job man, Sean, was appointed to drive Barry for the evening, so he took Elaine to the Bai Ram Singh club along Shanklin's Keat's Green, where there was late dining. The club was named after some Indian bloke who had done a spot of decorating for Queen Victoria. Like the Durbar Room at Osborne House, where the Queen had spent her holidays, the Bai Ram Singh was coated in ornate white papier-mâché decoration, with statues of elephants and peacocks and other Indian gods. As they waited for their food, Elaine told him all about university life and her plans to be a lecturer. They had a couple of dances. Barry liked to dance but the proximity of Elaine made him clumsy and he kept treading on her toes.

'Sorry.'

'Not to worry.' She laughed and he thought that this was how she treated the customers, always polite although what she was thinking was anyone's guess.

When it came time to leave, Barry's invitation to come back to his place was politely refused.

'Go on, just for a nightcap?' he pleaded.

'No thanks, really. My boyfriend will be waiting up for me.'

'Boyfriend? Then what did you come out with me for if you've got a boyfriend?' His initial disappointment made

Barry's tone petulant, although already relief was beginning to flood him. He had drunk rather a lot and a wild thought came to him. 'Why don't you dump him and move in with me?' That would show his brothers what he was made of!

Elaine looked amused. She even laughed. 'I don't know you. Rick and I are doing the same degree. Besides which, we get on well together.'

'Then why did you come out with me?'

She gave an endearing little shrug. 'To be honest, I was curious. I wondered what it would be like to be a gangster's moll, like in all the films – sorry.'

She didn't even wait for a lift home, just picked up her jacket, popped a kiss on his cheek, thanked him for the meal and walked out, leaving him feeling as if he was about twelve. He sat there for ages, trying to look calm and confident. To be honest, he was hugely relieved that she had gone and, on the plus side, she thought of him as a gangster. This thing with women, however, it reminded him of having to learn to swim. He remembered teetering on the edge of a diving board, his head already swimming with fear and his brothers teasing him.

'Go on Bar, jump!'

In the end he was pushed. He'd literally taken the plunge and survived without drowning, but he still didn't like swimming.

Meanwhile, invading every thought was the problem of how to find Vincenzo Verdi, aka Vincent Green.

—

Two days later and Barry was no nearer to finding a solution. It even kept him awake at night. If he failed over this then Harry would probably take away the few duties he had already entrusted him with. Everyone would know about it and he would be a laughing stock.

It was his night for picking up the takings at the Prince Leopold, along Sandown's seafront. It was a glorious evening, the sun lancing down its last spears of light onto the sea. The beach was nearly deserted and the enveloping hiss of the waves was broken only by the occasional echoing growl from the tigers in the neighbouring zoo.

Sean dropped him at the entrance to the club and he walked into the office, where he found the manager, Bernie Lowther, reading the paper.

'You seen this?' Bernie asked by way of greeting. He pushed the *Clarion* towards Barry. Barry didn't read too well but he struggled through the gist of the thing. What he saw caused his eyes to widen. It was rather a weird story about some bloke falling out of a tree and snuffing out another bloke passing by, but the dead bloke was none other than Tommy Hewson. It also said that the first bloke up in the tree was called *Vincent Green*. Brilliant! Barry thought that before he left for Spain Harry must have made contact with the hitman after all. What a relief. The paper even printed his address. He felt a huge weight lifted from his shoulders. All he had to do now was send him the cheque.

Back in the office later, he dug out the paperwork for the Swiss account and carefully wrote out a cheque for £20,000. Just to make his mark he thought he'd add a little note of his own: *Be more discreet next time.* Discreet was a word he had come across recently and, although he wasn't sure exactly what it meant, he thought it had something to do with being careful. Dropping blokes out of trees onto other blokes didn't sound at all discreet to him.

Satisfied with his evening's work, he placed the note and cheque in an envelope, carefully copied the address from the *Clarion*, stuck on a stamp and popped it in the post.

FIVE

Constable Alan Grimes let himself in at the front door of his home at No. 24 Prince Consort Crescent to be greeted by the aroma of cooking. From the kitchen he could hear banging and sizzling and a low commentary on the food's progress from his daughter Charity.

'Hello? What's this?' he asked, falsely jolly, poking his head around the door.

Charity, looking rather flustered, was chasing something unidentifiable around a frying pan.

'Chicken.'

'Chicken?' He perked up.

'Well, Quorn.'

'Quorn.' Charity, a great animal lover, had transformed the house into a meat-free zone. Since her arrival back at home a month ago, Alan had been treated to all kinds of culinary mysteries, some of which he would have been happy to forego.

He had just been getting used to being alone. Margaret, his wife, had died eight months ago, a blow because it was so sudden, a tumble down the steps of an escalator on a day trip to London, then complications, and then the awful news.

Both his daughters had come flying home to offer comfort. Charity worked in Guildford as manager in a branch of M&S. Prudence lived in Chelmsford and was married to Ray, who ran a builders' merchants yard. Prudence didn't work but looked after their two boys, Ralph and Geoffrey. Both daughters had been full of advice.

'You are coming up to retirement Dad, why on earth don't you sell up and come and live with us?' – this from Prudence. The thought of incarceration in Essex with Pru and her family made him gratefully but firmly decline the suggestion, no easy task in the face of her determination to look after him.

With an overdeveloped sense of duty and a strong competitive streak, Charity had then taken it upon herself to resign from her job and come home to stay. She had heard that a managerial vacancy at the local branch of M&S was expected to come up shortly, and by then she hoped to have Alan settled so that she could go out and leave him for a few hours each day. The fact that he in turn regularly went out to work seemed to have bypassed her.

Alan was an easygoing man, unambitious, as evidenced by his failure to rise above the level of constable, but it suited him. Country stations, rural constabularies, he had been content with sorting out petty misdemeanours, still favouring an avuncular telling off or an occasional clip around the ear until that had been well and truly forbidden. Now fifty-eight, retirement indeed beckoned, but he had not visualised spending it with Charity.

Charity of course was a nice girl, but she would interfere. His house had been completely rearranged in line with some obscure M&S policy on storage and stacking, and she had a trying habit of coming up with solutions to the occasional crimes that he was handling. They were nothing serious – a break-in, a taking away without consent – but immediately Charity was on the case. Often he was tired when he came home and didn't really relish explaining to her how it was illegal to electrify a doorbell or fix the brakes of a potential stolen car, even to catch a criminal.

Alan washed his hands and went into the living-cum-dining room to await tonight's surprise feast. The *Clarion* was on the arm of his chair and he picked it up. He was immediately drawn to the main feature.

Mystery Man Identified. It went on to reveal that the unidentified man on whom local poet Vincent Green had accidentally landed – and killed outright – was none other than the notorious gangster Tommy 'Gruesome' Hewson, wanted for torture, murder and robbery. Hewson had been active mainly in south London and latterly along the south coast. What he had been doing on their Island was a mystery. He had built up a reputation as a vicious killer and his trademark had become his

sidekick, a small white poodle. In view of evidence of its presence at various grisly crime scenes, the dog had been dubbed
the Angel of Death by the press. A picture of Gruesome, who
had served seven years for armed robbery, was featured centre
page. The RSPCA had declined to have the dog's mug shot
splashed across the papers.

Alan put the *Clarion* aside and hoped that Gruesome being
in the area did not indicate that a local crime wave was about to
hit. He had fourteen months left to serve and he had no desire
to spend it dodging the big boys.

Charity came in and honed in on the headline. 'Don't you
think it's strange,' she said, 'That a known killer should be accidentally wiped out by someone falling on him?'

'No. It was an accident.'

She shook her head and sat down in the other armchair.
'I don't think so, Dad. Perhaps somebody arranged for this
Hewson to be bumped off?'

Alan shook his head again. 'You haven't met Victor Green,' he
said. Someone more law-abiding would be difficult to imagine.

'I thought his name was Vincent?'

'That's the press for you, always getting things wrong.'

Victor was also scanning the *Clarion* and he didn't like what he
saw. The thought of sharing his house with the notorious Angel
of Death gave him second thoughts about offering the little
poodle a home, but then, thinking of Fluffy's mewling bark
and trembling demeanour, he couldn't believe it was possible
that he might be vicious. More likely Fluffy had been a victim
of Gruesome's domestic violence, forced to defend himself by
obeying his owner's evil commands: 'Kill Fluffy!' – only he
didn't think that Gruesome would have called him that. He had
probably given him a horrible name like Bullseye or Gnasher.
Thus reassured, he determined to go to the Dogs' Home on
Saturday and make his case.

He spent the remaining evenings hunting out the escape routes that Fluffy might unearth along the hedge. Victor had heard about people keeping dangerous dogs and failing to keep them under control. He resolved to buy a muzzle and a 'Beware of the Dog' sign to nail to the gate. He must ensure that he became a responsible owner.

On Saturday he presented himself at the Dogs' Home and filled in the application form. 'I came in before,' he said, to make sure he was regarded as first in the queue. 'I have fenced in the garden and I am ready for inspection, now if you wish?' By this time Fluffy had been at the Dogs' Home for seven days and no one had come forward to claim him.

The man taking down the details laid his pen aside. 'No need for that, Sir. Someone will pop along during the week just to make sure that everything is OK. If you would like to follow me we can go and fetch him.'

'Now?' Victor felt his heart rate increase with excitement as he followed the warden out to the kennels. As soon as he set eyes on Fluffy, any doubts that he had quickly vanished. Here was the sweetest little abandoned dog and now he was to be his. Fluffy seemed to remember him and wagged his tail, emitting his falsetto squeak. The final details were completed, and to his amazement and delight Victor found himself standing outside, waiting at the bus stop to take his new companion home.

It was soon clear that they suited each other. Victor found a piece of foam rubber and a particularly soft blanket and fashioned a dog's bed near to the radiator, not that it was on at the moment but come the winter he would need somewhere cosy. Rather disconcertingly, Fluffy peed against one of the kitchen chairs then went off to explore the rest of the cottage. Victor thought that perhaps he should buy a book on dog psychology. He knew that bed-wetting was a symptom of anxiety in children so the same probably applied to dogs. Once he was settled, hopefully the little accidents would cease.

That afternoon they went for two short walks, just to familiarise the poodle with his new neighbourhood. In the unlikely event that he got out, Victor wanted to be sure that he knew his way home. In Prince Regent Street they stopped at the pet shop and got a new collar and lead, and a nametag to be engraved with Fluffy's name and Victor's telephone number. Stocked up with pouches and biscuits and treats, the two went home and settled down to get to know each other.

—

Her father was working on Saturday and Charity was bored. As she was lining the rubbish bin with an old copy of the *Clarion*, she read again the story of Gruesome Hewson's bizarre death. Just recently she had overdosed on crime novels and this seemed to be just the sort of thing that a writer might have woven into one of his plots.

Through the window the sun enveloped the world in tempting warmth, challenging her to go for a walk. With nothing else to do, she decided to take the opportunity to patrol the area where Vincent – or rather Victor – Green lived. The idea of meeting a poet appealed to her. Immediately she thought of those portraits of Lord Byron, black wavy hair, a passionate mouth. She felt disturbingly restless. The *Clarion* had thoughtfully printed his address so she had no trouble in finding it. No matter what her father said, she was certain that there was more to Gruesome Hewson's death than an accident.

She hung around for a while then set herself a route to patrol so that hopefully she would get a glimpse of the now famous poet. Her father was adamant that what had happened to Gruesome was an accident but just in case it wasn't, it was up to her to prove it.

Just as she was having doubts, her patience was rewarded. On the third time she passed the house she saw Victor and a small white dog coming out of the gate. Charity felt instantly disappointed. The man looked light years away from either a poet or an enforcer. He was short and probably weighed no more than nine stone. His nondescript hair was parted on the side and a lock hung limply onto his forehead. At best his clothes could be described as old-fashioned. All in all he was not an inspiring specimen. Still, looks could be deceptive and Charity really had nothing better to do.

Straightening her back she followed them down the road, and when the dog stopped to investigate some interesting smell, she walked up to them and said, 'What a sweet little dog.'

Victor jumped and wondered whether he should warn her to be careful. Perhaps he should have muzzled Fluffy in case he was conditioned to attack any stranger who approached him? Before he could say anything, however, the woman had bent down and was stroking the poodle's curls. Fluffy responded by rolling over and exposing a pink stomach.

'He's so sweet!' Charity stood up and looked at Victor. He looked embarrassed and his cheeks began to glow with the sort of blush that would have done credit to a Victorian virgin. Undeterred, Charity ploughed on.

'What's his name?' she asked.

'Er – Fluffy. I got him from the RSPCA. He – he was orphaned.' He supposed that was an accurate description of Fluffy's status.

Charity was remembering the article in the *Clarion* and she looked anew at what she suddenly wondered might be the Angel of Death, then decided that that would be too much of a coincidence. Determined to see the case through, however, she fell into step beside Victor.

'I'm just out for a walk,' she announced. 'I've only moved here recently and I don't know anyone really.'

When he didn't respond, she added, 'I always think a walk is so much nicer if you have a dog, don't you?'

Victor nodded, unaccountably tongue-tied. His new companion was determined to pursue the conversation. She said, 'I'm not working at the moment so I have plenty of free time.'

'Oh.'

'I might look around and see if anyone would like their dog walked.'

Victor jolted inwardly at the turn events were taking. Wasn't this just what he was looking for, someone to come in when he was at work – someone to keep Fluffy company, take him for a stroll and generally see that he was well?

'I – I've got a few days off,' he volunteered, 'but then I've got to go back to work so I will have to find someone to …'

They looked at each other. 'If I can help at all,' Charity volunteered and gave him her phone number.

><

After finishing work at the police station, Alan called in to see Edna Fairgrove. He had only met Edna a few months ago, when she had come into the station to report that a man was sleeping rough in the bus shelter opposite her house.

'I don't want to get him into trouble,' she started, 'but it does seem a shame that he should be there. Perhaps there is a hostel that he could go to?' After a moment she added, 'And to be honest, I suppose there is a possibility that he will break into one of the houses in search of food.'

Alan agreed that it was indeed possible and said that he would look into it. Edna had seemed in no hurry to leave. When Alan had written down her details, she said, 'To tell the truth, I'm a bit nervous these days. My husband died six months ago and I can't get used to being on my own.'

'I know exactly how you feel,' Alan found himself saying. 'I lost my wife recently too.'

Edna Fairgrove was a comfortable looking lady, well covered but not fat, neat and tidy but not tarted up. Alan thought that she looked very nice.

'I'm just going off duty now,' he said, 'but I could perhaps escort you home?'

Edna's shoulders wriggled in a way that reminded him of a chicken that, after preening itself, ruffles its feathers. In fact, she reminded him of a hen altogether, soft and downy with bright amber eyes.

Alan refused Edna's invitation to come in for a cup of tea, but when he happened to bump into her in Sainsbury's a couple of weeks later, they both stopped for a cup of coffee before going their separate ways.

'I was wondering,' said Edna, 'if you might like to come round for a bite to eat sometime. Please don't misunderstand. It's just that I really miss having someone to cook for and you might be missing your wife's dinners?'

Her eyes were without guile. Alan felt that this was perfectly proper and a week later he came to Sunday lunch. It was lovely. The food was delicious. Edna's house was cosy but not too tidy, so he didn't have to worry about taking off his shoes at the door or perhaps dropping the odd crumb. While he was there, he went out into the garden and fixed the latch to the back gate for her.

'It was nothing,' he said in response to her thanks. 'Just think of it as payment for such a lovely meal.'

Over the weeks they had settled into a gentle pattern of occasional meetings. Alan did not feel pressurised in any way. They would sometimes sit in companionable silence in her front room, sometimes watch a comedy programme on TV or talk about the latest news. Sadly, this happy little routine had come to a halt with Charity's arrival.

On the second occasion that he told Charity he was going out to have a meal with a friend, she asked, 'Is this a woman?'

'As a matter of fact, it is. She's a widow. We've been having the occasional meal together.'

Charity was immediately bristling with disapproval. 'I don't know what Mum would think,' she said. Alan couldn't think of an appropriate reply that didn't suggest he had abandoned Margaret's memory. When he didn't answer, Charity added, 'Anyway, there's no need for anyone else to cook for you now, I'm here.' Reluctantly the Sunday dinners and mid-week roasts with Edna were abandoned.

That evening Charity had gone to a talk at the village hall about the Duke of Wellington, so it was Alan's chance to stay out without causing an atmosphere.

He knocked at the door and, after a few moments, Edna answered. She looked both surprised and flustered by his unexpected visit.

'Oh, Alan. I'm – please come in. I've got a friend here at the moment.'

'Oh no, I don't want to disturb you. I just thought I'd pop by and say hello.'

From the front door he could see along the passageway to the kitchen, and there at the kitchen table was a man. He was sitting in the place where Alan had until recently enjoyed Edna's meals and a wave of loss and disappointment filled him.

'As long as you are OK,' he said, backing away.

'Please, do come on in.'

'No, really. It was just …' Somehow he made his retreat and went home. At that moment, he realised just how much his little outings with Edna had meant to him, and now it seemed that there was someone else. Miserably, he thought that if only Charity hadn't come back then his peaceful trips with Edna would have continued, but then the guilt overcame him. His daughter had made a huge sacrifice to come and look after him. He should be grateful. The only problem was, he wasn't.

SIX

A queue shuffled its way slowly beneath the shadow of the towering brick wall that surrounded Parkhurst Prison. It looked at least twenty feet high, the top overhung on both sides, making it madness for anyone inside or out to even think of scaling it. On the inner side, spotlights as brilliant as the midday sun picked out every corner. The nearest neighbours some half a mile away complained about what they called light pollution, while across the road, the new mothers in the maternity unit of St Mary's Hospital longed to go home, then thought themselves lucky that their incarceration was of such short duration.

None of this interested Roger Rodriguez, generally known as Dodge, as he edged his way forward with the queue. It was raining, a soft drizzle that soaked into his fleece and insinuated its way inside his collar. The weather reflected his general mood for he felt abandoned, cast adrift to run the family affairs about which he knew nothing. Today was Thursday and he clutched in his hand a disintegrating piece of paper, a pass that allowed him one hour's visit with his elder brother Reginald, who was serving a ten-year sentence for fraud.

Dodge recognised the couple in front of him in the queue as regular prison visitors, not family or friends but professional do-gooders who made it their business to inflict themselves on the poor sods who had no one on the outside of their own. They were discussing something they had seen on the telly the night before. Dodge studied their backs, a middle-aged man and woman, both wearing tweedy clothes, confident of their place in law-abiding society. He thought that being visited by one of them must be like a punishment in itself. If he had his way he'd ban the lot of them.

They had reached the gate and the couple both showed their passes to the guard. He nodded at them, gave them a cursory running over with his metal detector thing and they stepped inside. Stage one. Dodge was next. The guard, a stocky man who looked as if a JCB wouldn't budge him, did not speak but took his pass with an expression that implied it was bound to be counterfeit. He looked Dodge over as if trying to identify him, even though there was nothing on the document to say what he looked like. The metal detector then roamed over his body. Was it his imagination or did the bloke deliberately poke it into his crotch? Without a word, just a single nod of his head, he gave Dodge permission to step over the threshold.

Inside there was more. Two dogs were waiting, hoping to find the merest hint of drugs. One of them began to bark and wag his tail, emitting an excited Eureka of discovery, and the man in front of the middle-aged couple was hauled out of the line. The professional visitors dutifully held up their arms while they were frisked, again a token gesture, and replied 'No' when asked whether they were bringing in anything illegal. This included things as various as arms and drugs, and any form of food and drink. *'I could kill for one of Ma's bacon sarnies'*; that was one of Reggie's habitual gripes.

A woman officer frisked Dodge and he hated that. It made him shiver when a woman touched him and his face burned as her hand hovered close to his private parts, but at last it was over and he was allowed to go forward, into the vast room where an hour's visiting was permitted.

Tables were spread out as if for a whist drive, with a chair on each side. The men expecting visitors were already seated, one at each table. Dodge saw Reggie immediately in the second row. He was a handsome man, Reggie, with his father's Mediterranean good looks, dark hair and liquid eyes. As a child, Dodge had adored him. Experience had taught him, however, that Reggie was of uncertain temper and could not be relied upon to be kind. He waved, then hastily put his hand down again. A screw stood near to his brother. Throughout the visit the warders kept up a patrol, but Dodge had noticed before that they always placed themselves nearest to the most important cons – and he knew that Reggie was important.

'Reg? How are you?' He sat down opposite his brother and waited.

Reg was wearing the uniform navy serge blouson and trousers with telltale stripes down the sides. His hair was cut shorter than Dodge knew he liked. Proud of his hair, was Reg. The assortment of gold that he liked to wear was also absent.

'Bruv.' Reggie acknowledged his presence and looked around him to make sure that the guard was not within hearing.

'Everything alright?' Dodge asked.

'Never mind about that, word on the street is that things are happening.'

'Things?'

'Us being banged up, Randy and me. Word is that those Hickman bastards are planning to move in.'

'Move in?'

'Stop repeating everything I say.'

Chastened, Dodge looked down at his hands. His brother always managed to make him feel a fool. He waited while Reggie looked around again, then leaned forward.

'They've got it into their heads that while we're away, our patch is up for grabs.' He breathed in deeply. 'Time to let them know what a mistake they're making.'

Dodge waited, unsure as to what was expected of him. He soon found out.

'It's up to you now. We need to send them a message. You need to get hold of someone, a fixer, teach 'em a lesson.'

Dodge began to panic. He had no idea who he was supposed to fix or how to go about it, or about anything else come to that.

'What do you want me to do?' he asked hopefully.

'Get in touch with someone.'

'Who?'

Reggie shook his head impatiently. 'I don't know who's around, do I? Use your gumption man. Get out there on the street and find out. See what Vincenzo Verdi is up to. He's the best.'

'Wh–what do you want him to do?'

'What do you think? Get him to take out one of Hickman's lot.'

'The Pretty Boys?'

'That's what they like to call themselves.'

'Any particular one?'

'Any one really. What about Mauler Maguire? He's a right bastard. He's given us trouble in the past. Yes, make it Maguire.'

'Mauler?' Roger's heart sank further. This was way outside of his league.

'How do I contact Verdi?' he asked.

'How do you think? Ask around. Someone will know where he's operating and if he ain't available, find someone else.' As an afterthought, he added, 'You might find that he's operating under the name of Vincent Green – *verdi* is Italian for green.'

Dodge sat in silence, lost. Eventually he asked, 'What about price then?'

'Twenty-five grand will do it. Use the Channel Islands funds.'

'How do I pay him?'

'Send him a cheque!'

After that they talked about general things. Dodge tried to sound positive, to set Reggie's mind at rest, but his brother was brooding and unpredictable. Dodge was glad when the visiting time was up.

Sitting on the bus on the way back, he felt the familiar churning in his stomach that he got when he didn't know what he was supposed to do. Reggie's twin brother, Randy, was more helpful, for he understood that Dodge didn't take easily to this kind of thing. Reggie would never explain things properly, whereas Randy would say, '*It's like this, Dodge,*' and make it simple. The trouble was, Randy was locked up as well and he wasn't seeing him until next week and Reggie had said that it was urgent. The churning notched up another degree.

Someone had left the *Clarion* on the train and he flicked through it listlessly, turning to the sports page. The local team was out of the Cup – no good news there then. He was about to put it aside when his eye was caught by the headline: *'Mystery Man Identified.'* As he read it he gave an involuntary gasp. Quickly looking around to see if anyone was watching, he read the article again. It was too late. What Reggie feared was already happening. The mystery dead man was their Tommy Hewson and he had already been taken out. There was something about a tree that Dodge didn't understand but the article did give the name of the bloke who had done it. It was Vincent Green – and Reggie had said that Vincenzo Verdi might use this name!

Surreptitiously, he tore out the article and put it in his pocket, his brain working overtime.

If Green was already working for the Pretty Boys then he couldn't do work for them as well, could he? This was something else he didn't know. He remembered Randy once saying that hitmen were always for sale to the highest bidder. He wondered how much the Pretty Boys had paid Verdi to dispose of Gruesome. He felt a peculiar mixture of fear because a gang war was about to start, but it was tinged with relief that Gruesome wouldn't be around to bother him any more. Gruesome had always teased him and behind the teasing was a barely disguised menace. Well, at least that was one less thing to worry about, not forgetting of course that Gruesome was supposed to be on their side.

He sat for several moments trying to think it all through. Perhaps he could offer Verdi more money to bump off Mauler Maguire? It was all too complicated. He wanted to go home and have his tea and watch the telly. He felt suddenly sad and home-sick. Dodge had lived all his life in the house he had grown up in with his Mum and brothers and Dad, until Dad had flitted off back to Spain and the boys had moved on. Before they had been sent down the twins had both got places of their own. Once they'd moved out there had just been Dodge and Mum, until she took sick and died. He missed her. For a moment he wondered what Dad would think. He thought about phoning him to ask his advice, but he'd been told never to discuss business over the phone because you never knew who was listening.

Then he had a bright idea. The *Clarion* had thoughtfully printed Vincent Green's address, so he would drop him an anonymous note asking to meet him. Once face-to-face, he might be able to explain the situation to him, see if they could come to some arrangement. He sat pondering his plan to see if there were any flaws but he couldn't think of one. Where would be a good place to meet? It needed to be somewhere public so that to anyone watching it would look like a chance encounter. He scratched around in his mind and then wondered about Shanklin Chine. People sometimes wandered along there admiring the wild scenery and the tumbling waterfall, so it wouldn't look too suspicious if they met up. He needed to set it up as quickly as possible so he decided to make it Wednesday.

When he got home he found a brown envelope and a sheet of paper, and in his best handwriting wrote: *Shanklin Chine, Wensday 8.o'clock. Be there.* He didn't sign it. As an afterthought, although he was sure this Vinnie wouldn't need reminding, he wrote *Keep it simple,* then, carefully addressing the envelope, he stuck on a stamp and dropped it in the mail.

SEVEN

The morning after meeting Charity, Victor took Fluffy for a walk along the cliff. Once again it was a beautiful day. Three hundred feet below the sea spread out along the sands, advancing and retreating, gradually edging nearer and then, at low tide, leaving a smooth, damp playground for children. To the south, rock pools sheltered an assortment of winkles and anemones. Victor thought nostalgically of his childhood days, his Mum brushing the sand from his damp toes and forcing his feet into gritty sandals. Their picnic had always consisted of salty cheese sandwiches and warm lemonade. For a moment he felt a poem coming on but Fluffy was busily doing his business on the path and he stopped to clear it up.

Other people were walking their dogs and it gave him a comforting sense of acceptance. This was what nice, normal people did in the mornings – those who didn't have to go to work. For the moment he didn't have to think about the office so he gave himself up to being one of the lucky ones.

Fluffy didn't seem very keen on chasing balls or fetching sticks. He was more concerned with his fellow dogs roaming the green. They came in all varieties, big bounding Labradors, busy spaniels, a frenetic Jack Russell and several Staffordshire bull terriers, the latter mostly belonging to a group of young men who gathered aimlessly around a bench. They didn't work either but there was none of the comfortable middle-class self-satisfaction about them, more a challenging stance that defied anyone to look at them twice. Fluffy was not keen on any of the dogs, but particularly the Staffies, and Victor had to pick him up when their attentions became altogether too much for him. The glares of the young men had a similar effect on Victor and he retreated to the other end of the green, where a better class of person seemed to be taking their exercise.

Fluffy had now got the hang of the situation and at the approach of any dog he set up a hysterical yapping, showing his small needle teeth. Victor wondered again about the muzzle but then, if faced with a fight, Fluffy wouldn't be able to defend himself. Dog ownership was not quite as trouble-free as he had imagined.

Walking home he thought about Charity, the girl he had met the day before. At the time he had been too flustered to pay her proper attention but from what he could remember she had looked quite a decent girl. He suspected that she was pretty too but he hadn't had the temerity to actually look at her face. What a coincidence that she should be looking for a dog to walk on the very day after he had acquired Fluffy. He had written her name and telephone number on the pad by his telephone so that he wouldn't lose it, and had once or twice fantasised about phoning her. He quickly stifled the thought that she might turn into the very Elizabeth that he was looking for.

Walking up the drive to his cottage, he stopped to empty the mailbox. There was the usual assortment of rubbish, a catalogue for useful gadgets and a shiny magazine sporting a tweedy man on the cover offering a range of country gentleman's clothing. Victor had once ordered some cavalry twill trousers from them and they had been pestering him ever since.

There was also a brown envelope with a handwritten address. As soon as he was indoors Victor opened it, expecting some offer for double-glazing or roof insulation, but inside was a single piece of paper. Written across the middle in spidery writing was the terse message: *Shanklin Chine, Wensday 8.o'clock. Be there.*

Spelling aside, he had no idea what it could mean. His first instinct was to throw it away but the tone of the note niggled at him. Finally, he resolved that it was a nice walk as far as the Old Village so he and Fluffy would go along the following evening and see what happened.

Dodge had often wondered about Vincent Green, aka Vincenzo Verdi, who was something of a legend in gang circles. He had of course never seen him but he had a mental vision of what he must be like. Perhaps it was the name that made him think of Lincoln Green, and he imagined him as a sort of Robin Hood character, wearing tights and shooting arrows at the enemy. Dodge could picture his face, chiselled nose, firm chin, flashing eyes. His manhood stirred. This was the sort of guy he'd love to meet, someone strong and athletic who would be there for him when life got difficult. The thought of actually meeting him in the flesh increased his heart rate, set his imagination rampaging. Together they'd become known as the Supermen, brothers in arms (and lovers in bed)? People would admire them for their skill and daring and speed. They'd dispose of all the bad people in the world and this included screws and prison visitors. All he had to do was meet him.

On Wednesday evening he went to a lot of trouble to look his best, proper suit and shirt, his hair slicked back and his shoes with the Cuban heels, just to give him a bit of extra height. He felt childishly excited, a boy expecting Christmas, a man meeting his hero. In his pocket he had a cheque already made out for £25,000, just in case Vincent expected to be paid in advance. He already guessed that you didn't argue with the likes of Vincent Green. The thought of this powerful figure made him go weak at the knees.

He was actually on the way to the door when there was a knock. Cursing, he opened it with the words, 'I'm just going out,' but they fell on the deaf ears of Groping Joe Windsor, who barged his way past him.

'You've heard about what's happened to Gruesome?' Joe started.

'I read about it in the paper. I'm sorting it.' Roger felt a familiar unease at the sight of Joe, oily, limp-wristed, his fingers always fluttering as if they were longing to reach out and grab him by the balls. When he was younger he had quickly learned to keep away from Groping Joe, had even shyly confessed to

Randy how the older man took every opportunity to get him alone, but Randy had said, "Fraid you'll just have to keep out of his way, Dodge. Reggie won't hear a word against him. He's one man he can rely on to do whatever is needed.'

Groping Joe said, 'You've got to get down to the nick and see Reggie. Fast. Get those brothers of yours to sort something out.'

'It's already in hand,' he said with an authority he didn't feel.

Joe took a step nearer. 'If this is the start of some rumble then I'm out. I'm getting too old for this. Besides, I like the softer things in life.' He looked Dodge over meaningfully.

'Don't worry. I'm fixing it.'

Groping Joe came right into the kitchen and a potent aroma of stale French scent wafted around the room. Dodge wrinkled his nose and stepped back.

'Joe, I've got to go. I've got an important meeting.'

'He'll wait.'

'He won't!'

'Then find yourself another boyfriend. There's plenty more out there.' Joe looked him up and down again in a way that was the stuff of Roger's nightmares. Alarmed at what Joe was suggesting, he added, 'How do you know I'm not meeting a girl?' Although meeting girls was way outside of his comfort zone.

But Joe was still preoccupied with the way that things were going.

'What you gonna do about this problem then? How you going to protect us?' With each question he moved forwards and Dodge retreated until his back was up against the washing machine. He squeezed to the side.

'I'm hiring someone.'

'You know they've got Vincenzo Verdi? Who's going to outwit him?'

Dodge didn't say anything about his plan to offer Vincenzo more money, in case Joe pooh-poohed the idea for he had no alternative plan. Meanwhile, the minutes were ticking by.

'Look, I'll see you tomorrow. It will all be sorted by then, I promise.'

Joe eyed him with a predatory gleam. 'Yeah? You gonna look after me then?' He gave a high-pitched giggle.

All the time Dodge edged towards the door, repeating, 'I'll see you tomorrow. I promise.'

Reluctantly Joe stepped back out onto the pavement, looking up and down the street with exaggerated care, as if expecting an ambush, then, with a last lascivious look at Dodge, he scuttled away down the road, sticking to the shadows as he went.

With a sigh Dodge hurried over to his car, a vintage red Jaguar that he had bought because he was a fan of Inspector Morse. He unlocked the door, slipping into the driver's seat and turning the ignition key. The car gave a cough and then nothing happened. He tried again with the same result.

Swearing loudly he scrambled out and lifted the bonnet, looking helplessly inside, for he really had no idea how the thing worked. Hopefully he got back inside and tried again, but it was no good. It was only at that moment that he realised that he had left the lights on and that the battery was stone dead.

Still cursing, he got out and began to run down the road. It was a good mile to the Chine. He'd never make it on time. He'd never make it.

He ran until his lungs heaved like bellows and a sheen of sweat covered his face and chest, soaking his armpits. At last he drew near to the hollow leading down to the entrance, in his hurry nearly knocking over a startled looking little man with a ridiculous white poodle. The dog yelped and the man picked it up and glared at him, but he ignored them. A little further on he turned, reached the gate and stopped to get his breath. As he went to walk on, he realised that there was something wrong. People were gathering along the pathway and pointing into the water. Seconds later he heard a police car and, with an instinct born of a lifetime's experience, he turned tail and hurried home to another sleepless night of indecision.

—

At seven forty-five, Victor and Fluffy arrived at Shanklin Chine. It was the Chine that had made Shanklin famous, turning it from a remote, fishing village into the place that adventurous Victorians loved to explore. Privately owned, a deep chasm in the cliff opened up to reveal a steep-sided wonderland where a waterfall rushed in its hurry to reach the sea. Green and glistening, visitors stopped in awe to experience the wonders of nature. The entrance kiosk was not manned so Victor walked straight in, keeping a grip on Fluffy's lead in case he slipped over the edge and into the ravine. His old fear of heights was back with a vengeance and he kept well away from the edge. The footpath had become a favourite shortcut from the village to the beach below but at this time of the evening it seemed narrow, poorly lit and secluded. The only evening walkers were likely to be lovers, looking for a bit of privacy. Feeling a little nervous, Victor wandered along until he came to a bench and a good view of the waterfall. He sat down, keeping Fluffy close in case he should go exploring too near the edge and fall into the rushing water. He imagined himself diving in to rescue the dog, a brave effort as he could barely swim. *Local Hero Saves Pet from Certain Death!*

A boy and girl walking hand-in-hand passed him. They were whispering and the girl giggled as they went by. He wondered if they were talking about him but then decided that he was being paranoid. Sitting back, he listened to the breathless tumble of the water. As he surveyed the lush foliage clinging to the sides of the chasm, the poet in him was stirred. This torrent started somewhere in the Downs, gaining momentum until it plummeted over the waterfall and raced to its extinction, mingling with the restless water of the sea below.

As he was trying to compose a verse, he became aware of a man creeping along, clinging to the shadows. He was big, shuffling, and he carried what looked like a sack. Victor sat very still, his heart beginning to thud. The evening gloom hid his presence. Fluffy was on his lap and he held him tight.

Looking around in what could only be described as a shifty manner, the big man appeared to be about to throw the sack into the water. Something flashed in Victor's mind, some memory of stories about people drowning kittens in this way.

'Excuse me!' he called out and the man jerked back, dropping the sack on the ground.

'Whaddayouwant?' He turned towards Victor and he was huge. Fluffy began to bark.

Seeing Victor's modest size the man bent to pick up the sack again, clearly intent on throwing it in the water. Victor ran towards him. He could see that the sack was moving and his compassion took precedence over his fear. 'If those are kittens, please don't drown them!'

The man turned and swung the sack like a weapon and Victor ducked, nearly missing his footing. At the same moment, Fluffy went into action. Yapping loudly, he flung himself at the man and bit him sharply on his rather grubby exposed ankle. The man gave a yell. As Victor staggered dangerously near to the edge he reached out to save himself, accidentally pushing the man. On the very edge of the ravine, he wobbled like a silent film comedian and, throwing his arms up in the air, tipped over backwards, down into the water.

Victor gazed into the maelstrom. There had been quite a bit of rain recently and the stream was a veritable torrent. Amid the froth, he caught a glimpse of the man drifting smartly over the edge of a weir. The water would be quieter there and no doubt he would be able to climb out easily. Victor imagined him dragging himself out, dripping wet and enraged. He wasn't going to hang around. Stopping only to pick up the sack, he grabbed Fluffy's lead and hastened back along the footpath. Someone hurrying in the opposite direction bumped right into him, nearly kicking Fluffy in the process. In spite of his anxiety, Victor glared at him and picked Fluffy up. Some people had no manners!

He continued to walk quickly, glancing over his shoulder constantly in case he was being followed, but there was no one in sight. He didn't slow down until he reached home and was safely indoors.

Panting heavily, he put the sack on the table and carefully opened it. Inside were two small kittens, one black and white and the other tabby. In spite of their rough treatment they appeared unhurt. Faced with daylight, they let out a pitiful mewling noise and tenderly Victor lifted them out, smoothing their fur and reassuring them that now they were safe. For want of anything else to do he warmed some milk in a saucepan and filled a saucer, placing it on the ground with the kittens. Fluffy watched with interest.

To his delight they both began to lap. Clearly they were weaned. He felt a moment of anger that anyone could do anything so cruel as to drown them. 'Never you mind,' he said to the pair, 'you are both safe now.' What he was going to do with them, he had no idea.

—

Victor spent the night listening for a break-in. At any moment he was certain that the kitten killer would find him, smash a window and then 'assault' him before taking the kittens away to certain death. He allowed Fluffy to sleep on the bed as a guard dog while the kittens were wrapped in a towel, which in turn was wrapped around a hot water bottle.

When morning came, Victor felt exhausted. To Fluffy's disgust, they did not go for a walk after breakfast. Instead he was allowed briefly into the garden while Victor kept a sharp eye on the gate.

When nothing happened, Victor eventually risked a short stroll as far as the corner shop. The *Clarion* was piled high just inside the door and the headline nearly caused Victor to miss his footing. '*Second Wanted Man Dies in Neighbourhood. Police Suspect Gangland Killing.*' Victor took a copy to the counter along with some more pouches of Doggybics for Fluffy and some tiny tins of special kitten food. Having paid, he hurried home to peruse the paper.

With a dry mouth he read how a second well-known gangster had died last night, mysteriously drowned in Shanklin

Chine. No one had witnessed the accident, although a young couple passing along the path by the weir remembered seeing a sinister man with a small white dog. The victim had been immediately identified as Bernard 'Mauler' Maguire, who was wanted in connection with several gangland killings.

Surely, *surely*, this must be a huge coincidence and the man who had drowned was not the same man who had accidentally fallen into the water? Really, in spite of its speed, the water was not that deep. Victor was sure that he had had nothing to do with it. Although he had lost his balance and pushed against the man, he was so huge that Victor's weight alone could not have unbalanced him. He wondered if perhaps he had hit his head and passed out. He should have dived in to save him. *Passer By Rescues Man from Drowning!*

His first thought was that he must go immediately to the police, but what would they say when they learned that he had walked away from a crime scene – only he hadn't realised at the time that it was a crime scene. Various scenarios played themselves out. Supposing someone had seen him near the weir? Following so closely on from the other accident with the tree, the police might well be suspicious, even arrest him? He sat down quickly. At the thought of going to prison, his nerve failed and he reached out to smooth Fluffy's curly fringe. Looking at the dog, a worst case scenario occurred to him. If he were arrested then what would happen to the little dog? He would be taken back to the RSPCA and when no one else came to claim him he would be put to sleep. He could never let this happen. There was nothing for it but to lie low and hope for the best.

The kittens, meanwhile, were tucking into a saucer of Kittychunks. Victor had found a seed tray in the greenhouse and filled it with dirt. With trembling hand, he carried the kittens to the soil and after they had eaten they dutifully performed. He praised them, assuring them that they were such dear little things. Here too was another reason not to be arrested. He had no idea whether they were male or female so he chose names that wouldn't make any difference, Tabby and Puss.

The rest of the day passed in fretful anxiety. He heard more about the weir incident on the local news. It seemed that Mauler showed no signs of having suffered any violence other than some puncture wounds on his ankle that might be marks from a hypodermic syringe. The police were pursuing their inquiries. The journalist, clearly enjoying himself, wondered about the mention of a white dog in the neighbourhood and hypothesised that the Angel of Death might be in business again.

The next morning, there was another brown envelope in the post identical to the one before. Feeling alarmed, Victor opened it to find a cheque inside again made out to V Green. It was drawn on the National Bank of Jersey. It was for £25,000. This was just silly. He unfolded the paper and read: *Next time, use a gun.*

The news of Mauler's demise reached Barry at The Earthly Delights. He read the *Clarion*'s report several times and the void in his chest felt increasingly huge. Mauler was one of their gang and he had no idea what to think. From the account it looked as if it might have been an accident, but the mention of the small white dog was worrying. Besides, what on earth would Mauler have been doing in the Chine?

The last time Barry had seen him he had been mumbling something about drowning some kittens, so perhaps he had gone to the ravine and fallen in? On the other hand, he could just as well have drowned them in a bucket. Barry shuddered. He didn't like killing things. In fact, he went to great lengths not to do so, always opening windows for trapped insects and setting humane traps for mice. When he caught any he sent the chauffeur off to drive them into the countryside and let them go.

Try as he might, he couldn't quite get rid of the feeling that Mauler's death on top of Gruesome's was too much of a coincidence. Assuming that before his brother Harry went to Spain he had indeed arranged for Vincenzo Verdi to take out Gruesome, had the Blues Brothers taken their revenge and hired someone to take out Mauler? Worse, if they had, then it must now be up to him to set in motion some sort of revenge, but what and how?

Meanwhile, the takings from the Bird of Paradise refused to add up. When Barry challenged the manager he threatened him either with his resignation or violence – 'take your pick.' Barry couldn't afford for him to leave and, as the bloke was built like a Centurion tank, he managed to calm him down, taking the figures back to his office to check them again. With luck the mistake would turn out to be his, so he wouldn't have to sort out this particular problem.

He hadn't heard from Harry or Gary since they left for Spain so he had no idea when they were coming back. Whenever it was, he needed to present them with a smooth-running outfit, not one with resignations and revenge killings. Sitting at his desk and twiddling nervously with his pen, he thought: whatever happens, I'll have to do something soon.

EIGHT

Constable Alan Grimes was plagued by heartburn. In the past he had noticed that it was always worse when he was worried, and just at the moment it looked as if trouble was brewing in the neighbourhood, or as Charity had put it, 'Looks like there's a turf war on your manor.' She really did read too many detective novels.

The death of Mauler Maguire had aroused the interest of the national press. Being a henchman for the notorious Island gang known as the Pretty Boys, Mauler had a long record of violence and mayhem. His death, so close after that of Gruesome Hewson, a heavy regularly employed by another local gang known as the Blues Brothers, suggested that Charity might be right and that professional hitmen had been brought in to dispose of the gangs' artillery. If this was the case though, their methods were bizarre in the extreme. In any case, Alan knew for certain that Gruesome's death had been an accident and anyone less like an assassin than Victor Green was difficult to imagine.

By sheer coincidence, it seemed that Mauler had also met with an accident. Normally Alan did not believe in coincidences. He toyed with the possibility that one or other of the gangs was planning to take over the other's outfit – but if they were, they were using some very inventive methods. He was also disturbed by the tiny detail that a small white dog had been present at the scene.

It was quiet at work and Alan, on desk duty, consulted the files, looking first for anyone who had a connection with the Blues Brothers. The list was a long one.

The brothers themselves were born to a Spaniard, Alfonso Rodriguez, and raised in Balham. Their mother Josie came from a well-known gang called the Enforcers and her marriage to Alfonso had been seen as an alliance, a deliberate step to strengthen gangland loyalties. Her boys, twins Reggie and Randy, were now in their thirties whilst the youngest, Roger, known as Dodge, had appeared on the scene some ten years later. They were what Alan always thought of as a collective nasty piece of work. Only Dodge had avoided prison and this was largely because he was too soft to be of much use as a gang member.

Looking up their present whereabouts, Alan discovered that both Reggie and Randy were doing time – one in Parkhurst and the other in Camp Hill because, being identical twins, there was a good chance that they would pull some identity swap scam. Among their known associates had been Gruesome Hewson.

Alan sat back to think of the implications. With Reggie and Randy both behind bars, perhaps someone had decided this was a good time to take over their operations. He checked to see if there had been any rumours of a new gang moving into the neighbourhood but found nothing.

Among their other known associates were Fingers Kilbride, so-named because he had lost two digits in an accident with some gelignite, and Nicos the Greek, who had a good line in drug smuggling. It struck Alan that here, in this beautiful paradise of the Island, was a veritable United Nations of rogues.

He thought again for a few moments about Victor. He was such a worrier, one of those little nervous men who wouldn't say boo to a goose. Not very prepossessing, young Victor – a nice lad, though. If more were like him there would be less crime in the world.

Victor had checked the telephone directory and Yellow Pages but there didn't seem to be any branch of the Banque Prive Suisse or the National Bank of Jersey in the area. That meant that the nearest place was probably London. He toyed with the idea of ringing Directory Enquiries but they would only give him telephone numbers. What he needed were addresses so that he could return the cheques by post with a note of explanation. Perhaps he should treat himself to a little holiday and actually go to Jersey and Switzerland? The idea perked him up and for a while he imagined the rugged coast of Jersey where people spoke French, and the Swiss mountains with chalets and cowbells tinkling in the wind and the people yodelling to each other from valley to valley. Then he realised that now he had Fluffy, he couldn't just up sticks and go. Perhaps in the future he could put him into kennels for a few days, but certainly not yet when he was so unsettled. Another time he might be able to ask that Charity if she would take Fluffy in for a week, or even come to stay while he was away. The thought of her in his cottage, perhaps sleeping in his bed, was too disturbing and he carefully stored the second cheque along with the first one. *Use a gun next time.* Whatever did that mean?

—◆—

Charity was bored. Vacuuming the house, putting things in the washing machine, planning a nice vegetarian meal for herself and her father nowhere near filled her time. Until she found a job she needed a hobby, something to exercise her mind. The death of Gruesome Hewson and the discovery of Mauler Maguire were just the sort of mysteries that inspired her. It wasn't that she had no faith in the local constabulary. On the contrary, she knew from her father that they were busy with a campaign to catch speeding motorists and another one to tackle litter louts. While they were thus engaged, she would see if she could discover anything that might help them with their enquiries.

As soon as she had finished her chores, she set off for Shanklin Chine to see if she could find any evidence the police might have overlooked. Walking along the footpath she felt a frisson of anxiety. This was the sort of place where people could easily lie in wait for innocent targets, tumbling them into the rush of the water. She fought down her anxiety and stood on tiptoe to see as far down as she could, but it was dark down by the water and there was nothing she could identify. For all she knew, another body might lurk down there. She stopped to listen in case someone might be calling out, but all she could hear was the peremptory command of a blackbird and the swirling hiss of the water. Walking on, she passed a place where a bench rested in the lea of some trees. Two young people sat on it, holding hands. They watched her progress until she had rounded the bend where the water emptied into the stream below. Here she was confronted with blue police tape, roping off the area. This was the point at which Mauler had been dragged from the water and given the kiss of life – to no avail – by a young constable who would rather not have done so. Apart from scrape marks on the bank there was nothing of interest, so Charity walked back the way she had come.

The young couple had gone, and opposite the seat she noticed footprints and stopped to examine them. It looked as if someone had been stamping around; then at the edge of the bank there were scour marks, as if somebody might have dug his feet into the ground to keep his balance. Could it have been here that Mauler stumbled into the water? She remembered that the newspaper had mentioned puncture wounds to his ankle. Perhaps he had been injected with anaesthetic so that he couldn't fight back. The mud at the edge of the bank bore other indentations – human shoes and what looked like a tiny dog's paw, or possibly a fox.

Pleased with her discovery she went across and sat on the bench, staring at the chasm and hoping for inspiration. The bench was quite rough and a close examination revealed a variety of threads caught in the wood from various garments. The trouble was, hundreds of people might have rested here. There was nothing to suggest that Mauler's murderer had been one of them, other than the report by the young couple that they had seen a sinister man with a white dog. To her mind, sinister men were tall and skeletal, clothed in raincoats and hats with brims showing only their wild, deranged eyes. She glanced over her shoulder in case anyone of similar appearance was creeping up on her. Rubbing her hand along the bench, she found some fine white strands of what could be fur. She placed it in her palm and it curled gently around. Perhaps this was a clue? The paper had mentioned a white dog. The couple mentioned in the paper had seen a sinister man with a dog. Could this possibly have come from the Angel of Death? Wrapping it in a tissue and slipping it into her handbag, she quickly stood up and hastened for the safety of the village. Whether she had discovered anything worthwhile she had no idea. Perhaps this detection lark wasn't as easy as she had at first imagined.

━

At the station, Alan had come across an interesting connection. The night before, one of the local old lags, Bertie Rhodes, had been brought in for vagrancy. It was really a humanitarian act on the part of the constable on the beat, because it had been an unseasonably cold night and Bertie was found huddled in a doorway looking rather the worse for wear. He wouldn't be charged. After a night in the cells and a cooked breakfast from the station canteen, he would be released with a caution – until next time.

Alan had had many dealings with Bertie over the years. To his knowledge, the worst that he had ever done was to nick a packet of fags from the corner shop. He felt sorry for the poor old boy. His release was usually accompanied by a handout of a fiver to get himself something to eat later in the day, and an encouragement to book a bed at the local hostel.

It was Alan who took Bertie what he thought of as breakfast in bed. The old man was curled up in his blanket, blissfully snoring.

'Wakey wakey.' He made a business of unlocking the cell door and took a deep breath of comparatively clean air before entering the foetid enclosure inhabited by the old man. Bertie grunted and grumbled and managed to sit up. He was not a pretty sight. A bath, a haircut and a change of clothes would go a long way to improving his appearance, not to mention his smell.

'Here we are, Bertie. Get this down you and then you can go – after we've had a little chat.'

The little chat followed familiar lines, don't sleep in the precinct, don't beg, don't nick anything and get yourself booked into St Rhadegund's.

Bertie nodded as if taking all the advice on board. As he creaked to his feet, he said, 'Guess who I saw last night, Mr Grimes.'

'I don't know, Bertie, who did you see?'

The old man hesitated. A longstanding nark, he wasn't in the habit of giving information without some monetary reward.

'Tell me who you saw and I might – I just *might* – find a few coins in my pocket.'

'Probably worth a tenner at least, Mr Grimes.'

'Well, I'll be the judge of that.'

Bertie whetted his lips and leaned forward confidentially. 'I was outside the bookies yesterday, just passing the time of day, and who should I see but,' at this point he leaned forward, giving Alan the full benefit of his perfume, 'Barry Hickman.'

'Who?'

'Barry Hickman. You know who I mean, Barry, Harry and Gary – sons of Larry Hickman?'

'You mean the Pretty Boys?'

'The very same.'

'What would Barry Hickman be doing?'

'That I don't know Mr Grimes, but it might well be worth your while to find out.'

▼

Alan stayed late at the station searching the files again for anything he could find about the Hickman brothers, aka the Pretty Boys.

Lawrence Hickman had been born along the coast into a respectable family but he was the traditional bad apple in the barrel and having left school barely able to read and write, he had miraculously discovered a talent for wheeling and dealing, launching himself into the petty underworld. Raised in this hothouse, his three sons, Harold, Garfield and Barton, alias Harry, Gary and Barry, had blossomed into a full-scale gang, providing dubious protection to south coast enterprises and importing an illegal, abused and unprotected workforce. Old man Hickman had retired to Spain, leaving Harry and Gary to run the show. Barry, the youngest, was generally thought to be missing a bit upstairs but he was a whiz kid with figures, useful if money laundering was part of your job description.

As he flicked through the dossiers, Alan noticed the name of Vincenzo Verdi. Now here was an interesting thought. There was some question as to whether or not Vincenzo Verdi actually existed. Some claimed that his name was a cover for an as yet unidentified hitman who, over the years, had taken out a whole range of people from bankers to East European spies to unfortunate witnesses who happened to have seen something and might be able to identify known criminals. He wasn't averse to knocking off fellow crims either, if the situation demanded it. As far as Alan knew, no one had ever actually seen him.

He ran the name over his tongue and it had a poetic rhythm – Vincenzo Verdi. Alan had been on holiday to Tuscany the summer before and had dutifully attended language classes beforehand. As a result, he knew that the Italian word for green was *verdi*. In the report on Gruesome's death there had been some mention of Vincent Green, the *Clarion* having misprinted the first name in mistake for Victor – could there just be some connection? If there was, he had no idea what it might be.

With little hope of finding anything, he looked in the telephone directory under Verdi but – as expected – found nothing. He consulted the electoral register just in case, but no one of that name was listed.

It was getting really late but before he left, Alan drew up a list of all the men he had identified.

The Blues Brothers	The Pretty Boys
Alfonso Rodriguez (62) (Spain)	Lawrence 'Larry' Hickman (72) (Spain)
Reginald 'Reggie' Rodriguez (34) (Parkhurst)	Harold 'Harry' Hickman (41) (Where?)
Randolph 'Randy' Rodriguez (34) (Camp Hill)	Garfield 'Gary' Hickman (37) (Where?)
Roger 'Dodge' Rodriguez (18) (London?)	Barton 'Barry' Hickman (21) (Nearby?)
Known Associates	
Tommy 'Gruesome' Hewson (42) (Dead)	Bernard 'Mauler' Maguire (51) (Dead)
Joe 'Groping' Windsor (58) (Where?)	Angus 'Fingers' Kilbride (48) (Where?)
Leon 'Frenchie' leFevre (38)	Rupert 'Gentleman' Craven (37)
Suspected Hitman	
Vincenzo Verdi (aka Vincent Green) (Where?)	

Alan studied his list. Was there some significance in the fact that both Papa Rodriguez and Larry Hickman had retired to Spain? Did they have any contact? When were the Rodriguez boys due to be released from gaol? What were the Hickman boys mainly engaged in these days? And Vincenzo, also known as Vincent, where was he now and what was he doing? He had as many questions as you like, but very few answers.

Pushing the papers into his desk drawer, he set off for home and another of Charity's curious culinary concoctions.

NINE

Her father was late so Charity had plenty of time to mull over the mystery of the two accidental deaths. As far as she could see there was no obvious link between Hewson and Maguire, other than that both men had been known criminals. The other thing that just might be significant was that on both occasions a white dog had been present at the scene of their deaths.

Charity felt understandably unnerved at the thought of a dog called the Angel of Death. As far as she could make out, it was a miniature poodle – and Victor had a miniature poodle. Miniature poodles were not exactly synonymous with acts of violence but even so… She must ascertain exactly how long Victor had had Fluffy and where the dog had really come from. She must also establish whether Victor might have been the sinister man lurking in the vicinity of Mauler Maguire's drowning.

When Alan arrived home he seemed distracted.

'Long day,' she observed. 'A lot going on at the nick?'

'Yes and no. I've been on the desk but there were some facts I wanted to verify.'

Charity wondered whether to tell him about her trip to the Chine and the discovery of some strange marks and the white dog hairs, but decided to keep it to herself for the moment. Wouldn't it be great if she could solve the mystery of Mauler's drowning, discover a crime that the police had so far failed even to identify.

Meanwhile, still distracted, Alan packed back a second helping of lentil and pesto risotto without apparently even noticing.

The next morning, Alan found himself unexpectedly attending a post-mortem. It hardly ever fell to him to do so, largely because he was not technically a part of CID. Today, however, the actual detectives were otherwise engaged and he was told to report to the mortuary.

The victim turned out to be Mauler Maguire and the station had thought that, in view of his criminal tendencies, it might be wise for one of their number to be present in case of any later repercussions.

Alan was not very good with dead bodies. The living he could cope with pretty well, but the particular tainted smell and the waxy deadness of a cadaver invariably made him feel ill.

The pathologist was a pretty girl who looked as if she should still be in school. Alan thought that it was wrong that a woman should want to do such a job. He tried to imagine how he would feel if Charity had decided to go into forensics. As it was, he had been quite disappointed when she had settled for a job in retail, even in a managerial role. She was a bright girl, was Charity. She had been to university and studied economics. What was she doing working in a High Street chain?

Now that she had come home, he nursed the fragile hope that he might be able to persuade her to find something more rewarding – if he could persuade her to do anything at all. She seemed to have got it into her head that he needed looking after and, without wishing to hurt her feelings, he had yet to find a way of telling her that he quite enjoyed being on his own.

Alan's marriage to Margaret had been happy enough. They had met when she came as a clerical assistant to the station, not a police role but a civilian one. He had liked her quiet manner, the way she smiled. He had asked her out, began to date her and then they had quietly agreed to get married. It wasn't a great romance, none of the nonsense talked about in films and novels, but it had been nice and comfortable and they had been blessed with their two daughters.

He wondered how the girls had turned out to be so alike and yet so unlike either of their parents. Both were assertive, opinionated and, to be honest, bossy.

It had been something of a relief when they finally left home and he and Margaret were left to muddle along together.

Margaret had plenty to keep her busy. She helped in the hospice shop, she knitted and sewed garments for her grandchildren, she read an inordinate number of books, went to the WI and helped on their stall at fêtes. In their own quiet way they had been happy, until Margaret had made the fateful trip to London and fallen on the escalator. He still didn't understand exactly what had happened later on, but a weak artery or something had suddenly ruptured and within minutes Margaret, apparently on the road to recovery, had died.

All these thoughts occupied Alan so that he didn't have to concentrate on Mauler's body, now sliced from throat to groin, the contents taken out one by one – like delving into a dressing up box – and stored in what reminded him of Margaret's Tupperware collection.

The pathologist, Eunice, broadcast a low-voiced commentary. Mauler's lungs showed signs of water inhalation and it was this that had killed him. In other words, he had drowned. His liver and kidneys were in a sorry state, he had varicose veins, his skin was plagued with psoriasis, he had suffered various broken bones over a number of years, and shortly before his death he appeared to have been bitten on the ankle by a small dog. Eunice carefully measured the space between the puncture marks, the depth of the wounds, and recorded it all as evidence.

Alan forced himself to listen. There were no signs of violence other than the bitten ankle. Was it not just an accident? Could the bite have caused Mauler to lose his balance and plunge into the weir? He was pretty certain that the coroner was going to introduce an open verdict.

He forced himself to look at Mauler's face before his skull was sawed open and his brain extracted. Even in death he looked pugnacious, aggressive. It was hard to imagine that he ever had a mother, might even have had a girlfriend. Now, he was going to carry any secrets he had to the grave.

While Alan was in the mortuary, Charity decided to extend her field of enquiries. It was a fresh, bright morning and she guessed that Victor would be taking Fluffy for a constitutional so, using the local Co-op as an excuse, she set out to parade in its vicinity until she spotted them.

Victor came along the road dressed in lightweight flannel trousers and a green cardigan. Fluffy's red lead clashed with the orange shopping basket that Victor carried. She noticed that on his feet he had open-toed sandals with black socks and at his neck, a blue-green cravat. This, she assumed, was Victor's idea of casual wear for the summer. She was training herself to notice details. In fact, as she took up a position a yard or so behind Victor, she recited to herself a minute description, just in case she was called upon to give evidence.

'Five feet four or five, about 120 pounds (she usually worked in stones but they used pounds in American detective novels), mousy brown hair worn a little long and parted on the side (left). Light brown eyes, rather myopic (she had noticed that he wore brown-framed glasses for reading). Slim build (very slim). A habit of licking his lips before he spoke. Slightly sticky-out ears.' She recorded that he carried his shopping bag looped over his left arm – might this mean that he was left handed? – this was something she would need to identify.

At this point, Fluffy stopped suddenly for one of his routine sniffs and, nearly bumping into the back of her quarry, Charity made herself known.

'Hello, going for a walk?'

Victor turned round, went pink and began to stutter. 'J-j-just a tr-tr-ip to the sh-shops.'

Charity tried to put him at his ease by saying, 'I like to come to the Co-op. I like their ethical trading. It's the same with M&S – where I used to work – humanity isn't sacrificed for the sake of profit.'

Victor looked a little surprised but he said, 'I l-like the Co-op washing-up liquid.'

They had reached the shop and Victor went to tie Fluffy up to one of the rings thoughtfully set into the wall. Fluffy, realising that he was about to be abandoned, set up a castrati-like whimpering that was almost off the scale.

'Would you like me to stay with him,' Charity offered, 'so that you can look around?'

'That's very kind. I – I hadn't realised that having a dog could be such a tie.'

'You haven't had him long then?'

'No, just this week.'

Aha, that was one piece of information cleverly extracted.

Charity untied Fluffy and picked him up and, pacified, he watched his new master go through the door of the Co-op. In an inspired moment, Charity tugged a small clump of wool from Fluffy's coat and carefully secreted it in her pocket in case she ever needed to compare it with the dog's hair from the bench.

Victor eventually emerged with his bag full of shopping. 'Th-that's very kind of you. I-I'll be going home now. Th-thanks very much for looking after him.'

Charity saw her chance for further investigation slipping away so she said, 'I'm going your way. I'll walk back with you, that is if you don't mind?'

'No, of course not.' She thought she detected a hint of pleasure around the eyes.

On the way back, Charity kept up a stream of conversation. She was wondering how to ask more significant questions but nothing useful came to her then, as they turned into Victor's road, she said, 'Well, this is a thirsty morning. I could really do with a cup of tea.'

For a moment she thought that Victor wasn't going to take the bait but as they slowed down at his gate, he blurted out, 'Would you like to c-come in for a c-cup of tea?'

'That would be lovely.'

Victor took down his mother's best china cups and saucers, and the floral china teapot instead of the brown one he normally used. There was a matching milk jug, a tiny sugar bowl, and he remembered to put out the slop basin and strainer, for he always used leaf tea instead of the teabags his mother had been so much against. There were a few Rich Tea biscuits in the tin and he found a pretty rosebud plate and a doily from the linen drawer.

Once it was all laid out he warmed the pot, spooned in the requisite amount of tea leaves and waited the appropriate time for the tea to brew.

Charity watched the proceedings with fascination. The only place she had witnessed something similar was in an old-fashioned teashop that her mother had occasionally taken her and Pru to when they went on shopping expeditions into town. She had rather liked the way the waitresses wore black dresses with little lace pinnies, and the tables had embroidered cloths.

Once Victor had poured out their tea, she began to think of ways to extract any useful information.

'Are you enjoying your holiday?' she asked.

'Oh yes, it's so nice not to go to work.'

'You work at the tax office?' She had picked this up either from her father or from the newspaper – she must be more careful and remember the sources of her information.

Finding her so easy to talk to, Victor admitted that he would really like to give up work and stay at home with Fluffy.

'What would you like to do?' she asked.

He thought for a while. 'It would be very nice to go abroad, to Italy perhaps.'

'Have you been abroad before?'

He shook his head, a little embarrassed by his lack of adventure.

'Do you go out much here – in the evenings for example?'

'Not very often – at least, now I have a dog I take him for a walk most evenings while the weather is nice.'

'Where do you take him?'

'Oh, just round about.'

This wasn't getting Charity anywhere so she said, 'I expect you've been to Shanklin Chine?'

To her delight, Victor definitely looked rattled. Quickly she added, 'I like walking along the path there, down towards the shore. I like the sound of rushing water, don't you?'

He nodded, still looking troubled.

'Have you taken Fluffy there at all?' she pressed on. 'Only if you have, I do urge you to keep him on the lead. If he fell into that water...'

'Oh, I do – I will.' Victor seemed grateful for her advice.

So he *had* been there. She was tempted to mention the drowning but she didn't want to arouse Victor's suspicion. Instead she asked, 'How did you come to get a dog then?'

'Well,' clearly pleased to talk about it, Victor told her all about the accident when he had landed on Mr Smith – 'only his name wasn't Smith. He seems to have been some sort of criminal.' He shook his head at the way things had turned out. 'Fancy that, and him being in our road.'

Charity nodded and listened to the saga of Victor going to the RSPCA and being concerned for the orphaned Fluffy's welfare.

'It was the least I could do,' he said. 'Besides, I have always dreamed of owning a dog.' He looked suddenly wistful.

It was at that moment that Charity noticed a movement in the corner, and from a blanket neatly folded against the skirting board, a small kitten suddenly woke up, stretched and came across to investigate. Seconds later a second one joined it.

'Oh my goodness, you've got some cats too. Did you get them from the RSPCA?'

'No. There was a terrible man, he was going to drown them. I – I said I'd take them home.' He faltered as if perhaps he had said too much but Charity was already on her knees cuddling the kittens to her.

'Aren't they adorable?'

For a while she played with them, then she finished her tea and announced that she must be going.

Victor saw her to the door. Just as she was going through the gate he heard himself ask, 'I say, I don't suppose you would l-l-like to c-come to the cinema?'

Caught by surprise, Charity in turn heard herself say, 'That would be very nice.'

TEN

Victor searched the local paper to see what was on at the Regal. They were having a Marlon Brando week and there was a film on called *Last Tango in Paris*. This sounded perfect. Victor liked musicals, especially the sort he had once watched with his mother where hordes of girls in slinky dresses and feathers high-kicked in unison on elegant stairways. He had always fancied himself as a bit of a Fred Astaire, largely because Fred was a slight, slim man who clearly appealed to the ladies, particularly as he could dance. In private, Victor had practised his turns and toe-tapping until he thought that if he were ever called upon to perform he would give a pretty good account of himself.

He had arranged to meet Charity outside the Regal at six o'clock. During the afternoon he took Fluffy for quite a long walk so that the little dog would be tired and not mind spending the evening alone. He wasn't sure what he should wear. Walking back along the High Street, a tired poodle in tow, he took time to study the clothes displayed in the shop windows. The male models were attired in the sort of trousers that looked as if they were meant to be worn on safari, with short-sleeved shirts in interesting shades of sand. In a mad moment he tied a protesting Fluffy outside, popped into *He World* and browsed. He was on holiday after all; he wasn't going away somewhere expensive and therefore he could afford to indulge himself in something new. For a moment, he remembered the £45,000 worth of cheques filed away in his desk. Supposing somebody broke in and stole them? He really should put them somewhere safe and the safest place was clearly the bank. Having decided that, he then took time to select a new pair of trousers and a shirt.

The shop sold rather rakish caps too, with peaks designed to keep the Saharan sun out of your eyes. There wasn't much sun about at the moment but, having tried one on, Victor thought that the style really quite suited him, and rather self-consciously he placed it on the counter with his *Safari Sun* chinos and *Cairo Nights* shirt. Having paid for them, he went home to prepare for the night out.

Charity prepared a tofu salad for her father, popped it in the fridge and left a note on the kitchen table telling him that she had gone out for the evening.

What to wear was a bit of a challenge. At work she had always worn a uniform, a rather smart suit with the company logo emblazoned across her left breast. She was also quite addicted to jeans but she felt that tonight called for something a little more feminine. She had a skirt in what had been advertised as electric blue, but having bought it she had always found it difficult to find a top to match it. The same thing still applied, and she spent ages standing in front of the mirror gripping the skirt with one hand and a series of blouses and T-shirts with the other. In the end she settled for a rather staid long-sleeved blouse in a blue sufficiently different to contrast rather than clash. At a quarter to six she left the house and walked to the cinema.

Victor and Charity were both silent as they descended the steps of the Regal at the end of the performance. Outside it was dusk and people wandered aimlessly around the town. A queue was already forming for the next performance of *Last Tango in Paris*. Neither Charity nor Victor looked directly at them, or at each other.

Victor had never felt so embarrassed in his life. He had been expecting some singing, an orchestra and a love story. Instead… He wondered what Charity must be thinking of him, taking her to something like that. He would never be able to spread butter on his bread again without remembering the humiliation.

Charity was quietly smiling to herself. She could hardly imagine people meeting anonymously in their village, hiring flats and having sex orgies. In Paris it must be different, so suave and sophisticated. She fancied Marlon Brando like mad. In fact, the film had really quite stirred her up. Victor of course bore very little resemblance to the star of the film, but...

Victor thought that he should walk Charity home. He struggled desperately for something to say, some safe observation that would bypass the film. Meanwhile, the silence was growing intolerable. The way to Charity's house meant actually passing his own front door and, as they drew level, Charity spoke for the first time.

'How about inviting me in for a cup of coffee?'

Victor hesitated. This would mean extending the already unbearable silence but he couldn't see what else to do. Hopefully Fluffy and the kittens would divert their attention, give them something different to focus on.

Inside, the animals came to meet them. While Charity took off her jacket and flung it across the arm of a chair, Victor went to the kitchen to prepare the coffee. He only had a jar of instant and he wondered if she was expecting one of those percolators that had recently appeared in a series of television adverts where a young couple were always popping into each other's flats to borrow sugar or something. The idea of popping into flats brought him back to the film and he felt extremely hot.

As he was pouring boiling water into a jug to which he had already added several spoonfuls of coffee, Charity poked her head around the door.

'I don't suppose you have anything stronger, do you?'

For a second he thought that perhaps she had been watching him and that he hadn't added enough coffee but then, following her eyes, he saw that she was looking at his bottle of wine on the work surface. He had fortified himself with a glass before leaving for the cinema, and it was just as well that he had.

'Of c-c-course.' At last he managed to make a sound and fetched two wine glasses.

As they sat in the lounge with Fluffy squeezing onto the sofa and Tabby and Puss playing around their feet, Victor thought what a splendid girl Charity was. He had taken her to a terrible film, subjected her to the most embarrassing experience, and yet she was behaving as if nothing had happened. Taking courage, he looked directly at her.

Charity was leaning forward, teasing the kittens with the handle of her bag. Together they stalked it, pouncing and then retreating, falling over each other in their excitement. Her neatly cropped brown hair looked smooth and glossy and, as she bent forward, he got the merest glimpse inside her blouse. She wore a very white cotton bra with lace around the top. Victor's face burned with heat.

He didn't look away quite fast enough and Charity, sitting up, met his eye. For a moment she simply stared at him then, taking a sip from her glass and placing it on the table, she said, 'Well?'

'I—,' Victor's hands were shaking. He dared not pick up his own glass for fear of spilling the contents all over the place.

'Shall we?' Charity stood up and to his amazement she began to undo her blouse. 'Come on,' she encouraged, 'that is unless you don't want to?' As an afterthought she asked, 'You aren't gay are you?'

He shook his head, transfixed by the sight of her slipping off her blouse and beginning to unfasten her skirt. Like an elephant who has seen a mouse, he quickly drew his legs up onto the sofa, dislodging Fluffy, who gave a yap of protest. Taking this as an invitation to join him, Charity sank onto the sofa and began to struggle with the waistband of his *Safari Sun* chinos.

'I say!'

Charity seemed to be deaf. She was certainly a single-minded girl and at the moment her objective was to get Victor out of his trousers.

'Come on then,' she turned her back to him, inviting him to unfasten her bra. In the face of her calm authority, he began to fiddle with the catch, unsure as to how such contraptions worked. Meanwhile, something amazing was happening inside his trousers. Charity's neat little fingers had invited themselves in and were doing unthinkable things to his private parts.

Overcome by nature, Victor followed Charity's gentle slide onto the carpet and buried the biggest, strongest erection he had ever had into the appropriate part of Charity's anatomy. She held him so tight that he could barely breathe, shouting words of encouragement as he rose to the occasion. Victor in turn issued a series of squeaks, although he wasn't entirely sure which came from him and which from Fluffy, who was leaping around excitedly, entering into the fun.

Afterwards, Victor lay on top of Charity in a trance. Nothing even approaching this had happened to him in his entire lifetime. He had imagined it often enough, politely climbing into bed with his fantasy girl Elizabeth, but this – this was out of this world. He began to wonder how well he had performed and if Charity might be disappointed. He had a sudden, rather disturbing image of her as his schoolmistress, standing over him with a cane, saying, 'Victor, that just isn't good enough. You are going to have to stay behind and do it again until you get it right.' The very prospect roused his newly assaulted manhood into another life of its own.

Charity felt better. Victor wasn't the first lover she had had and certainly not the best. That accolade definitely went to Mr Burton who had taught her geography – and a lot more besides. Still, Victor was OK. He was biddable and obliging and for the moment that was enough. It was only as she was easing him off her and looking for her knickers that she remembered he was a suspect in her enquiries into a possible murder case.

ELEVEN

Dodge sat at the head of the table in the Blues Brothers' office. It was located in a department store they ran in Shanklin High Street called Something for Everyone. Local people referred to it just as Something. *I'm just popping down to Something to get a new kettle* – you name it, Something sold it. Apart from anything else, the store was a very convenient front for all their other enterprises.

Although the office was only small, Dodge felt dwarfed and out of his depth. His planned meeting with Vincenzo Verdi at Shanklin Chine had failed and he was now at a loss as to what to do next. He couldn't remember actually having asked Vincenzo to take out Mauler Maguire but he must have done so, for Vincenzo had acted very promptly – although how he knew that Mauler would be at the Chine was another mystery. Anyway, he had dutifully sent him a cheque for a job well done. Now he wondered what might happen next.

It struck him that this whole turf war thing was ridiculous. Both gangs had operations all over the Island so surely there was plenty to go round for everyone? Why couldn't they just settle it without all this killing? It was then that he had another idea. It was so novel that he had to go over it several times in his head to make sure that he wasn't going completely mad. The sensible thing to do was to arrange a meeting with both Vincenzo Verdi and Barry Hickman and see if they could sort something out between them! He thought about it for ages and imagined going into the prison and telling Reggie that there was no longer anything to worry about because he, Dodge, had sorted it all out.

Inspired by the prospect, he rang down to the front desk and got a telephone number for Leon 'Frenchie' leFevre, who knew most of what was going on locally.

'Leon, Dodge here. I don't suppose you have a contact number for Barry Hickman, do you? There's a bit of business I need to sort out.'

'I 'ave an address.' Frenchie's strong accent sounded like something out of a radio play. 'Ze Pretty Boys, they 'ave a bureau, vairy smart.' He spent a few moments rustling among some papers and came back with it.

'Thanks, Frenchie,' said Dodge. 'Everything alright with you?'

'*Tres bien*, Rogeur. Tonight I go to Paris to see my mother.'

'Good. Well, have a good trip.'

When the call was over, Dodge took two brown envelopes from the desk and two sheets of paper. He needed to set this meeting up quickly, but where and when? Monday night looked like a good time, but where? He suddenly thought of Rylstone Garden. It was a place he had often been with his mother because she liked the flowerbeds. It was reasonably isolated but, at the same time, meeting there shouldn't attract attention. On each sheet of paper, he wrote *Rylstone Gardens, Monday night, 7 o'clock*, put the papers into envelopes, addressed one to Barry, one to Vincenzo, and took them to the post.

Victor surfaced the next morning from a vivid, not to say embarrassing, dream. It was only as he lay gathering his senses that he became aware of an array of aches and strains around his person and slowly the details of the evening before came back to him. The memory left him breathless.

Once Charity was dressed he had walked her home, his legs feeling as if they belonged to someone else. She had held his hand as they walked and chatted gaily about her life. It was at this point that he had discovered that her father was none other than the nice policeman, Alan Grimes. The realisation threw him into free-fall, for what on earth would Mr Grimes think if he knew what Victor had done to his daughter – although to be honest it was more a question of what she had done to him.

On the doorstep Charity had grasped his face with both hands and twisted her mouth over his as if she was trying to extricate a cork from a bottle. Carefully he tested his lips, but they seemed to have survived the onslaught.

Resolutely he kept his eyes closed, trying to untangle the assortment of implications. Gradually the overriding thought was that, as from last night, he was a different person, no longer a shamefaced virgin but a man of the world. With that happy thought, he threw back the covers and went in search of tea.

Having freed himself from the attentions of Fluffy and the kittens by filling their food bowls, he settled to thinking about the wider world. Today was already Thursday. He had only three more days before he would be back to work. There were certain things that needed to be sorted out, the most pressing being the question of what to do with the two cheques.

At first he considered simply taking them to his bank and asking to deposit them in his current account, or perhaps to open a new savings account so that while he was waiting to contact the true owners, they would be gaining interest. He would, of course, hand the interest over once everything was sorted out. Gradually, however, he began to see the flaws in his plan. What would Miss Hutchinson, the bank clerk, think if he tried to pay in this unbelievable amount? Called upon to explain himself, it could be very humiliating, until he hit on the idea of pretending that this was an inheritance being paid in instalments. Satisfied with his plan, straight after breakfast he and Fluffy set off for the High Street.

There was quite a queue at the bank and he felt rather self-conscious, suspecting that the person standing behind him would be able to see over his shoulder. Outside, Fluffy was giving a good imitation of a banshee. Victor smiled sheepishly at a lady who clearly thought that he was some sort of heartless monster, leaving the poor little thing to pine, but there was nothing to be done.

As he waited, Victor considered his options. He didn't want a rumour to start circulating that he had come into money.

Perhaps he should ask to see the manager and be ushered through into a private office, but Mr Barber was a remote figure and Victor didn't quite have the nerve to ask for his attention. As it happened, another bank clerk had opened her window, and by the time Victor reached the counter he was the last customer. His face a ripe shade of tomato, he handed over the cheques along with his paying-in slip to Miss Hutchinson. 'B-Bit of an inheritance,' he managed to stutter.

Miss Hutchinson looked at the cheques and then at him, surprise at the very least registering on her rather homely face. 'My goodness Mr Green, what a lot.' After a moment she excused herself and returned a few moments later with the said Mr Barber.

'Mr Green, perhaps you would like to come through to my office?'

By now Victor's heart was steaming away. so he could hardly hear over the pounding in his ears. It took him a moment to register that Mr Barber was being unusually engaging, a positive Uriah Heap in fact.

'Please, please take a seat. Can I get you coffee or anything?'

This was the first time he had been offered anything other than a distant although polite good morning, so he nodded his head. Mr Barber pressed a buzzer on his desk and barked out an order. With remarkable speed. a young lady wearing the bank's uniform trotted in with a tray of coffee and biscuits.

'Right, now.' Mr Barber settled himself behind his desk. 'This is quite a sum of money, Mr Green.' As Victor was about to defend himself with mention of a previously unknown aunt in Cheltenham coupled with a surprise win on a Channel Islands lottery, Mr Barber continued, 'Perhaps you would like to think of investing it? A bond perhaps that will yield good interest?'

'I –, I don't want to tie it up for too long,' Victor said, finding courage from somewhere.

'Ah-ha, planning to indulge ourselves are we? A fast car? A little trip abroad maybe?'

This sounded like a good idea so Victor agreed, only half listening to Mr Barber's plans for housing the embarrassing cheques. Within twenty minutes it was all settled and he walked out with a new bank account and a temporary chequebook.

'So nice to do business with you Mr Green. If there is anything else you would like help with,' so saying the unctuous Mr Barber saw him to the door

Relieved of the responsibility of the money, Victor could now plan the rest of his day.

Fluffy greeted him as if he had been sent away to Siberia and had only just managed to get back. Embarrassed, Victor picked him up and carried him to the end of the street while his face was immersed in canine spittle.

When he arrived home it was to see the post van driving away, so on the way up the drive he opened the box. There was another of those white envelopes. They were beginning to annoy him now. In response to the last one he had gone along to the Chine but no one had met him there. Instead, that awful man had tried to drown the kittens and then fallen into the water. Thinking of Tabby and Puss, he had to admit that he was glad that he had been there, otherwise… he shuddered.

Forgoing the use of his paperknife, he ripped the envelope open with his finger. As he entered his front door, a sheet of folded paper tumbled out. There was no cheque, just another typed line. *Rylstone Gardens. Monday night.* 7 *o'clock.*

For two pins he would have thrown it away but he still had to make contact with the elusive correspondent. Perhaps this time he would be lucky.

Once Charity had completed her household chores she walked round to see Victor. She hadn't been expecting much from the evening before but in the event it had turned out quite well. Victor wasn't exactly her dream man but he was alright – a little stuffy, generally too thin – except, surprisingly, where it mattered. That had indeed been a pleasant discovery. Since she had split up with her boyfriend Sebastian, a fellow manager at M&S, she had been celibate. It wasn't a state she favoured for long. Clearly Victor didn't have much idea but she could soon lick him into shape, perhaps even literally. Her blood pressure went up a notch or two.

She knocked on the door with the lion's head knocker and Victor came to meet her, looking flustered.

'Have you been out already?' she asked, seeing that he was wearing his brogues.

'Just a little business at the bank.'

They walked into his kitchen and he rather hurriedly swept up the morning's post and secreted it behind the mantel clock. Remembering her original goal, she wondered if it was significant. Victor went to make tea and so, to keep in practice, she described to herself what he looked like. There were a few additional details she could now name but it seemed unlikely that they would ever come in useful, not unless he turned up as a mutilated corpse and she had to identify him by what remained of his torso. She realised that she hadn't noted whether or not he was circumcised. Unlikely as it seemed, one day that might turn out to be an important clue. She must remember to find out.

Victor returned with the tea tray and they discussed the rest of the day. As Charity suggested various activities, he began to wonder whether they were discussing the rest of his life. Were they perhaps engaged now? Surely the degree of last night's intimacy demanded some sort of commitment? He imagined walking into the office on Monday and announcing, 'By the way, while I have been on leave I got engaged.' No doubt there would be congratulations and speculation as to who the lucky girl might be. He thought about Pamela and wondered if she would be disappointed. Could she have nursed a secret love for him all this time and he had never noticed? Perhaps he could console her, tell her that somewhere out there was the perfect man for her but that it really wasn't him.

'What do you think?' asked Charity.

'Pardon?' He realised that all the time she had been talking. She gave an exasperated tut and said, 'Why don't we go out somewhere, take the dog and have a picnic.'

'That would be very nice.' He sensed that this was how it was going to be – her making plans and him going along with them. It wasn't exactly what he had dreamed of but it was certainly better than what had gone before. He said, 'I shall be back at work on Monday.'

'Then I'll come round and see to Fluffy and the cats.'

'Would you? That would be perfect.' Perhaps perfect wasn't quite the right word but Victor was wondering what they might take for a picnic. Meanwhile, Charity seemed to have changed her mind and was suddenly rather ruthlessly struggling with his trouser zip. Given the choice of cheese sandwiches in the park or her groping fingers, he certainly knew which he preferred.

The next two days of his holiday passed in a frenzy of sex and walkies. On Saturday he tentatively announced, 'I'm afraid I'll be rather busy tomorrow preparing to go back to work.'

Charity looked surprised. 'What have you got to do?'

'Well, there is some washing and ironing and I need to clean the house…'

'I will do that.'

For a moment Victor felt that he was losing a barely acknowledged battle of wills but then he asserted himself. 'I don't want you having to look after me. Besides, I like to have a quiet Sunday so that I can read the paper and…' He didn't know what else he might do that required being on his own for the entire day but he craved some solitude.

'I see.' He could tell that Charity was offended but while they were on the subject he had something else to say. 'I'm afraid I won't be able to see you on Monday either because I have to go to a meeting after work.'

'In that case I could come round and take Fluffy out and cook you a meal.'

'No, really. I have my lunch at the canteen and I can take Fluffy with me in the evening. I don't know what time I will be back.'

He thought of Rylstone, the designated meeting place with his mysterious benefactor. It was a secluded cliff-top park perched above the Chine. A quaint chalet suggested that it had once been a private residence. The garden was open to the public until dusk. Here he and Fluffy could lie in wait for whoever might turn up.

'Is there someone else?' asked Charity in a brittle voice. 'If there is, I'd rather you said so.'

'No, of course not. It's just that…'

With a rare moment of insight, Charity visualised what had been his normal routine – staid, stolid, set in stone – and perhaps secretive? Her arrival seemed to have thrown his life into disarray. 'It's alright,' she heard herself say. 'I'm sorry if I have been too pushy.'

'You haven't. It's been – wonderful, but I…'

It could so easily have developed into a quarrel. They might at this point have done what Victor thought of as breaking up, but instead, Charity said, 'Well, if you don't have anything better to do on Tuesday after work perhaps we could go to the cinema again?'

'That would be lovely.' Victor took her hand and squeezed it. 'You are a splendid girl, Charity.'

Overcome with emotion, Charity launched herself into his arms, thereby setting in motion another molten surge of passion on the rug that hopefully would be sufficient to see her through until Tuesday.

Alan had the weekend off and enjoyed having a rare Saturday to himself. Charity had thoughtfully baked some sort of casserole and left it in the fridge, and rather guiltily he left it and sneaked down to the chippy for a longed-for piece of cod. It seemed that Charity had found herself a boyfriend, and having her attentions directed somewhere else was a bit of a relief.

On Sunday he planned a round of golf and then a Sunday roast at the Tudor Restaurant. The taste of flesh would be a welcome change from beans and vegetable protein. Regretfully, he thought about Edna's Sunday roasts in her calm, peaceful house, where he had read the papers and drunk a half of beer while she quietly sat and sewed. Still, he should be grateful for having such a devoted daughter.

As he was about to go to bed on Saturday evening, Charity arrived home. She looked breathless and dishevelled.

'Had a good evening?' he asked. 'I was just going to bed.'

Charity seemed to be fighting with some internal demon. She said, 'I will be at home tomorrow father to look after you.'

His heart sank. 'Charity, there is really no need. In fact I have arranged to play golf with Sam Walters and then we are going out to lunch together. You go on out and do whatever it is you are doing.'

Charity looked increasingly crestfallen.

'What's the matter?' Alan came over and touched her on the shoulder. 'Have you fallen out with someone?'

She shook her head, miserable for no very good reason. 'It's just that I came home to look after you and now I seem to have deserted you.'

'Nonsense. You go out and enjoy yourself. A young woman like you should be having a good time.' He squeezed her shoulder. 'Is the young man anyone I know?'

'It's – Victor Green.'

'Victor? Splendid, a more reliable chap you're never likely to find. Why don't you invite him to tea one day?'

Charity thought of her enquiries. To regain some of her self-respect she reminded herself that Victor was on her list of suspects, although at the moment it was a list of only one. She assured herself that she wasn't taking him seriously as a boy-friend – was she? It was more of a Mata Hari scheme to find out what she could about the deaths of two associated gang-sters, both in mysterious circumstances. Victor had been there at the first and a man with a small white dog seemed to have witnessed the second. There was a mystery here and it had to be solved. She straightened her shoulders. Right! She would ask

Victor back to tea and listen to what he and her father talked about. Perhaps, accidentally, Alan would force him into revealing some clue. She made up her mind. Time to stop being distracted by Victor's body: time to put him back where he belonged on the list of the Isle of Wight's Most Wanted.

TWELVE

Barry sat alone at the boardroom table and looked through the day's post that Sonia had plonked down in front of him with barely disguised contempt.

'You can fetch me a coffee,' he said, wondering whether to remind her that while Harry and Gary were away, he was in charge and he could, if he felt so inclined, dismiss her on the spot. In reality he would not dare to do so, because for some reason Harry seemed fond of her and he would get it in the neck if Harry came back to find that she was gone.

He opened the letters one by one, putting them into piles to be dealt with. The last one stopped him in his tracks. It contained just one line summoning him to a meeting at Rylstone Gardens on Monday – no signature. He wondered if it might be from Vincenzo. On the other hand it might be an ambush set up by the Blues Brothers. Something told him that this was significant though; it might even be a chance to avert a wholescale war.

It was then that he realised that he couldn't go. He already had a meeting with one of Harry's contacts, bringing in some stuff from Turkey. With Harry in Spain, he simply had to be there. Damn. He really wanted to go and perhaps at last get a look at Vincenzo Verdi. For a long time he sat and wondered what to do, then he decided that the next best thing was to send someone in his place. He thought long and hard, but so many people were out of commission for various reasons that the only person he could come up with was Fingers Kilbride.

Fingers was not a good choice. He never washed, and outside his area of expertise as a safe blower he was unsociable, grubby and generally uninspiring, but he couldn't think of anybody else. So, Fingers it would have to be. Pressing the intercom on the desk, he said to Sonia, 'Get me Angus Kilbride.'

'What are you planning to do with him?' He ignored the sarcasm in her voice. Biting down his irritation, he said, 'Tell him to be here at six o'clock on Monday – without fail.'

On Monday, Fingers arrived at the office at a quarter to six to be sent directly to the boardroom, where he found Barry putting on his jacket.

'I've got an important job for you,' Barry started.

Fingers stared suspiciously at him. 'I'm dead worried Mr Hickman, first Gruesome and then Mauler. 'Ave you sorted anything out yet?'

'It's all underway.'

Fingers was silent, fulminating. Barry said, 'I want you to go to Rylstone Gardens. You know where that is?'

Fingers gave an uncertain nod of his head.

'Well, you don't have to do anything, just see who's there – and take a photo of anyone who comes in, with this.' He held out a camera.

Fingers looked at it as if it might explode in his face. Barry felt impatient.

'Look, all you've got to do is look through here and press this button here. It has a zoom lens – see? You just move this lever and you can photograph someone close up from a long way away. That's all you've got to do.'

Fingers shook his head as if he was being asked to swim with crocodiles. 'Who's going to be there then?' he asked.

'Probably no one. You don't need to speak to anyone, just get a description and take some photos.'

Fingers shook his head more vehemently. 'I can't.'

'You can. Look, there's a ton in it for you if you do it.' More gently, he said, 'There's absolutely nothing to worry about. You'll be quite safe. Nothing can go wrong.'

Victor got up early on Monday morning and took a rather surprised Fluffy for an early morning walk. Before leaving for work he left a door key under the flowerpot for Charity and, with some misgivings, set off for the tax office.

'Hi Victor, good holiday?' He was greeted in a friendly manner by Rob, who had been overseeing his work while he was away.

Victor agreed that he had had a good break and Robbie filled him in on any developments during his absence. 'Do anything interesting?' Robbie asked.

I had sexual relations, with a woman, Victor thought to himself, allowing a secret smile. No doubt his new-found passion with Charity was something that Robbie was familiar with, but it gave Victor a warm feeling to be part of adult male society, something he had rarely experienced before.

Pamela actually made him a cup of coffee and seemed to hang around quite a lot. Looking at her he wondered if he had been right, and that all along she had had some sort of feeling for him only he had been too blind to see it. He studied her as a man of the world might do. Under her old-fashioned blouses she was a quite a pleasing shape, nothing provocative, but beneath the prudent garments there was no doubt a well-endowed woman. Her legs, hampered by the sensible lace-up shoes, curved in all the right places too. Disapproving of his own thoughts, he turned back to a very inventive tax return, deciding to call Mr O'Shaughnessy in to discuss his claims. He gave Pamela a relaxed and friendly smile. He wondered what it would have been like to follow his daydream through and announce that he was engaged, but, to be honest, he didn't think he was really ready for such a step. He wasn't sure what would follow, a wedding? Planning guest lists, choosing a honeymoon destination, Charity preparing to move in with him – after the ceremony, of course. He imagined her ordering new furniture, throwing out things that had been in the house ever since his childhood. No, he really wasn't ready for that.

He left the office at five sharp so that he could race home and pick up Fluffy, ready for the rendezvous. He hoped that he wouldn't find Charity still there waiting for him and expecting an explanation. In the event, the house was empty except for Fluffy and the kittens. The cats were blissfully asleep, food still in their bowls, and Fluffy was clearly quite relaxed and probably hadn't had too much time on his own to begin to feel abandoned.

Victor decided not to change. His work clothes were more official somehow and he needed some degree of authority to find out what was going on. He washed his face and hands and cleaned his teeth, and wondered about boiling an egg before he left, but then decided to make himself some sandwiches. He could eat them sitting on a seat in the gardens. It was a lovely spot and a nice evening and he would enjoy that.

Looking in the cupboard he only seemed to have peanut butter, but that was OK. Carefully he sliced the bread – he never bought ready sliced – spread it thinly with local farm butter and covered it with a thick layer of crunchy peanut butter. Delicious.

It took him less time than he expected to get there. He wandered in at the entrance along the cliff top. The evening was perfect. A dying sun cast its last blessings across the sea below as if sprinkling an inheritance of diamonds, dancing on the waves. Victor fished out a notebook to write down the image of the sunset, just right for a poem. There was no one else in the garden.

The garden's flowerbeds were secluded by fir trees. From the top branches, the scraping call of rooks echoed across to meet the hiss of the sea. Glancing at his watch, Victor realised that he was too early. He found himself a rather ornate garden seat on the sunny side of the wall and sat down to wait.

As the Monday rendezvous approached, Dodge felt increasingly nervous. He had prepared a speech to address to both Vincenzo and Barry. As the time grew near, however, it seemed less and less likely to work. Dodge hadn't met either of them before.

He was always nervous with strangers and in this instance so much depended on making the right impression.

By mid-afternoon he was so anxious that he decided to call in at one of their warehouses to check on some stock. At least it would give him something to do. As he drove out of town he began to regret the decision. The warehouse was a deserted barn of a place on a disused industrial estate and, being isolated, there was no one to notice any comings and goings. At the same time the place was eerily silent and it gave Dodge a creepy feeling. He nearly turned back, but the stock really did need checking and he couldn't think of anything else to fill the time.

Inside, everything was covered in a layer of dust. As he worked it got up his nose and clung to his fingers. Just after four-thirty he had had enough and decided to go home and change, ready for the evening meeting. Heading for the exit he practised his speech to himself until he reached the top of a narrow wrought iron staircase. Quite what happened next he didn't know but somehow he missed his footing, tumbling down twenty-one steps to the concrete floor below. The next thing he knew, he was lying in the dark well of the stairs and from somewhere a torrent of pain was engulfing him. He moved his leg and the pain turned to agony. Damn it! Damn it! He knew for certain that he had broken his ankle. This was a disaster. To reach a telephone he would need to climb the stairs again and he was in far too much pain to move. He tried shouting but there was no one around. Unless he was very lucky, he was going to be stuck here until next morning.

—■—

Victor sat for a while enjoying the evening sunshine and then he began to unpack his sandwiches. At his feet, Fluffy amused himself by sniffing around the area as far as his lead extended. The dog must have had several long walks during the day, for after a few moments he curled up under the bench and went to sleep.

A man wandered in at the other end of the garden. He looked round with rather exaggerated care and then began to walk slowly with his hands in his pockets. First he stopped to study the lobelia then, after looking round again, he took out what looked like a camera and stared at it, turning it this way and that before apparently turning it on. A little further on, he reached out and sniffed at a misty pink rose before pointing the camera very roughly in the direction of the flower and snapping away. Victor covertly watched his progress, planning what he should say. The man did not look in the least like he had imagined. He had been expecting someone well dressed, executive, the sort of person who might have dealings with thousands of pounds.

'I think there has been a mistake,' Victor practised to himself, 'but don't worry, the money is quite safe,' or perhaps: 'I'm so sorry but I seem to have received some mail that wasn't meant for me.'

The man drew closer. Victor noticed that his clothes looked shabby and none too clean. Surely this wasn't the man he was supposed to meet? He glanced at his watch. There was still two minutes to go before seven. This was just some tramp taking advantage of the opportunity to enjoy a wander in the sun.

Suddenly the stranger flung himself down onto the bench beside Victor, glancing covertly over his shoulder. Victor flinched but kept his cool. He wondered if he was going to demand the money. Reassuringly, Fluffy, still half-asleep under the bench, gave a growl. Victor shortened his lead and imagined that Fluffy was a police dog that he could release at a moment's notice and set on his attacker, dragging him to the ground. Fluffy jumped onto Victor's lap.

The man was studiously silent, looking to the entrance to the garden as if he too was expecting someone else and was in two minds as to whether to leave. Victor felt that he must take charge of the situation.

'Beautiful evening,' he offered.

His companion appeared not to have heard. Victor wondered if he might be deaf, or even daft, for he was mumbling quietly under his breath.

The sandwiches were open on his lap and, in a sudden spirit of friendliness, Victor held them out. 'Would you like one?'

The stranger glanced down at them, then at Victor. Victor nodded encouragingly and waved the package closer.

With a suspicious glower the stranger reached out and grabbed one. Victor saw with shock that the man's hand was badly mangled, as if he had had an accident with some machinery. Ever polite, he looked away.

Hungrily, the man packed the sandwich back. For the first time, he looked directly at Victor, with Fluffy sitting alertly on Victor's knee. The dog's appearance seemed to unnerve him and he stared at Fluffy as if he was some sort of ghost. Without saying anything, he got up and hurried for the exit, glancing anxiously back over his shoulder.

No sooner had he moved than Fluffy, now wide awake, gave a yap and set off in pursuit, and, to Victor's horror, made a dive for the man's ankle. As his teeth made contact, the man let out a howl and kicked out with the injured foot. Fluffy gave a yelp and flew through the air, landing several yards away. Picking himself up, he hurried back to Victor's protection.

Victor was shocked to think that in an unguarded moment he had loosed his hold on Fluffy's lead with such consequences. 'You must stop doing that,' he admonished the little poodle.

He felt relieved that the man had now disappeared, half expecting him to come back and challenge him about his dangerous dog. Thankfully, he didn't do so and gradually Victor relaxed – until he remembered the reason for his presence in the garden. Well, at least it would be much easier to meet his companion with no one else around. He held on to Fluffy securely to prevent any further mishaps.

The sun was beginning to disappear behind the horizon in a haze of purple and orange, and the temperature dropped markedly. Victor glanced at his watch – ten past seven. He – whoever he was – was late.

He noticed that Fluffy had done his business right by the leg of the seat and, glancing round to make sure that no one was watching him, he bent down and scooped it up in a tissue, depositing it in the now empty sandwich bag. Victor had only made two sandwiches and he was still hungry, although he felt a certain feel-good factor at having shared his meagre meal with the tramp. Along by the exit there was a dog dirt box, and fastidiously he walked along and dropped Fluffy's donation into it. He was intending to go back to the seat but at that moment the park attendant poked his nose round the gate.

'Last one, Sir?' He glanced down the length of the garden.

'I was just waiting for someone.'

'We close in a few minutes.' The attendant went down to check that there was no one hiding in the bushes, then came back and hovered meaningfully near the gate. As the hands of his watch crept up to seven-thirty, Victor felt angry. Here was another journey he had wasted. Just wait until he caught up with whoever had sent him the note. He would certainly give him a piece of his mind.

Annoyed, he made his way back down towards the village. At the junction ahead there was some sort of commotion and what looked like a police car. A group of people were huddled around something. Victor changed his mind and went back the way he had come. If he cut through the housing estate he should be home within half an hour.

THIRTEEN

Charity invited Victor home to tea on Wednesday.

'Come straight from work,' she instructed. 'I'll pick Fluffy up in the afternoon and bring him over so that you needn't worry about him.'

'Thank you.' He fought down the feeling that his life was being organised to the nth degree.

Charity had come round to his house after work on Tuesday and grilled him about the mysterious meeting that he had had the evening before.

It was too complicated to explain; besides, he suspected that if ever she knew the whole story she would immediately take charge of the mysterious money and for the moment he wanted to keep the business to himself.

'I just met up with an old business colleague,' he said, uncomfortable in the role of liar.

'A man?'

'Of course.'

Victor then raised the question of paying her for her role as dog walker. She wouldn't hear of it. In fact, she said that she was offended that he should even think of such a thing.

'I thought we meant something to each other, Victor. I don't know how you can even suggest it.'

'We do, I —,' he stumbled out something about having to pay if it was someone else and as she wasn't working etc., but she pooh-poohed his explanations away.

'I am perfectly happy to pop round every day while you are at work.' The matter was settled.

He arrived at her father's house clutching a bunch of flowers and a bottle of wine. He wasn't sure about the wine, whether Mr Grimes – Alan – might disapprove, but it was Charity who answered the door and swept the gifts from his arms, putting the flowers in water and the bottle (Chablis) in the fridge. Personally, Victor preferred red wine but he knew that Charity was a dry white wine drinker.

'Come on in and take your jacket off. Put your feet up and relax. I'm afraid father is delayed, some development at the nick.'

She treated Victor to a corkscrew kiss and fondly gave his genitals a little squeeze, a hint of what was to come later.

Fluffy tripped out of the living room and came to meet him with tiny trills of delight. Victor bent down and picked the dog up, he smelt of roses. Seeing him sniff Fluffy's coat, Charity said, 'I gave him a bath and trimmed some of his hair. You should take him to a dog stylist.'

Dog stylist? Victor had no idea that there was such a thing. Now he looked closer, he could see that the pom-pom on the end of Fluffy's tail definitely looked more spherical and his top-knot had a positively bouffant look.

'Thank you,' he said lamely. This was becoming a habit, thanking her for doing something he didn't want done in the first place.

She escorted him to the living room and settled him in a chair, fetching him a glass of wine and the paper. He suspected that if this was his home she would take off his shoes and put on his slippers for him. Whilst being mollycoddled was nice in small doses, he wasn't sure he wanted it as a way of life.

'I won't be long.' She kissed the top of his head and retreated to the kitchen.

Victor took a long gulp of the wine. It was very cold and he knew that later on it would repeat on him, but the other day Charity had expressed her preference for a *cold Chablis*, so that was what they were drinking.

Victor read the *Clarion*'s lead story about the council's plans to re-route a bus that was causing controversy. *'Save the Number 7'*, the headline demanded. The number 7 ran in a different area so made no difference to him, but he liked to know what people had to say.

He turned the page and noticed a small piece headed *'Mystery Man Still Not Identified'*. On Monday evening, an unnamed man had collapsed at the junction of Prince Leopold Lane and Rylstone Hollow. The police were asking for anyone who was missing a friend or relative, or knew anything about the incident, to get in touch. Victor turned the page, thinking that it was on Monday that he had been in the area. With a sudden realisation, he wondered if the man who had been on his way to meet him had met with an accident. That would explain his failure to turn up. He wondered if he should go to the police station and explain that he had been meeting someone who hadn't arrived, but then he imagined the questions that they would ask him. 'What did he look like, Sir? What was his name? Where did he live? Why were you meeting him?' Victor couldn't answer any of these and he fought shy of explaining about the money because it would just sound ridiculous. He decided that, after all, he could not help the police with their enquiries.

Idly he wondered what he might do if the man coming to meet him really had died and no one came forward to ask for either of the cheques back. Well, he'd cross that bridge when he came to it.

At that moment he heard the front door open, the sound of boots being wiped on the doormat, and low voices. Fluffy flew to the kitchen to discover the nature of the intruder. Victor heard Alan say, 'What on earth's that?' Disloyally, Victor wished that Fluffy didn't sound quite so much like a strangled soprano.

A few moments later, Alan came into the living room clutching a glass of red wine. Victor cursed himself for not having been a bit more assertive and asking for red himself. Alan shook his hand and asked how he was.

'I apologise for being late,' he said. He looked troubled and Victor waited apprehensively, in case the older man started expressing misgivings about his relationship with Charity. He could not, of course, know about *Last Tango in Paris* and what had followed but even so, it was an uncomfortable moment.

Alan gave a big sigh and sank into the other armchair, trying to ignore Fluffy, who was investigating his trouser leg with what looked suspiciously like evil intent.

After a moment, Alan asked, 'I don't suppose there have been any repercussions since your accident?'

'Repercussions?' Victor thought for a moment, but apart from inheriting Fluffy he had largely managed to put the incident out of his mind.

'Bit of a mystery at work,' Alan said. 'You might have read about that man who collapsed near Prince Leopold Lane? Well, we have got a positive identification and it's a bit worrying. His name is Angus Kilbride, generally known as 'Fingers' and he's a nasty piece of work.' Alan looked like a man wondering whether to say anything in the confessional, then, seeming to decide that Victor was someone whom he could trust, he added, 'The fact is, he's the third member of two rival South London gangs to die in this area.' He gave a sniff. 'What is even more disconcerting, they have all died in mysterious circumstances.'

Charity clattered in with an assortment of cutlery and busied herself at the table.

Alan continued. 'The first one, whom you had the misfortune to land on, was Tommy Hewson – he was a known associate of a gang known as the Blues Brothers. Then there was Bernard Maguire – Mauler – who drowned in the Chine. He worked with another gang, the Pretty Boys. Now there is Fingers Kilbride, another member of the Pretty Boys' outfit.' He sighed. 'Fingers is so-named because he is what they call a Peter Man, a safe blower. A few years ago he managed to take off his own fingers when some gelignite went off by mistake, but that didn't seem to slow him down.'

Victor had a sudden vision of the hand reaching out to take one of his sandwiches, the missing digits. He gulped.

'H-h-how did he die?' he managed to ask.

'That's the thing. He seems to have had some sort of seizure. The pathologist called it toxic shock. Poor chap had a nut allergy and somehow he had eaten peanuts just before he died. Fatal.' Alan shook his head at the mystery of life.

Victor had just raised his glass to his mouth and nearly choked on his wine. He was back in the park sitting on the bench, offering one of his peanut butter sandwiches to the tramp who had joined him.

'Are you alright?' Alan saw his expression, the sudden pallor. 'I say old chap, you're not going to pass out are you?'

Victor shook his head to try and clear the spinning vortex in his mind. It was the Chine incident all over again. He tried to remember anything about the tramp other than that he had looked shabby and smelled. His manner had been shifty and Victor had no idea what he might have been doing wandering around Rylstone Gardens. But the sandwich, that was the worrying thing. He had accidentally given the tramp something that had killed him. He tried to reassure himself. Surely Fingers must have known that he shouldn't eat nuts? Perhaps he was so hungry that he didn't even think about it.

'Victor?' Charity was frowning at him. 'Come along, tea's ready.'

Somehow he got to the table and toyed with what Charity announced as sosmix burgers.

'Come on, eat up!' Her tone demanded obedience.

Victor's head was in such a whirl that he longed to go home and hide until he could think of some explanation for what had happened on Monday evening. Gradually it was dawning on him that he had inadvertently become a serial killer. He realised that he must keep himself under control, try to behave normally until he had had a chance to think through all the implications. Across the table Alan and Charity were quiet, pretending to concentrate on their food, trying to ignore his change of mood.

Under the table Fluffy was investigating Alan's shoelace and getting a little too friendly with his ankle. The policeman gave his foot a shake and Fluffy flew off with a squeal. Alan looked embarrassed, saying, 'Whoops, think I accidentally kicked him.' As if to make amends, he asked, 'Where did you get him?'

'Victor got him from the RSPCA,' Charity answered on his behalf. She was having her own thoughts, amongst which was the increasing likelihood that Fluffy was indeed the Angel of Death and that Victor, quiet biddable Victor, was a foreign spy or secret agent or hitman or something. After an initial frisson of fear, the excitement began to bubble up. Was she..., could she be a gangster's moll? She glanced at her father. She must think of Alan's reputation. How would it look if it turned out that his daughter's lover was the most wanted man in Britain? She looked across at Victor, chasing a piece of sosmix around his plate, and she gave his ankle a nudge under the table. He looked up like a startled rabbit and she smiled broadly at him.

Shall I let him know that I know, she thought? The idea of being bedded by Britain's most wanted man was the most exciting thing that had ever happened to her!

When the meal was over, Victor offered to help with the washing up, anything to keep him occupied, but Charity wouldn't hear of it.

'You stay here and talk to father,' she insisted. Victor had no choice.

As Alan seemed so preoccupied with his own thoughts, Victor decided to instigate a conversation. Perhaps he could find out how much the police knew and whether they had any suspicions as to his involvement in the crime.

'You must f-f-find your work ex-exciting,' he offered.

Alan made an effort to be a good host. 'Most of it is just routine, writing reports, filing information.'

'Ha-have you any idea what m-might have h-happened to the g-gangsters?'

Alan leaned forward. 'Let me tell you about the two gangs. The Pretty Boys are so-called because they are brothers and think they are good looking. A worse trio you would be hard put to find. Two of them, Harry and Gary, have been in gaol for arson and armed robbery but they are on the loose at the moment. Their father, Lawrence Hickman – Larry – moved to Spain some time ago as he's wanted over here and daren't come back. The youngest brother, Barry, isn't as cunning as the others but he's good with money.'

Alan leaned closer and lowered his voice. 'This is only a theory, but I think the Pretty Boys are trying to take over the territory of the Blues Brothers and I'll tell you why.'

Victor's eyes grew large and his heart started thudding. Hearing about all this from the inside was exciting – until he remembered that in some way he seemed to be implicated, at which point he felt faint again. Fortunately, Alan was too engrossed in telling the story to notice. He continued: 'This brings me to the Blues Brothers. Two of them – Reggie and Randy – are twins, the sons of Alfonso Rodriguez, a Spaniard. Like Larry, he lives in Spain but his boys, Reggie, Randy and the youngest one, Dodge, are well known for running drugs and protection rackets. At the moment, Reggie and Randy are both banged up – in different gaols mind you because other-wise they'd be pulling some scam. My suspicion is that while the two older Rodriguez boys are in gaol, the Hickmans want to take over their patch.'

Victor thought about it for a while before asking, 'What m-makes you think it is the Pr-pr-pretty Boys?'

Pleased that Victor seemed to be following the story, Alan said, 'Well, the fact is that Gruesome is an associate of the Blues Brothers, while Mauler and Fingers were both members of the Pretty Boys' gang. My guess is that both gangs have hired a pro-fessional to take the others out.' He paused for thought.

This was too much for Victor to take in but Alan was speak-ing again. 'My theory is that one of them has hired Vincenzo Verdi for the job. He's known to be one of the best – and the thing is, the police have never been able to track him down. He just seems to turn up on the scene, carry out a killing and then vanish the way he came.' With a sigh, he added, 'We have no idea who the other gang might have hired but it looks like there will be trouble ahead.'

He looked to Victor for his reaction. 'Fancy,' he managed to murmur.

Alan nodded. 'So, we have a bit of a dilemma. We've never had much trouble on the Island with organised crime but we do know that the Blues Brothers have included our area in their theatre of operations.' He looked troubled again. 'If this is turning into a gang war, then a lot of local people might be caught in the crossfire.'

At that moment, Charity came in and plonked herself on the arm of Victor's chair, putting her arm around his shoulders. Her breast touched his cheek and he jumped. At the thought of any later encounter of the romantic kind he quailed. He desperately wanted to go home. Alone.

Somehow they stumbled on through the evening. Alan and Charity made most of the conversation, Victor struggling hard to concentrate and to appear normal. To his relief, Alan didn't become the heavy father and ask him what his intentions were towards his daughter. He already knew about his job so he didn't need to ask about his prospects. What he didn't know was that Victor had accidentally been instrumental in three deaths and the outcome might be a bloodbath. Vitcor felt faint again.

'What's the matter, aren't you well?' Charity sounded just a tad irritated.

'B-bit of a headache,' Victor said.

'Well, perhaps you had better have an early night. I'll walk home with you.'

'No!' The word came out far too quickly.

Alan said, 'Charity, Victor is quite capable of getting home on his own. No one is going to assault him.'

Assault. That word again. It covered a multitude of things, all of them unpleasant.

Charity, clearly annoyed at her father's interference, came with Victor to the door, helped him on with his jacket and brushed some invisible specks from his shoulders. For a moment Victor thought that she was going to do up his buttons for him, but instead she stepped back and inspected him like a mother seeing her child off to school.

'Well, I – I'll see you,' he started, hoping that it wouldn't be too soon.

Charity held up her face to be kissed. When he went to peck her on the cheek, she twisted his head around and applied herself to his lips, pressing her pelvis close to his. 'Don't worry,' she whispered, 'your secret is safe with me.'

Secret? He leaned against the doorframe for support, then took Fluffy's lead and escaped into the night.

FOURTEEN

The security guard found Dodge the next morning. He was lying in a pool of urine and sobbing to himself. 'I've been here all night,' he wailed. 'I'm thirsty. My leg really hurts.'

The man sent for an ambulance and they carted him off to hospital. His leg was X-rayed, but it was only sprained and a bandage was applied. He was, however, kept in overnight because, having got so cold, they thouht he might have hypothermia.

Although he was exhausted, Dodge kept fretting, wondering what had happened at the meeting the evening before. He thought they would have wondered where he was, until he remembered that he hadn't signed the note. That meant that Barry Hickman and Vincenzo Verdi had been forced into a private meeting. He wondered what they must have talked about. Perhaps they had agreed to join forces against him and his brothers? Perhaps he had caused the very thing he was trying to avoid and now the Blues Brothers would be annihilated. He started to cry until a nice male nurse said, 'You've had a shock. I'll get you something to take.' After that he felt better, but he knew that he must get out of hospital and find out what was going on.

He was discharged that afternoon with some painkillers, and a crutch to help him get around. They ordered him a taxi and when he got home the first thing he did was to ring Something for Everyone, just to check if there were any messages.

He recognised the voice of the girl who answered the phone. She did the store's accounts. 'Mr Rodriguez, where are you? I was worried, especially in view of what's happened.'

He started to explain about his accident then, he said, 'What *has* happened?'

'Do you know a man called Angus Kilbride?'

'Yes, what about him?'

'Well, he seems to have died on Monday night down near Rylstone Gardens. I just thought that after the other deaths…'

Roger couldn't think fast enough. Surely this couldn't be another coincidence? Perhaps Barry Hickman had taken Fingers along for protection and Vincenzo had wiped him out? His first instinct was to rush down to the office but then he remembered his leg and that he was stuck.

'Thank you for telling me,' he said to the girl. Slowly he came to a conclusion. It couldn't have been Barry Hickman who killed Fingers because he was one of their own. That definitely left Vincenzo. Gradually it dawned on him that this was yet another commission that Verdi had carried out on the Pretty Boy's behalf and this time Dodge was certain that *he* hadn't actually asked him to do so. Perhaps this was what hitmen did, act on your behalf whether you had told them who the target was or not. Anyway, you didn't argue with a hired assassin. Reluctantly, he thought that he had better pay up before Vincenzo came to look for him. His hands were shaking as he wrote out yet another cheque. In spite of struggling with the crutch, he forced himself to hobble to the postbox on the corner. He felt angry with himself for paying up and yet he was too afraid not to do so.

Back at the flat, he made a coffee and sat on the sofa with his bad leg stretched out in front of him. All the crazy events swirled around in his head. Certain things were becoming inescapable. If the problems were ever to be sorted, it seemed that the hitman was the real fly in the ointment, the obstacle preventing any peaceful solution. Perhaps the time had come for someone to take Vincenzo Verdi out.

Barry's meeting with Harry's Turkish contact had not gone well. The man was asking for more money and threatening to go elsewhere if he didn't get his way. Barry tried to think what Harry would do in his place – beat the guy up probably, but he was bigger than Barry and besides, he couldn't stand violence. In the end, he had agreed to an interim increase while making it clear that it was still under negotiation.

He slept badly, wondering what Harry would say when he came back, wondering what had happened at the rendezvous at Rylstone Gardens. He did not hold out any great hopes that Fingers had discovered anything useful. In all probability he would come back with a series of photos of either the sky or headless subjects. He didn't look forward to seeing Fingers and being treated to that awful stench of unwashed clothes and rotting teeth.

When he arrived at the office on Tuesday morning Sonia, for once, didn't look sulky. Instead, he thought that she looked quite worried.

'Have you heard what's happened?' she asked.

'No?'

She came round the desk. 'It's Fingers, something happened to him last night. He collapsed in the road out Greystones way. He's dead.'

'What?'

'He died. They think he had a reaction to something he ate.'

Barry sank into the nearest chair. The bastards! Fingers must have been poisoned. He immediately thought that this was a set-up organised by the Blues Brothers – only Dodge Rodriguez couldn't have known that it was Fingers who would be coming instead of him. If he had gone himself... he couldn't bear to think about what would have happened if he had gone himself.

Sonia said, 'Here's something to cheer you up though. Apparently young Rodriguez had an accident yesterday and he's broken his leg. He was stuck all night in a warehouse.' She gave a little giggle.

Barry felt that he couldn't take on board one more piece of information but gradually the truth filtered through – if Dodge hadn't been at that meeting, then who had? He came to the conclusion that that only left Vincenzo. He must have set up the meeting himself and it must have been he who had taken out Fingers. A horrible mixture of guilt and anger consumed him. If he hadn't sent Fingers he would still be alive. If he had gone himself, he would be dead!

Right, he thought, time for this to stop. It was going to be dangerous but it was definitely time that someone took out Vincenzo Verdi.

Walking home from Charity's house, Alan's news circled like a whirlwind in Victor's head. What on earth was going on? How had he come to be involved in what seemed to be a serious gangland feud? As he walked, he half expected a sinister figure wielding a dagger to step from the shadows. How did you defend yourself against a knife? Why had he never attended self-defence classes? He knew the answer without even asking the question. Small, skinny, timid, he had long ago recognised that if anyone ever attacked him he would simply give in. He had a vision of himself on his knees, pleading for mercy. It was a shameful image, and if he was to survive he needed to learn how to fight back.

He reached home safely, then wondered if a member of the Blues Brothers or the Pretty Boys might be waiting for him. Perhaps they knew who he was, where he lived, and had been staking him out? What would he do if they jumped him?

He fumbled in the mailbox and carried his post indoors, turning on all the lights as he went and pushing doors wide open before he entered a room. The house seemed reassuringly silent. Fluffy did a quick tour of inspection and finished up some Doggybics that were still in his bowl. The kittens had clearly retired for the night. There were no unwelcome intruders.

Taking off his jacket, he pulled the curtains shut before sitting at the table and looking through the mail. Oh no, not again! One of those unwelcome envelopes greeted him. This time it was a white one. His hands began to shake as he sliced it open. As before, there was a folded sheet of paper and this time it also contained an enclosure, another cheque for £25,000 drawn on the National Bank of Jersey. Gradually, an unbelievable connection was forming in his mind. Could these mysterious payments really be some sort of pay-off for having disposed of members of the two gangs? Did some mysterious company arrange murders and he was somehow on their books? Victor tottered to the sink and poured himself a drink of water.

He turned back to examine the piece of paper but this time it was blank. Did that mean that this was an end to it? Had all the villains been bumped off? Perhaps the gang had decided to employ someone else who used more conventional methods like a gun with a silencer or a grenade through a window. Carefully, he went round the house and locked every door and window.

That night he left his bedroom door open so that if anyone happened to creep up the stairs, then Fluffy would be sure to hear them and give the alarm. He wished that he had shutters on the windows but it was a bit late for that now. He wished that Fluffy was a Rottweiler or a Doberman. He wished that he was braver. He wished that he had a gun and knew how to use it.

The phone was by his bed and he wondered whether to leave the bedside lamp on so that he could quickly dial 999 if the need arose. The light might guide the intruder to his room though. Feeling distinctly scared, he turned the light off and leaped into bed, pulling the duvet up to his ears, then lowering it so that he could hear any noise, however slight.

His last thought before falling asleep three hours later was that something was going on here and he was way out of his depth.

Charity poured herself another glass of wine and sat down in the chair so recently vacated by her lover. She was all of a tingle. There was so much that she didn't know about Victor and for the moment it seemed that everything she discovered only added to the mystery. He was no longer a rather nondescript, timid tax officer, but a master of disguise, living a double life. She rippled with pleasure.

Across from her, Alan was holding the *Clarion* but not really reading it. Eventually, he said, 'I think it might be better if you stopped seeing young Victor Green.'

She looked up in surprise. 'Whatever for?'

Alan looked troubled. 'I didn't say anything while he was here but there are some details that the public don't know.'

She frowned and, putting the paper aside, he said, 'There have been the usual enquiries in the neighbourhood of Rylstone Gardens and when asked, the park attendant said that there was a man with a small white poodle hanging around the gate at closing time. His description fits Victor.' He looked at her to see her reaction but her expression was unreadable. He added, 'When they did the post-mortem, Fingers had puncture marks on his ankle, exactly like Mauler Maguire. The pathologist thinks they were bite marks made by a small dog.'

Charity's eyes widened. Then perhaps Fluffy *was* the Angel of Death! It was no good, she had to find out exactly where Victor had been on Monday night. She paused in her thoughts. On the one hand she longed to be the one to unmask a master criminal but on the other, she was talking about her own boy-friend. Perhaps she could persuade him to go straight? One day when she and Victor were married and had two children, a boy called Alan after her father and a girl called Victoria for her mother, her father would say to her, 'I wonder what became of Vincenzo Verdi? He just seemed to disappear. Perhaps he died?' She smiled to herself.

'Charity, are you listening to me?' Alan couldn't interpret her expression. He was expecting her to argue with him, to say that she wouldn't give him up, to say that her father had no right to tell her what to do, but the smile? Now he was truly at a loss.

FIFTEEN

The combination of a sleepless night and the discovery that he had been implicated in three deaths meant that Victor didn't feel well enough to go to work the next morning. He was consumed by the knowledge that sooner or later someone was going to come and *'take him out'* or *'finish him off'* or *'see to him'*. However you put it, his life must now be in danger and he didn't know where to turn for help.

He phoned the office to say that he thought he had the flu, giving a rather convincing cough for good measure. 'Well, let us know how you are tomorrow,' the receptionist said. She was a nice, motherly lady who never tired of telling him that her daughter was about the same age as him. It hadn't occurred to him until now, but it seemed that her daughter might be another young woman looking for a husband and her mother had him lined him up for the role. 'If you need any shopping or anything, I could ask Elizabeth to pop in on her way home,' she offered. Elizabeth – strange that the girl should have the very name that he had invented for his private Madonna.

'No, really. I have a friend coming round later.' He left her to make of that what she would.

He crawled out of bed to let Fluffy into the garden, anxiously watching through a crack in the door in case someone was lurking nearby to take the dog hostage. He tried to imagine what he would do if Fluffy was kidnapped. He imagined saying, 'Let the dog go, take me instead,' but he wasn't sure that he was willing to swap his own life for his sometimes-difficult pet. When Fluffy finally came back in Victor locked the door, fed him and the cats, made a cup of tea and retreated upstairs.

If anyone broke in he would barricade the bedroom door and phone the police.

As he feared, Charity arrived at about ten to take Fluffy for a walk. From the bedroom he could hear her clunking around downstairs, talking to Fluffy, and from the sound of drawers opening she was generally tidying up and making herself useful. It wasn't until he gave an accidental cough that he heard her stop in her tracks and call up, 'Is anyone there?'

'It's me. Not too well,' he called out. As she came to investigate he quickly added, 'I shouldn't come too close – I might be infectious,' but Charity was a hardy girl and not afraid of the odd germ.

She placed her hand on his forehead, pulled down the lower lids of his eyes and told him to stick out his tongue. Obediently he did so.

'Hmm.'

Lying in bed he felt particularly vulnerable to her attentions. It seemed that the same thing had occurred to her and, having been denied the evening before when he had come to tea, she clearly decided that now was a very good time indeed.

'Charity, please!' Victor hung on to the cord of his pyjama trousers but she slapped his hand and said, 'Don't be silly, I just want to see if you have a rash anywhere.' He knew when he was defeated.

Charity seemed in good form. She kept calling him darling and muttering something about standing by him no matter what. She mounted him like a runner in the three-thirty at Kempton Park while, like a Victorian wife, he lay back and submitted. When she had sorted him out, she said, 'I think you had too much to drink last night, that's all.'

He was too exhausted to argue. In all fairness, though, he wondered if he should warn her that he was expecting someone to come round and *'snuff him out'*, but that would call for an explanation that he just wasn't up to giving. 'I think I'll just try and sleep,' he offered, and Charity went off to take Fluffy for a constitutional.

'Did you see anyone?' he asked on her return.

'See anyone?'

'Anyone outside – you know, lurking about.' Quickly he added, 'I saw something in the *Clarion* about a spate of burglaries. I thought perhaps someone might be casing the joint.' She gave him an indulgent little smile. 'Don't you worry yourself about that. Besides, you've got the dog.' As an afterthought, she added, 'Anyway, I can stay the night, keep you company.'

'No! I – I wouldn't want you to catch what I've got.'

It was hopeless. She spent the day cleaning in corners, rearranging the kitchen, then the bedroom. She had all his clothes out of the wardrobe and advised him strongly to get rid of certain items: 'Really Victor, no one wears these any more.' To escape, he closed his eyes and pretended to be asleep.

At her insistence, Charity did stay the night. Victor realised that he had never actually slept in a bed with anyone before and he didn't like it. Whichever way he turned, part of her anatomy always seemed to be in the way. She flung an arm across his chest, trapping him and, later, her leg insinuated its way between his and he was treated to another attempt at what she called 'making love', but his manhood had a mind of its own and defied her.

'Never mind. All men have that problem at some time.' She gave him a little pat, turned over and began to snore.

By morning, he made sure that he was up and dressed and ready to go to work.

'You aren't thinking of going to the office when you're ill?' She gazed at him soulfully from the bed.

'I must. We're short-staffed. I need to be there.' Before she could argue, he raced down the stairs and made his escape.

Charity spent the day walking the dog and looking for clues. When Victor came home from work there was nothing about his demeanour to suggest that he had spent any part of the day carrying out another gangland killing. She dished him up a *lentil surprise* and grilled him closely about his activities, but learned nothing useful. Thinking of her father, she decided that perhaps she should just go home. With luck Alan may have something new to impart.

'Are you sure that you'll be alright?' she asked, thinking that perhaps Victor wanted her to stay.

'Of course I will.' He yawned meaningfully. 'I'm a little tired. I could do with a night's uninterrupted sleep.'

She arched her eyebrows, then smiled. 'Alright. I expect I can manage without you for a whole night.'

Was it her imagination, or did he look relieved?

When she got home Alan was out. She knocked up another *lentil surprise* and scanned the late edition of the *Clarion* to see if any murders or executions had taken place in the area. If they had – well then she really should tell her father of her suspicions. In the event, there was nothing of any interest.

SIXTEEN

Having made up his mind that something must be done about Vincenzo Verdi, Barry went over a list of available operatives at the office. They seemed to be very thin on the ground. He was looking for someone – anyone – whom he could trust to undertake this very important mission. He had made up his mind. He was going to send one of the Pretty Boys to bump off the hitman. For ages he thought about all the implications, all the qualities needed for this most difficult of tasks. However, he couldn't think of one person whom he could trust with this job. An awful truth dawned on him. If it was going to happen, then he would have to do it himself.

The very thought reduced him to a jelly but there was nothing for it. He had never killed anyone before. In fact, he had never killed anything. The idea of bashing Vincent over the head or throttling him or running him through with a dagger made him feel faint. There was only one way that he would be able to do it and that was with a gun.

He went across to the drinks cabinet. He knew that the cupboard had a false back and lurking behind the panel was a selection of firearms. Fortunately, Barry had fired a gun before. When he was young his father had insisted that he should learn to shoot, and he used to go along to a firing range and eliminate numerous cardboard figures. He had been good at it too. He had enjoyed playing at soldiers, being the hero of one of his own make-believe stories, but it was just that, a game. He prided himself on having been a good shot but it was years since he had even handled a gun.

Opening the cupboard and removing the back panel, he looked at the assortment of deadly weapons in the alcove. After some deliberation, he picked out a lightweight automatic and a magazine. He wasn't familiar with this particular model, and it took him a while to work out how to assemble it, but at last there was a satisfying click as he pushed the last component into place.

At that moment there was a knock on the door, and he scrabbled to push the gun back into the cupboard and close it.

'Come in!'

It was Sonia.

She was wearing a very tight top that caused her boobs to wobble like two strawberry blancmanges. No wonder she had been a success at The Earthly Delights.

'I've just heard from Harry,' she said, stretching herself and almost purring at the thought.

Barry felt indignant. He was a child again competing for the attention of his eldest brother. 'Why didn't you put him through to me?'

'Because he rang to speak to me.' She threw a derisive glance at him, her mouth set in a self-satisfied smirk. He longed to wipe it off her face, but remembering the gun lurking just inside the cupboard he thought that he should get her out of the room as quickly as possible. If he wasn't careful, he might be reduced to using her for target practice.

'Well, what did he say?'

'He says they're coming back on Sunday – and that you shouldn't do anything until then. He'll sort everything out himself when he gets back.'

Stung by her tone, he answered, 'There won't be any need. It will all be settled by then.'

━

Over the weekend Dodge had been considering his options and had come to the conclusion that Frenchie was the only man he could safely employ to take out Vincenzo Verdi. He considered the situation at length and there was no doubt about it. Vincent/Vincenzo had to go. If he was out of the picture then perhaps he and the Pretty Boys could negotiate a settlement, but as long as a hitman was waiting in the wings, looking for work, there was little hope of getting back to normal.

Leon leFevre had just arrived back from Paris. He had been to see his mother who lived in a retirement home for nuns. It seemed that after Leon's birth she had seen the light, and as soon as he was old enough she had sent him off to a boarding school and taken her vows. She was now known as Sister Serenity.

In answer to Dodge's call, Frenchie came over to see him. He was a small, dark man with a black moustache that looked as if it had been pencilled on. It twitched in time with his rather beaky nose which he a habit of wrinkling when he was concentrating. He looked like a curious mouse.

'How was Paris?' Dodge asked as an opening.

'Formidable.' Frenchie kissed his fingertips flamboyantly.

'Good. I'm glad you're back because I have a very important job for you. I'm trusting you not to let me down.'

Frenchie looked at Dodge with raised eyebrows. 'Really, mon brave. What is it that you wish for me to do?'

'I want someone disposed of, as soon as possible.'

Frenchie pulled a face. 'That is not my line of work.'

'I know that but it's important – and I think you would be better at it than me.'

Frenchie shrugged, a Gallic gesture that was one of his mannerisms. 'So oo is zis person?'

'Vincenzo Verdi.'

'Zut! You are serious?'

'Very serious. Frenchie, if we get rid of him we can all get back to business. He's the one causing all the trouble at the moment.'

Frenchie pulled another face. 'Ow much?' he asked.

'Twenty grand.'

Frenchie considered. Clearly the thought of the payment was doing its work. 'I – I will shoot but nothing else, no knife, no strangles, nothing touching.'

'That's fine. Do it any way you want, as long as it's soon.'

Two days had passed without incident and Victor was beginning to feel safe again. By pleading a bad back he managed to avoid Charity's most intimate attentions and he felt that life was really beginning to get back to normal. It was a shock, therefore, when he took Fluffy out for his evening stroll on Thursday and suddenly became aware that he was being watched.

The first thing he noticed was a man in a black beret standing in the doorway of Bicycle World. He was leaning back in the shadows and did not look in the least like the sort of man who would want to buy a bicycle. Victor tightened his grip on Fluffy's lead and hurried on a few yards, stopping to look in the window of Mothercare. For a moment he was distracted because they had some rather nice quilted blankets that would be ideal for Fluffy and the kittens, then he remembered the man across the road. Carefully, he positioned himself in such a way so that he could see the pavement opposite reflected in the plate glass of the window. Sure enough, the man with the beret had moved down a few shops and was now staring in the electrical appliances shop window.

As Victor went to move on down towards the High Street he became aware that there was also somebody on his side of the road, a young fair-haired man who seemed distinctly nervous. He wore an unseasonably large raincoat and he appeared to have a spinal curvature because he was bending over to the left while his right hand was tucked into his side. Victor wondered if the poor chap was deformed.

Victor went to hurry on but Fluffy chose that moment to empty his bowels, so he was forced to a sudden halt while the dog hopped from leg to leg to find the right position, his pompom bouncing in the air. He then made a big show of scraping the ground around his deposit.

'Fluffy, hurry up!'

The man in the beret moved away from the electrical appliances shop window and promptly dived into Wholefoods R Us. The young Quasimodo also hesitated then crossed the road, ending up on the same side as beret man.

Victor felt guilty but he didn't stop to clear up after Fluffy. Instead, he dragged the little dog along rather faster than he wanted to go, still heading for the High Street.

As Victor walked faster, so did both men on the other side of the road. He didn't think that they were together and neither did they seem to be aware of each other, but Victor was very aware of them both. This was a long road and the High Street still looked very distant.

He began to jog and, glancing over his shoulder, he saw beret man shuffling along faster than before. The younger man was also gathering speed, despite his awkward gait. He seemed to be encumbered by a large object under his raincoat and Victor wondered if he might wear some complicated brace – or maybe he had bought something from the furniture shop on the corner and was struggling to get it home.

Apart from the two men there was no one else in the road. He was alone with two potential attackers. Losing his nerve, Victor hoisted Fluffy into his arms and began to run for the junction and the traffic lights.

Behind him he heard two sets of echoing footsteps increasing in speed. Now, blind panic set in and, racing for the main road, he hurled himself across the pedestrian crossing. Fortunately the traffic light was red, although just as he stepped off it the amber light began to flash. Without stopping to look back he turned left, preparing to dive into the first pub or café he came to. Before he had gone two yards he heard an unholy screeching of breaks and, behind him, a sickening thud and gasps from people walking nearby.

Resolutely he kept walking, longing to know what had happened but not daring to look round. At last he came to the Bear and Biscuit and pushed the door open with a trembling hand.

Inside the public house it was quite busy but he saw a table over in the corner. Buying himself a large gin at the bar, he hurried across to lose himself among the drinkers. Fluffy was in danger of being trampled by the evening drinkers and took refuge under the table, whimpering to himself.

A few moments later a couple came in. The man was holding the girl by the arm, reassuring her. To the bartender he said, 'Nasty accident up at the lights. Some bloke ran straight out under a lorry. Bit of a mess.' He patted the girl on the arm and ordered her a brandy. 'We didn't stop to see what happened,' he continued. 'There were plenty of witnesses and Sandra here is upset.' He gave her a reassuring squeeze and they sat at a table a little way away. Victor could not quite hear what they were saying. He took a large gulp of his gin and his overriding thought was to wonder what had become of the second man.

For perhaps half an hour he sat and stared at the door, hardly daring to blink in case he spotted one of his followers, but no one remotely resembling either of them came in. Victor risked getting himself a second gin, and as it did its work he began to rethink the situation. Had the men been following him? Buoyed up with Dutch courage it seemed much less clear. Perhaps it was his imagination. Perhaps when he started to run the men had hurried for quite separate reasons of their own. Calmer now, he decided that he would not mention this to anyone. After all, he could hardly ask for police protection, could he? The more he thought about it the more unlikely the whole thing seemed. Best to go home and get a good night's sleep. A little unsteadily, he got to his feet and tucked Fluffy under his arm, just as the dog had spotted an inviting ankle. Deprived of his fun, Fluffy weed down Victor's jacket.

━━●

Further down the road, Barry Hickman walked shakily into the Tub and Thumper and ordered a large whisky. He was shaking so much that he could barely stand.

'You alright mate?' The bartender gave him a curious look.

'Just saw someone run over on the crossing,' Barry blurted out. 'Lots of people saw it. I – I felt sick so I didn't stop.'

'Poor sod,' the bartender said. 'It never pays to jump the lights.'

Barry struggled to get some change out of his pocket, being

encumbered by the automatic rifle tucked beneath his jacket. He had quickly realised that this was not the weapon of choice if you were stalking someone in a busy street. Somehow he doled out the right money and picked up his whisky. He needed to sit somewhere quiet, where no one would notice him, but the place was quite crowded. He managed to slide onto the end of a bench, the rifle jabbing him in the thigh. He had a sudden panic in case it accidentally went off, and he couldn't remember actually assembling it. Perhaps it wouldn't fire at all. If Vincenzo Verdi had turned on him then he wouldn't have had a chance to get a shot in first, not with the gun stuffed down inside his jacket.

Vincenzo had been something of a shock. Barry had been expecting someone lithe yet muscular, moving with an easy grace and blending easily into the shadows. This had been a little runt of a man with floppy hair and accompanied by a ridiculous looking poodle. At the thought of the poodle, he suddenly remembered Gruesome. He had had a dog like that, a sort of crazy trademark. Hadn't they called it the Angel of Death? Coming back to what had happened to that guy at the crossing, something cold and dark seemed to envelop him. Supposing it was the dog that had the power, some demonic ability to bring about the destruction of his enemies? Fortunately he had been behind that other guy, the one who had copped it. He wondered briefly who he was, probably some innocent bystander. Strange the way Fate picked out its victims. If Barry had been in front... at the thought, he shook so much that his teeth began to chatter. Getting rid of Vincenzo Verdi was going to be a mammoth task.

SEVENTEEN

Alan was called to a road traffic accident in the centre of town. Some chap had jumped the lights at a pedestrian crossing with lethal consequences. He hated these sorts of cases, a moment's misjudgement and a tragedy of enormous proportions.

The lorry driver who had hit him was in a bit of a state. Someone had found him a chair and he was sitting by the side of the road with a blanket around his shoulders. The victim was also covered with a blanket, stretched out diagonally several yards from the crossing where he had been thrown by the impact. One of Alan's colleagues was turning the traffic back and a bottleneck was fast building up.

The driver, whose name was Arthur, kept trying to explain. 'The lights had changed, I'm certain they had. I started to move forward and he just jumped into the road.' He looked around him for support. To Alan, he said, 'D'you think it might have been suicide?'

Young Isabelle Peters, a new constable, was on duty with him and rather than give her the job of touching the body he sent her to take statements from the bystanders. Girding himself up for the unpleasantness of the task, he bent down and eased the blanket back.

He wasn't much of a specimen, this victim. His eyes and mouth were still open, as if at the last moment he had been aware of the lorry and was about to emit a shriek of alarm. He looked as if he had put his hands up to ward off the impact, realising too late what was happening, and his arms were still raised up towards his face. Apart from a trickle of blood around his left ear, there were no signs of injury.

Alan carefully inserted his hand into the victim's coat pocket and managed to extricate a wallet and some other pieces of paper.

The writing on them was all in French. Taking in the man's appearance, it seemed indeed likely that he was from across the Channel. The thought came to him that at least he wouldn't be the one to have to break the bad news. He eased the man a fraction so that he could reach his other pocket, running his hand down his side. He felt something bulky and solid at his hip. Pulling it half out of the pocket, he found himself holding the butt of a pistol. Quickly he shoved it back again. His job was only to see if there was a next of kin he could contact. Guns were something else.

Alan turned back to the crowd. The man who was comforting the driver said, 'I got the impression he was chasing someone. There was a little chap racing up the road ahead of him and he just caught the lights.'

'What happened to him?'

'He just kept going. We were all too shocked by what happened to pay him much attention.' As an afterthought, he said, 'Perhaps he didn't realise what happened.'

'What did he look like?'

The comforter thought. 'Little, skinny, a bit pansy-ish really. He had a titchy little dog with him.'

'What – what colour was it?' Alan felt his throat grow dry.

'A little white poodle thing.'

Alan's heart seemed to plummet in his chest. This was just too much of a coincidence. What the hell was going on? To the witness, he said, 'I'm sorry, Sir, but we might need you to come to the station to make a statement. What you saw may be significant.' To himself, he added very significant indeed.

—◣—

Dodge had stayed at the office. Before Frenchie set out on his mission, he said to him, 'Make sure and let me know how it went, won't you?' He was having second thoughts about the whole thing. It was alright in the films but in real life, killing someone wasn't so easy. Supposing Vincenzo Verdi got in first and shot Frenchie? All they would have achieved was to put the hitman on his guard and make it even more difficult to get him out of the way.

The evening dragged and he heard nothing so at last he decided to go home. As he drove towards his neighbourhood, he saw that there was a large diversion sign down by the High Street and a Police Accident notice. Cursing, he turned off and faced a convoluted journey just to get on the other side of the main road. People really should drive more carefully.

It was then that he wondered if Frenchie had topped Verdi down near the junction. Surely he wouldn't be so stupid as to shoot him in a public place? If so, there was a good chance that he had been caught and arrested. At the thought he swerved, narrowly missing a gatepost. He slowed right down, trying to concentrate, but whichever way he looked at it, if Frenchie was in custody, sooner or later he was going to break and tell the cops everything.

Another thought occurred to him. Supposing Vincenzo had spotted him and taken him prisoner? It wouldn't take him long to get out of Frenchie that it was Dodge who had set it up and then he would become the focus for Vincenzo's next killing. God, this was awful. There must be a way out.

The next day he was going to visit his brother Randy in Camp Hill. He felt a sense of relief. Somehow he'd manage to tell the whole story to his brother and ask him his advice. He'd have to be careful though, make sure the screw didn't cotton on. He arrived home without any further incident and went straight to bed.

The next morning he got up early. He could have been driven to the prison but he thought that he would rather give himself thinking time on the bus. On the way he could rehearse exactly what he was going to say, decide what he needed to know.

On the journey he had plenty of opportunity to think about the events of the day before. He still hadn't heard any news of Frenchie. He no longer trusted his judgement and it would be a relief to ask Randy's advice. Randy would know what to do.

At the prison they went through the usual routine of showing papers and being frisked. Camp Hill was a newer prison, lighter, less gloomy than Parkhurst, and catered for less dangerous guests. Essentially though, the place had the same smell of men and cooking, overlaid with whiffs of cannabis that somehow managed to find its way into every penal institution. Dodge guessed that it was Randy who had been sent here rather than his brother because Reggie was generally viewed as the driving force behind their nefarious activities. Twins they might be and physically the original two peas, but in personality there was a softer, more restrained side to Randy. The prison ethos was gentler too, an attempt to treat even hardened cons with respect and kindness in the belief that it might rub off on them. As a result, there were no uniform tables separating visitor from prisoner, just a series of comfortable chairs neatly spaced in pairs.

Randy was waiting for him in a seat near to the window. Although it was no doubt heavily reinforced and possibly even electrified in some devilish way, the window gave the impression of a light, sunny room with a vista onto an undulating field. They were in a peaceful rural setting.

'Dodge!' Randy looked genuinely pleased to see him. The screw nodded indulgently as they embraced, keeping an eye on them yes, but not obtrusively. Randy looked quite animated.

'Our appeal comes up on Monday.' He bristled with nervous excitement. 'Our barrister has got new evidence. Witnesses have come forward to prove that we weren't there when the robbery was committed.'

But you were, Dodge thought, then decided it was best not to pursue that train of thought.

Randy stopped to draw breath. He grinned. 'All being well, before the end of next week we'll both be out.'

'That's wonderful!' Dodge did not want to spoil his brother's euphoria by filling him in on recent events.

'I saw Reggie last week,' he started.

'How is he?'

'Well. He didn't know about the appeal.' Try as he might, he could not cast aside his worries. He hesitated, then blurted out, 'There have been a few incidents lately. Reg thinks that the Pretty Boys are trying to move in on our territory — he wants me to take steps to sort it out.'

Randy's face clouded. 'Yes, I heard about Frenchie.'

'Frenchie?'

'Yes, the accident. It was on the news.' He shook his head. 'Good man, Frenchie. He'll be missed.'

Dodge was glad that he was sitting down. Black waves crashed through his head and he had to hold on to the arm of the chair to stop himself from sliding to the ground. 'Was he shot?' he managed to ask.

'Shot? No, he was run over apparently, on a pedestrian crossing of all things.'

Dodge was breathing heavily to ward off the blackness.

'Dodge?' Randy leaned towards him.

'Something wrong?' The omniscient screw came forward.

'Nothing, Sir. He's just feeling a bit faint that's all. It will pass.'

Dodge made a huge effort to take control of himself. 'I'm alright, thanks,' he managed to say, sitting up straight.

As soon as the warder withdrew, Randy asked, 'What in hell's going on?'

In a low voice it all tumbled out, the death of Gruesome so closely followed by Mauler, then Fingers — and now this. Quietly, guiltily, Dodge explained his decision to take Vincenzo Verdi out.

Randy drew in his breath at the wisdom of the plan.

'Have you ever met Verdi?' Dodge asked, a disturbing sense of guilt mixed with his earlier fantasies about the elusive hitman.

'No. I don't think anyone has. That's how he operates, through banks, institutions, keeping his identity secret.'

Dodge remembered the original report in the *Clarion*, how they had even printed his address, but he didn't say anything. It was just another niggling doubt in his mind. Meanwhile, the enormity of Frenchie's demise began to fill his thoughts.

Randy said, 'Look Dodge, if Reggie and I are going to be home in a week, perhaps you should just keep a low profile. We'll sort everything out when we get home.'

Dodge nodded. This was the best news he had heard in weeks.

Charity was having second thoughts about her relationship with Victor. He was forever trying to fob her off with some pretext about bad backs and early starts and having things to do. Besides, the sex wasn't up to much and she really didn't like Fluffy. He was a stupid, snappy little dog, always peeing and yapping. She had more or less made up her mind to stop seeing either of them when Alan came home from work looking particularly drawn and grey.

'Bad day?' she asked, dishing him up a nut roast with bean sprouts and spinach.

'Bad enough. Nasty accident down on the High Street.' He was frowning, his thoughts in another place. Eventually he gave a sigh of monumental proportions and said, 'The damned thing is, witnesses say that the victim was chasing a little bloke with a white poodle.' He looked up to see her reaction.

She showed very little other than to blink rapidly. 'Have you managed to speak to him?' she asked, her voice made brittle by the tension in her throat.

He shook his head. 'He disappeared. The thing is, there's no evidence that a crime has been committed here. According to everyone who saw it, the guy just ran out into the road. The other thing is that his name is Leon leFevre and he's yet another known associate of the Blues Brothers.'

Rapidly Charity began to reverse her strategy. Yes, she did want to get rid of Victor as her boyfriend but her original plan to follow up the mysterious case of this secret assassin must now be her priority.

Aloud she said, 'Leave it to me. I'll find out what Victor was doing tonight if it kills me.'

Seeing her father's alarm, she added, 'Don't worry, only joking.'

■—■

The *Clarion* was having a field day. Somehow their reporter had got wind of the fact that the ubiquitous white poodle had been at the scene of this latest accident and it ran as its front-page headline: '*Angel of Death Strikes Again!*' It also featured a photograph of a large, very superior white French poodle that was about ten sizes bigger and bore no resemblance whatsoever to Fluffy. The caption read, '*If you see this dog, be very afraid!*'

At home Victor was coming to the conclusion that he would now be under siege. Step outside the gate with Fluffy in tow and someone would spot him. Before he could draw breath he would be accosted, arrested, questioned, perhaps imprisoned for a series of crimes, none of which he had committed. The worst one could say was that he had landed on Gruesome Hewson and that Fluffy had nipped the ankles of both Mauler Maguire and Fingers Kilbride. In fact, the worst scenario was that Fluffy would be put down as a dangerous dog.

As he considered the possibility, Victor's thoughts on that particular outcome were mixed indeed. He had looked forward to having the dog as a companion, felt sorry for him in his abandoned state, but the reality was that he had dirty habits and was at best of uncertain temperament. Walkies were no fun in case Fluffy took it into his head to bite a passer by. At the same time, Victor always had to be on the alert in case another dog came near and threatened Fluffy with actual bodily harm, in which case the poodle promptly went into meltdown, yelping for Britain before he was even touched. No, dog ownership was not at all what it was cracked up to be. Besides, Victor had a strong desire to go away somewhere, get away from it all, but with the dog he was trapped. If the police took action then he would be powerless to stop it. It wouldn't be his fault if Fluffy was found guilty and despatched to meet his maker. Perhaps he should go to the station and confess to everything? At the very worst he could only see himself being charged with failing to report an incident – well, several incidents, but surely the sentence would not be too long? But then of course, on the downside, he would lose his job at the tax office, lose his civil service pension – no, perhaps it was not such a good idea after all. He and Fluffy seemed doomed to struggle on together.

As these thoughts assailed him, there was a knock at the door and it opened immediately with the call of 'Yoohoo!' It was Charity.

For once he was glad to see her. It crossed his mind to tell her everything. Whatever her failings she was unbeatable when it came to taking control of a situation and she would know what to do. The sly thought came to him that if he went to gaol then perhaps he could palm Fluffy off onto her, thereby being released of his burden.

Charity came into the living room and removed her jacket, throwing it across the arm of a chair, a gesture that reminded him of their first date when… He must not think about *Last Tango in Paris*.

'How are you?' he asked, for want of anything better to say.

'More important, how are you – not too busy? Back not hurting? Not got to get up early in the morning?' She hadn't intended to say any of this and the edge of sarcasm in her voice put Victor on the defensive. No, what she must do was to win his confidence.

To make amends she kissed him on the cheek and said, 'Sorry darling, feeling a bit edgy that's all.' From her handbag she produced a bottle of red wine. 'Thought you would like this.'

'Thank you.' He took it with surprise and she waited expectantly until he hurried off to the kitchen to open it.

One of the kittens was sitting in the dirt box while the other fought a life and death battle with the string from the loose cover of the sofa, unravelling it bit by bit. Fluffy had already come over to say hello, wagging his tail in the expectation that Charity's visit meant a walk. She wondered why he enjoyed walks so much when all he seemed to do was live in fear of other dogs.

Victor came back with two glasses of wine and placed them on coasters on the coffee table. Charity considered her strategy.

'What did you do last night?' she asked, hoping that the enquiry sounded casual.

'Nothing. I stayed in.'

Lie number one. 'Didn't you even take Fluffy for a walk?'

'Oh yes, we just went down the road.'

'Where to?' Did she sound calm and merely polite as if she was making small talk or would he recognise that he was being grilled?

She saw Victor's expression change and physically he stiffened. 'Why are you asking?'

'No reason, I just thought that you might have popped out somewhere, that's all.'

Defensively, Victor said, 'I popped into a pub for a drink.'

'You? On your own?' Too late she recognised the disbelief in her voice.

Lie number two. 'I was thirsty,' he replied.

Trying to regain control of her role, Charity asked, 'Which pub was that then?'

'I can't remember.'

She was about to challenge him as to the impossibility of having forgotten so soon when she realised that this wasn't getting her anywhere. Instead she said, 'I only thought that if it was somewhere nice, perhaps you and I could go there sometime.'

'It was just in the High Street.'

'Near where that accident happened last night?'

'I don't know. What accident?'

'Just some chap ran out in front of a lorry at the traffic lights.'

She took a huge gulp of wine and put her glass down again before coming across to him and placing her hands on his shoulders. 'Victor, you do know that you can trust me, don't you. With anything.'

She felt him lean away from her until his back was pressed against the back of the chair. His hands gripped the arms until his knuckles were white. 'Charity, I don't think…'

'Just relax now. I am going to make you feel a lot better…'

In spite of himself, the hypnotic movement of her fingers transported him into another place. Just as he was abandoning himself to a daydream where he was being held prisoner by the minister for Social Services, whose name he had forgotten but who was busty and bossy and might well have caned the juniors in her department, Charity stopped. His eyes jerked open. She was looking down at him. He couldn't interpret her expression. 'Please,' he whimpered, desperate to get back to the minister. Charity said, 'Victor, we'll continue after you have told me the truth.' Her hand gave him a gentle tug to remind him of what he was now missing.

'Tell me,' she said, sliding her leg across his and raising her skirts in promise of more delights to come. 'Are you Vincenzo Verdi?'

'What?'

'Are you Vincenzo Verdi, the hitman? Go on, you know you can tell me.'

'Charity, of course I'm not.' He struggled to sit up but she had him pinioned beneath her.

'Do you swear, on Fluffy's life?'

'Fluffy? Oh course I swear. How could I be a hitman? I've never handled a gun in my life.'

'You promise?'

'I promise.'

'That's alright then.'

Ten minutes later and Victor didn't know whether he felt better or not. As Charity slipped from his lap and smoothed down her skirt, she said, 'You'll really have to try and hold on a bit longer.' He felt like a pupil who had just taken a test and received the verdict of 'could do better.'

EIGHTEEN

The Singapore Airlines flight from Sydney had just landed at Heathrow airport. The journey had lasted for nearly thirty hours as there had been an unscheduled stop at Hong Kong but at last it touched down just as the sun was setting.

The first class passengers trouped off looking travel-worn. Altogether there were about a dozen, a cosmopolitan mixture of Chinese, Asian and Europeans all distinguished by a certain veneer of wealth that separated them from the general masses.

Among them was a man in his early forties wearing charcoal grey trousers and a black shirt. In spite of the long journey, he alone of his fellow travellers looked cool and at ease. He was of average height but distinguished by his impressive athletic carriage, not muscular so much as lithe. He might have been a dancer. His head of sleek black curling hair showed the first signs of grey at the temples. His passport bore the name of Guido Morelli. He was known in five continents as Vincenzo Verdi.

Guido, or more properly Vincenzo, had just returned from a successful assignment in Canberra. It had been easy. Fly in, stay a couple of days as a tourist to stake out the place, carry out the commission then move on to Melbourne for more tourism and fly back to the UK. He travelled lightly, just a black shoulder bag with shaving gear and some clean underwear. Everything else, wardrobe, weapon, was acquired on site. By the time he reached his hotel, a sum of £60,000 sterling would have been paid into his Swiss bank account.

Vincenzo flagged down a taxi and sat in the back, pointedly shutting himself off from the driver in case he felt inclined to pass the time of day. While he was away he had heard a rumour that his name was being banded around along the south coast. His first task was to find out what was going on.

At the Royal Cascade in Mayfair he had a suite permanently booked in the name of Giuseppi Milano. It was plush yet discreet and he had been left in peace there for the best part of two years. These rumours made him edgy and he wondered whether the time had come to look for another base, perhaps on the continent this time. The taxi dropped him off in Camberwell, where he picked up a passport from a run-down little shop in the name of Milano, where he had a private letterbox. It gave his occupation as pasta merchant, a legitimate reason for criss-crossing Europe. Taking another taxi he went to the hotel. As requested, the broadsheets from the last two weeks were waiting in his room. He took a shower, changed into clothing permanently hung in his closet, raided the drinks bar, sent down for some smoked salmon sandwiches and settled down to catch up on the latest news and rumours.

It soon became clear that something was seriously amiss here. Although the reports were brief, two South London gangs, the Blues Brothers and the Pretty Boys, appeared to be embarking on a gang war on the Isle of Wight and already several people had died in mysterious circumstances. It was these circumstances that worried him. If these were all contract killings made to look like accidents, then their bizarre nature made him feel very uneasy indeed. Goof old-fashioned shootings and stabbings were much more reliable. His name was being hinted at as the hitman working for at least one gang. Tomorrow he would take a little trip to the Isle of Wight and see what was going on.

The hotel arranged the hire of a Mercedes and it was delivered to the door at 10.30 the next morning. As soon as the paperwork was sorted out he drove south.

He caught the ferry from Portsmouth. As the grey stone of Southsea Castle and the red brick of the barracks faded away, he went on deck to watch the shipping. It was a busy waterway, everything from container ships to tiny dinghies criss-crossing the ferry's path. The whole was bathed in a soothing crystal light, calming him, focussing his thoughts.

From Fishbourne he drove to Shanklin, cutting across country and through narrow, hedge-lined lanes. En route he passed through the village of Havenstreet. Before he left London he had checked out the Isle of Wight and discovered that there was a steam railway there. He stopped just long enough to glance over at the metal monsters lined up in the marshalling yard. A thrilling shriek from one of the funnels sent a tingle along his spine. Trains had been his passion since boyhood. If he hadn't taken up his present profession he might well have been an engine driver.

Arriving at Shanklin he located the road where the phantom Vincenzo Verdi was supposed to be living. It looked innocuous enough but hardly the place where an international assassin was likely to find anonymity. Even as he watched, a flutter of lace at the neighbouring window alerted him to the dangers posed by nosy spinsters. His best source of information would be the office of the local newspaper, the *Clarion*, so he made his way there.

The reception area of the newspaper office provided tables and chairs where readers could scan various editions of the publication. Vincenzo sat quietly, making notes from different dates. Here he found a wealth of incredible speculation. It seemed that using the English version of his name, Vincent Green, the mysterious assassin had dropped initially from a tree onto a local thug. His name and address had even been conveniently printed in the paper. 'Princess Alice Cottage, Queen Victoria Avenue.' He had heard that Queen Victoria had once taken refuge on this Island and the locals seemed to have taken her to their hearts. Looking in his local map book, he checked out all the major roads to and from the town, just in case he needed to make a speedy exit.

As he was writing, a man came in to place an advert in the Friday edition of the paper. He clearly had time to spare.

'What's new then lad, have they found the Angel of Death yet?' he asked the cub reporter at the news desk. The youngster, spotty, gangly, was happy to oblige.

'It's all true, what they say. This Vincent Green who killed Tommy Hewson has been seen in the vicinity of all the jobs – *and* he's got a white poodle.'

'Has he now? He's really a hitman then?'

'Sure as eggs.'

The visitor asked, 'Why haven't the police picked him up then?'

The reporter leaned forward conspiratorially. 'Evidence. I've heard they haven't actually got any proof that he's done anything wrong.' He nodded to show the significance of this discovery. 'Must be bloody clever, that's all I can say.'

'Makes you wonder if any of us are safe in our beds.'

Vincenzo chose that moment to leave. His thoughts disturbed him. Was it really possible that someone using his name was successfully carrying out a series of killings and making them all look like accidents? He wandered aimlessly along the High Street. Another thought occurred to him. Who was paying this guy? Was it the Pretty Boys, or the Blues Brothers, or even both? He'd done jobs for both of them in the past. His face grew taut. Was some bastard ripping him off, taking a fee that should be coming his way? If so, he was one foolish cat, one very foolish cat indeed.

A familiar sensation began to spread through him, shutting him off from the outside world, focusing his mind on a single objective. There was a job to do here. He turned in the direction of the car park where he had left the Mercedes, honing his thoughts until they cut through everything except the need to take decisive action – so decisive that there was no going back.

Groping Joe Windsor called round at the Department Store to see if he could catch Dodge, but he was not there. He had always felt a sort of proprietorial interest in young Dodge ever since he was a toddler. There had always been something soft and malleable about the boy. Groping Joe's fingers fluttered at the thought of finally getting to grips with that young flesh, although he had to be careful. His was an unfortunate affliction – this need to cosset and cuddle young boys and men. They were hardly ever willing, so he had developed an additional strategy for getting his own way by simple force of intimidation. In its own way it added another piquant dimension to the pleasure. This wasn't a risk he could take with Dodge, however, in case he grassed to one of those brothers of his. Pity.

Groping Joe was often at a loose end these days. Ever since Reggie had been banged up he hadn't been called upon to do any work. He and Reg understood each other, not that Reg was any more interested in his advances than Dodge seemed to be, but they had a healthy respect for each other's little foibles.

Being at a loose end, Groping Joe decided that he would go and case the house owned by Vincent Green, see if he could come up with any information that might be useful to the Blues Brothers – and earn a few bob for himself in the process. With each recent accident he had grown more in awe of this Vincent's skill in disposing of unwanted obstacles, and he really wanted to see this legend for himself. Who knows, he might even be one of Joe's ilk – what he always thought of as the brotherhood. His imagination went into overdrive.

He walked up Queen Victoria Avenue and strolled past Princess Alice Cottage, glancing covertly up the path. The house appeared to be empty and Joe had a vague notion that Vincent worked as a tax officer, clearly a masterly cover for his real activities. An idea occurred to him, and, looking up and down the lane to see if he was being watched, he scuttled up the drive. For a moment he wondered whether he should simply ring the front doorbell, but then he decided against it. Princess Alice Cottage was screened by a tall hedge that separated it from Empress Frederick Cottage next door, so with little risk of being seen, Joe opened the back gate and stepped into the garden. He found himself in what was almost a caricature of a cottage garden, tiny lawns, herbaceous borders, heavily scented roses, honeysuckle; every sort of flower that he thought of as old-fashioned. It was all looking rather overgrown and for a wild moment Joe wondered if Vincent Green might not like to hire him as a gardener. Joe would almost be willing to come round here voluntarily – and who knew, perhaps he and Vincent might develop a relationship?

Breaking away from the fantasy, Joe looked through the kitchen window, forming a tunnel with his hands to cut out the glare. He could see very little and inside everything appeared to be quiet. He sidled towards the back porch and turned the handle of the door. It did not respond to his push and clearly it was locked.

Just as he was standing back to scour the upstairs and see if there was a handy window that had been left open, all hell broke loose. With a shrill yapping noise, a cloudy white blur flew through the cat flap in the back door and raced towards him. Caught off guard, Groping Joe made a dash towards the gate, but before he got there he felt a sharp pain in his right ankle as the small dog sank his teeth into him. It was the last thing that he remembered.

—

Vincenzo Verdi, alias Giuseppi Milano, alias Vincent Green, drove towards Queen Victoria Avenue, parking in a side road called Duchess of Fife Close with which it formed a junction. He had a troubling feeling that what he was about to do was disastrous. In the past he had always made it a rule to plan out his strategy, to spend as little time as possible in the location of a crime and to be absolutely certain that no one would remember seeing him. Already, he had broken several fundamental rules. What he was about to do was not planned. He had already spent time at the offices of the *Clarion* where he *would* be remembered. It was broad daylight and anyone might have witnessed him park the Mercedes – after all, it was a top of the range model and, as such, very noticeable in this modest little community. There was still time for him to change his mind but every nerve, every fibre, was now filled with the thought of the task ahead.

He willed himself to be invisible, sticking to the shadows of the overhanging hedges, gliding silently along the deserted lane until he was back at the address he was looking for. Right opposite was the entry to a footpath, overgrown and clearly very little used. Quietly, he backed between the two hedges and surveyed the cottage opposite. It gave him a perfect view of the pathway and the fence into the garden beyond.

In the lime tree in the front garden, a wood pigeon was cooing contentedly. Looking at its lopped branches, Vincenzo thought that this must be the very tree where the so-called Vincent Green had dropped onto Gruesome Hewson and taken him out. He grew tenser, listening for anything untoward. The curtains at the window next door were drawn. Further in the distance the drone of a lawnmower broke through the background hum of insects. Vinnie breathed deeply to calm himself, slipping his hand into his pocket. Carefully he withdrew the latest, state-of-the-art revolver, ridiculously slim, conveniently fitted with a silencer and telescopic sight. He kept it secreted under the flap of his jacket while he watched, all the time his senses honed to recognise any change in the background sounds of the neighbourhood. Everything was quiet.

Then, he saw what he was looking for, a man in the back garden of Princess Alice Cottage. He wasn't what he expected. He looked grubby, shifty, all the attributes that would mark him out as a suspect. He had expected the so-called Vincent Green to resemble himself. There wasn't time to dwell on it though, for here was his chance to act and be away from the town within the hour. He withdrew the revolver and raised it in the shelter of the hedge, taking careful aim.

Just at that moment a commotion broke out in the back garden. A little white dog came flying out of nowhere and the impostor Vincent Green began to run towards the gate. Too late. Vincenzo had him in his sights, his finger was on the trigger and he squeezed.

He did not wait to see more than his victim topple forward. Hastily slipping the gun back into his pocket, he strolled nonchalantly back towards the main road and to the safety of the Mercedes. Mission completed.

Charity was late. She had slept badly thinking of the evening with Victor. Following her little subterfuge she was now convinced that he was not the hitman, but this left her with a dilemma. She recognised that part of his attraction had been an element of danger, a fantasy that he was more than he seemed, instead of a rather puny tax officer. This being the case, she made up her mind to dump him. She realised now that she should have said something to him last night but she hadn't, and now she felt that she had to fulfil her promise and go and take Fluffy for a walk.

Walking round to the cottage she noticed a rather stunning Mercedes parked at the side of the road. What caught her eye was the registration plate, CAG 27. This happened to be her initials, Charity Alice Grimes, and her age. She imagined owning a car like that – not that she had actually learned to drive, but even so. The driver was sitting inside, holding the steering wheel and staring ahead. Charity gave him a second look. Dressed in a dark polo neck, he looked like the hero in a TV advert for chocolates or coffee, slim, handsome, with beautiful dark wavy hair. She gave him a third look and thought: Yes; that is a bloke I would definitely dump Victor for. At that moment the car pulled away from the kerb, a smooth purring sound that equally had Charity purring inside.

She wandered along Queen Victoria Avenue, daydreaming about having a handsome, suave, sophisticated boyfriend with plenty of money. As she drew near to Princess Alice Cottage she could hear Fluffy barking. It occurred to her that the sound must drive the neighbours crazy. It was amazing that no one had complained. She turned into the drive and called out to the dog. 'Fluffy, hush!' The poodle was by the gate, jumping up and down, growling and yapping alternately. 'Fluffy, what are you barking at?'

As she opened the gate, she saw exactly what Fluffy was barking at. Charity screamed.

NINETEEN

Victor was having a bad morning at work. He had arranged to interview Mr O'Shaughnessy at 10.30 and the Irishman arrived both peeved and late. Remembering Robbie's black eye, Victor escorted him to the interview room but left the door open a fraction so that in the case of trouble, those in the outside office would hear. There was also a panic button under the desk, although until this moment he had never expected to use it.

'And what the Divil would all this be about?' asked Mr O'Shaughnessy. 'Are you saying that I'm lying, is that it?' He shoved his tax return across the table, challenging Victor to find fault with it.

'Of course not, but there do seem to be one or two discrepancies,' Victor glanced nervously at his notes. 'For example, this claim for running two cars for your business – how many men do you employ?'

'Now you know very well I'm not employing anyone. Who do you think I am? I work for meself, don't I? I'm just a simple labouring fella.'

'Then I don't quite understand why you need two cars.'

Mr O'Shaughnessy looked at him as if he was truly an idiot. 'And what's me wife supposed to do while I'm at work, sit at home all day?'

Victor took a deep breath. 'You are only entitled to claim for a vehicle you actually use for work, not for your wife's run-around Mr O'Shaughnessy. The same goes for tax, insurance, running costs. You can only claim those for your work vehicle.'

'Well me wife works too, isn't it herself who looks after me books?'

'But she does this from home so she hardly needs a second car. Which brings me to something else. How come the salary you pay her is nearly as much as what you claim to earn? And while I'm about it, I assume that Mrs O'Shaughnessy fills in her own separate tax return as well?'

Mr O'Shaughnessy sat fulminating on the other side of the desk. He looked as if at any moment he might explode. To break the tension, Victor drew his attention to the notes that accompanied his tax form. 'These are meant to help you,' he suggested.

'And how am I supposed to be understanding all that?'

'I thought that was the reason why you employed your wife to do it for you.'

Victor immediately wished that he hadn't taken this opportunity to score a point, for O'Shaughnessy growled, leaned across the deck and waved his fist in Victor's face.

'Are you suggesting me wife's thick?'

'Thick? No, of course not. I simply assumed that she must have some knowledge of tax self-employment, otherwise, why would you employ her to do your books?'

To Victor's great relief there was a knock at the door and Pamela poked her head into the room.

'So sorry Mr Green but there is an urgent call for you.'

Excusing himself, Victor hurried from the room. 'Who is it?' he asked in a low voice.

'A lady. She sounds very upset.' Did he detect an edge of sadness in Pamela's voice at the thought that he might have a woman at home?

As he walked over to the desk Victor thought that perhaps while Charity was out, Fluffy had slipped his lead and been crushed by a car. Naturally she would be very upset.

'Hello?'

Rather than being merely upset, Charity sounded hysterical. 'Victor, you must come home. Now! There – there's a dead man in your garden.'

'What?' He automatically sat down, not quite believing what he was hearing.

'There's a dead man in the garden. I think Fluffy has killed him.'

'Are you sure he's dead?'

'Yes! There's blood on the path and on Fluffy's coat. He must have mauled him.'

'I'll come straight home.'

To Pamela, he said, 'A bit of a crisis. I think my dog has attacked someone.'

'Oh dear Victor, I'm so sorry. Is there anything I can do?'

He reached for his jacket on the back of his chair by his desk. 'Well, you can get rid of Mr O'Shaughnessy for me. Just tell him to take his form home and read the notes before he sends it back. And thanks, Pamela.' He gave her a smile and she blushed pleasingly. She had taken her glasses off and really looked quite pretty.

Victor hurried for the bus stop. Fortunately, the number 2 came along in a few minutes and he was home within half an hour. Charity was at the gate and as he turned into Queen Victoria Avenue she came running to meet him.

'Oh Victor, it's terrible. He's just lying there. His eyes are wide open and he looks terrified. There's a black spot on his forehead where he must have hit his head on something, and there's blood on his leg.'

Victor put his arm around her shoulders, trying to calm her. He still felt that this must be some kind of mistake.

Charity had shut Fluffy indoors and the garden looked peaceful. It wasn't until he reached the top of the path and looked over the garden gate that Victor realised Charity was right. A man was spreadeagled across the lawn, gazing into infinity. He was indeed, clearly dead.

Victor felt helpless. To Charity he said, 'Why don't you go and phone the police, or for an ambulance – just dial 999 and report what's happened.'

'But what about Fluffy? Won't you get into terrible trouble for keeping a savage dog?'

He nodded sadly, brave in the face of adversity. 'We must still do the right thing,' he said, and patted her reassuringly on the shoulder.

As soon as Charity was indoors, Victor moved closer and looked at the man. He had never seen him before. He wondered if he was an opportunistic thief who had realised that the house was empty and came in to take his chance. Well, if that was the case then one could hardly blame Fluffy for attacking him. He had only been defending his territory after all.

He looked closer at the mark on the man's forehead – a hole situated right between the man's eyes. He frowned. Slowly, shockingly, a series of television police dramas flickered through his mind. Crooks were shot, taken out by professional gunmen. There was a sound like a whack and then the victim fell forward with a black hole between his eyes. This stranger lying in his garden had been murdered!

━━

In Victor's kitchen Alan, in his role of village bobby, was comforting Charity while an Inspector had taken Victor into the sitting room. In the garden, a medley of police and medical men stumbled over each other in their anxiety to get the job done. Cameras clicked, people struggled into white suits. The garden looked like a stage set for a moon landing. Inside, Fluffy had retreated onto Victor's lap and growled at anyone who came near, baring his tiny yellow teeth as a warning.

'But I don't know this man. I have been at work all day,' Victor wailed for the nth time.

'It is possible that you killed the victim before you went to work and left him there for someone else to find,' said the Inspector. He wasn't a local man, and Victor thought of police dramas on TV where a fast-tracked officer upsets the locals and reads poetry in his spare time. He had the feeling that this man would force him to confess, even though he was at a loss as to what had happened.

Remembering the hole in the man's forehead, Victor said, 'But I don't have a gun!' This single piece of information must surely be his saving. He had no idea how a gun worked. You couldn't just point it and fire. It had to be loaded. Was there a safety catch? He didn't know. He would never dare to pick up a gun and point it at anyone, let alone pull the trigger.

'Who said that the victim had been shot?' asked the Inspector triumphantly. 'I would like you to come down to the station with us, now.'

'Are you arresting him?' Charity had suddenly appeared from the kitchen. At the sight of Victor's plight she had reverted to her role of mother hen. 'If you are then you must read him his rights and supply him with a solicitor.'

'Charity.' Alan came through from the kitchen looking embarrassed. 'We know this gentleman,' he said to the Inspector. 'It is very unlikely that he has anything to do with this crime.' At the back of his mind he was remembering Gruesome and the rumours of the Angel of Death. Could they all be wrong?

'We aren't arresting him, Miss Grimes, we are just asking him to come to the station so that we can explore all the options of what might have happened here.'

Once she had calmed down, Charity in turn explained exactly how she had found the corpse, how she had heard Fluffy barking and how she happened to arrive late to take the dog for a walk.

'So if you had been on time you might have seen the perpetrator?'

'I might have been the victim!' She sounded shrill.

'Did you see anyone in the neighbourhood? Notice anything unusual or suspicious?'

Charity thought of the chestnut Mercedes, the gorgeous man behind the wheel. That wasn't exactly in the vicinity although it was only two minutes' walk from Victor's house. She shook her head. A sudden exciting plan began to form in her mind. She would think through the details later.

As his legs were so shaky, Victor was escorted down the drive by two of the officers, one holding each arm. At least he didn't have a blanket over his head. Across the road he saw Mrs Randall staring at the scene. There was something predatory in her eyes, waiting to pounce on every detail and gobble it up ready to regurgitate later.

At the station, the police surgeon examined Victor. His heartbeat was unnaturally fast and his blood pressure was sky-high. He complained of a pain in his chest and of feeling sick. A blood sample was taken, causing him to feel faint as well, while his hands were dusted with some powder, his fingerprints recorded, scrapings taken from beneath his nails and a cotton bud wiped around the inside of his mouth. He was deprived of his clothes, including his underpants, and given one of those spacesuits with paper slippers to sit in.

'All routine, Sir,' the officer assured him. When all of this was completed he was given a cup of tea.

Painstakingly, Victor went over his story again and again, how he had taken Fluffy across to the field as usual, how he hadn't noticed anything untoward in the neighbourhood. He suddenly remembered that he had spoken to Mr Jellicoe at the bus stop and they had both boarded the bus together.

'Ask him,' he said triumphantly. 'He will be able to confirm that I left home at the usual time.' Meanwhile, Victor confirmed yet again that he had never before seen the man in his garden.

'I have always obeyed the law,' he insisted. 'I haven't got a gun – why on earth would I want one?' His tone grew petulant and he was aware of echoes of Mr O'Shaughnessy claiming his innocence in the tax office. Victor had once said to a client, 'Ignorance of the law is not the same as innocence.' Now he blurted out, 'I don't even drive a car and I have never, ever been in trouble, not so much as for a parking ticket or a fine for speeding.'

The officer nodded that he understood and wrote it all down.

Elsewhere, Groping Joe's body was being examined and his fingerprints had been matched. Now the police had a name. Now they knew that Groping Joe was yet another local gang member who had died, this time clearly not as the result of an accident.

The surgeon confirmed the time of Joe's death and it was clear that if Victor was telling the truth, it must have happened long after he left for work. Someone was sent to interview Mr

Jellicoe, who had just returned from work and was having his tea. Between mouthfuls he confirmed the conversation he'd had with Victor as they boarded the bus. Another officer visited the tax office, catching them just on the point of going home, and established that Victor had arrived on time and that his behaviour had been perfectly normal.

At last, the interviewing officer asked, 'Do you have anyone you can stay with for a few days, Sir?' Victor was struggling for an answer when Alan, who had just come into the room, said, 'It's alright Mike, he can come home with us.'

Once the formalities were over, Charity was allowed to go to Victor's cottage with her father and fetch some clothing for him. They then collected him like a piece of left luggage from the station and drove him home.

Charity sat in the back with him and held his hand as if he was a small boy. For ages his mind seemed to be a void, hiding from the awful events of the day, then he thought of something. 'Where's Fluffy?' he asked.

'They've taken him away.'

'Who? Where?'

'The dog pound. They want to examine him, check the bite marks and that sort of thing.'

Victor remembered Mauler and Fingers, both with Fluffy's fangs embedded into their flesh shortly before death. If they interfered with him, Fluffy would wriggle and yelp and show the very behaviour they were looking for. Poor little dog, he would almost certainly condemn himself and be found guilty.

As if picking up on his thoughts, Charity said, 'Well, it looks as if the only thing they can charge you with is keeping a dangerous dog.'

His earlier thoughts about being free of the burden that was Fluffy now came back to haunt him. It was all his fault. He should have looked after his pet properly, understood those early traumas that made him wee or bite whenever he got excited. With understanding, Fluffy could surely have been cured? Thinking of his failures, Victor began to cry.

TWENTY

Doctor Delaney called and prescribed a sedative to help Victor sleep.

'Would you like me to sign you off for a few days?' he asked when he had heard the full story. He was beginning to think that Victor must be incurably accident-prone.

Victor shook his head. He would be better off at work, have less time to think. Besides, he needed to go back and make sure that Pamela had been alright after facing Mr O'Shaughnessy.

'Well, have a day off tomorrow,' the doctor suggested. 'And if you change your mind, ring the surgery.'

The sedative meant that Victor slept well. Released from his worries, he had a strange dream about being secretary to one of those ladies who served in the Shadow Cabinet. He had to stay late to prepare a speech for her. Victor had never considered fancying her before when he had seen her on the telly. She was a woman of uncertain age with a rather restrained dress sense and a high-pitched voice that was liable to grate on one's nerves. In the dream she made Victor take off his trousers because she had spilt champagne down them and insisted on sponging them off. He awoke with an uncomfortable erection and a sense of embarrassment.

Alan had insisted that Victor have the spare room that was right next to his. It was a relief to realise that for tonight, at least, Charity wouldn't take it upon herself to offer him comfort of the carnal kind, although he was surprised to find that his earlier exhaustion had vanished. Cosy and still sleepy, he tried to get back to his office in the House of Commons so that he could get his trousers back.

Charity was up very early. As Alan was on a late shift, she made an excuse to go shopping and trotted down to the police station. The sergeant on the front desk was well known to her and, taking a deep breath, she said, 'George, father asked me to come down and ask if you could look up a car registration for him.' The sergeant, placid, patient, nodded his head.

'If it won't take long, I'll wait for it,' she said. She wrote down the registration of the chestnut Mercedes and sat down to wait.

It wasn't long before George was back. 'Registered to a car hire company in London,' he said. 'Diplomatic Limousines.'

'That's fine. I'll tell father.' She wondered whether to ask him not to say anything to Alan when he came on duty, but this would only arouse both men's suspicions so she left it.

As soon as she could, she contacted Directory Enquiries and they gave her the number of the main office of Diplomatic Limousines. The next step would call for some ingenuity but she was a resourceful girl and, putting on her best voice, she rang the number.

'Good afternoon, Winterbottom Police Station here. An article has been handed in to us by a young person who saw it fall from a car. It drove away without the driver noticing but he has probably been in touch with you since to see if you have found it?'

'Do you have his name, Madam?'

'Afraid not. The young person was alert enough to get the car registration though, so perhaps you can let me know who you hired the vehicle to yesterday, then we can return the item in question.'

It was easy. No one checked to see if there was even such a station as Winterbottom nick. No one asked for anything in fact, but the girl at the other end came back with the information that the car had been hired by a signor Giuseppi Milano who was staying at the Royal Cascade Hotel in London. Charity thanked her and rang off, bristling with anticipation.

When she got home, Victor was up and had done the washing up.

'How are you feeling?' she asked, kissing him on the cheek.

'Fine, I thought about going home.' Victor was keen to see what was happening and for once Charity did not try to overrule him.

He found that his garden was fenced off with blue and white tape and the front door sealed with yellow and red tape. Clearly he was not yet allowed inside. He stood outside looking help-lessly at his home, longing for its solitude. He was aware that the curtains across the road hurriedly fell into place when he glanced around. No good hanging around here or Mrs Randall would be phoning the police.

He did not want to go back to Charity's but he couldn't see what else to do without causing offence. Instead, he caught the bus and went to the office, just to pass the time.

The first person he saw was Pamela and she positively leaped from her chair and came over to meet him.

'Oh Victor, we were so worried when we heard what had happened. The police came round just as we were leaving yes-terday and it was all on the local news last night. They said you'd had a burglar and that you had shot him.'

The whole idea seemed suddenly absurd and he began to laugh. 'I don't think I'd be wandering around if I had killed someone,' he said. 'They don't know who the man was or who killed him, but it definitely happened while I was at work – and it certainly wasn't me.'

Pamela smiled her relief and went to make him a cup of tea. He watched her with increasing interest. Was it his imagination or was her skirt a little shorter, and tighter? Her blouse was cut unusually low for her so that the very top of her breasts were just visible when she moved in a certain direction, while her hair, her lovely hair, was tied back at the nape of her neck and snaked down to her waist.

'You look very nice,' he heard himself say.

'Thank you, Victor.'

She brought his drink over and set it on his desk.

'How did you get on with Mr O'Shaughnessy?' he asked her.

'Oh fine, I calmed him down and said that you had had an emergency and he's going to bring the form back when he's had time to consider it.'

'Well done.'

They both fell into an awkward silence then Victor said, 'I don't suppose you might like to come to the cinema with me one evening?'

Her face turned a beautiful shade of pink. 'I'd love to.'

It was on the tip of his tongue to say 'Tonight,' but then he remembered where he would be staying so he said, 'As soon as this business with the burglar is sorted out, let's make that a date.'

As soon as Victor went out, Charity raced upstairs to change her clothes. She fumbled through the assortment of skirts and dresses hanging in the wardrobe until she found something that was both flattering and suitable for travel, then she quickly changed. Going downstairs, she wrote a note and left it on the kitchen table. *Popped up to London to see an Exhibition. Will ring later. x x*

Within the hour she was on the train to Waterloo. Sitting in the carriage, she felt more exhilarated than she had ever done in her life. This was a wild, crazy thing to be doing but it made her feel alive. Perhaps she was wrong. Perhaps the Mercedes had absolutely nothing to do with the shooting in Victor's garden but something told her that it did. If she didn't act today then Giuseppi Milano would probably have left the hotel or even the country. It was her only chance to meet up with him. This might be her opportunity to change the course of history – if not of the world, then at the very least her own.

At Waterloo she took at taxi to the Royal Cascade Hotel. She was glad that she had dressed with such care. Even from the outside it was obvious that residents would think nothing of spending their entire clothing budget on a handbag or a pair of shoes. Girding herself ready to enter the lion's den, she went inside.

'May I help you, Madam?' The slender young man behind the reception desk, wearing a black shirt and trousers, small bow tie and a striped waistcoat, looked Eastern European. He was dark and neatly polished.

'Yes, I want to see one of your guests, a Mr Milano?' For a moment everything seemed to stop – sounds, her breathing, everything – while the young man consulted the guest list.

'Is Sr Milano expecting you Madam?'

'Yes.' She nearly said no but she didn't want to give him a chance to say that he wouldn't see her.

As the young man consulted the register, Charity managed to see his room number. He picked up the telephone but she said. 'Just hang on a moment, will you, I'd like to visit the powder room first.'

'Certainly, Madam.' He pointed the direction across the foyer and through heavy glass doors.

Charity gave him one of her most confident smiles and followed his instructions. Once through, she continued down the corridor until she came to a lift that she took to the sixth floor. Giuseppi's room was number 618.

Now was crunch time. She had to get this absolutely right, leave no loopholes, allay his suspicions. A nagging voice reminded her with some force that if she was right then this was a professional killer, so should she prove to be in the way, he would have no qualms about disposing of her. Carefully she rehearsed her lines and, with a shaky fist, rapped on the door.

There was no reply. A lady pushing a trolley laden with linen and toiletries worked her way along the corridor. In one of the empty rooms, a vacuum cleaner droned. Trying to calm her heart, Charity knocked again, louder. Just as she was about to give up and retreat to the foyer to rethink her plans, the lock clicked and the door opened a fraction.

'What ees it?'

'Mr Milano, might I speak with you please. It is quite important.'

'Who are you?'

'My name is Loretta Bird.' The name came from nowhere, it just floated into her brain and emerged from her mouth.

'I know you?'

'No, you don't, but it is important. Might we speak inside?'

The door opened wider, revealing the man she had seen in the car yesterday. He looked as if he had just stepped from the shower and his hair was plastered in damp ringlets against his skull, while the towel around his waist revealed an alluring streak of black hair descending beneath its folds. Charity felt suddenly hot.

The man stood back and indicated that she should go through. The size of the apartment took her by surprise. She was not in a bedroom but a lounge with armchairs, desk, and a view across the Thames to die for.

'How beautiful.'

Giuseppi tightened the towel around his waist. 'Please, sit down Miss – Bird.'

He remained standing, watching her with eyes the colour of liquid tar, his face expressionless.

Charity took the plunge. 'Mr Milano, you hired a chestnut-coloured Mercedes yesterday, registration CAG 27. You were spotted in the vicinity of a murder.'

'You are police?'

His accent, velvet, alluring, almost diverted her from her purpose, but she remained focussed. 'No, I am not the police.'

'Then I no see why you ask. This dead man, ee is your husband?'

'No!' She felt affronted to think that he could even imagine that she was related to Groping Joe. She also realised that she had not mentioned that the dead person was a man. This alone confirmed his guilt.

Calming herself, she said, 'Mr Milano, why did you kill Joseph Windsor?'

By way of response he looked at her, a quizzical smile causing his beautifully crafted mouth to twitch.

'You think I am killer?'

'I think you are Vincenzo Verdi, a hitman.'

Giuseppi laughed a throaty sound and Charity struggled to keep her cool. She said, 'Before we go any further I should tell you that I have left a full account of everything that I know with a complete description of you and the circumstances of what happened yesterday. If I don't arrive home by this evening, the police will be informed.'

His eyebrows rose in response. 'You think I kill you Miss Bird?'

For a second she had forgotten the name she had given him, but then she nodded.

He suddenly flung himself into another armchair, laughing. The towel opened dangerously and she found it impossible to look away. His legs were bronzed and muscular and shaded with silky black hair. She looked at his bare feet and longed to kiss his toes.

Giuseppi said, 'I tell you, I promise on life of my mother, I never, ever kill lady or child.'

She believed him. It was a few moments before she realised that he had not included men in the list. Nevertheless she found herself relaxing into the chair, an actress on an exotic film set with a leading man to die for – although not, of course, literally.

He said, 'Signora Bird, what is it that you want? You are wanting money?'

'No!' Again she felt indignant that he should impugn her motives in this way. She said, 'My father is a policeman.'

'Ah.'

'No, it is not as you think. I simply wanted to get to the bottom of a series of killings in our neighbourhood. They have been carried out for two rival gangs but apart from yesterday's they have all looked like accidents.'

'And you, you think I am killer?'

'Are you?'

He smiled. Such even, white teeth, such an erotic pink tip to his tongue. 'Signora, I give you my honour, honour of my mother, I know nothing about deaths that look like accidents. I swear.'

Looking into his eyes his earnest gaze washed over her. She nodded, believing him.

It was his turn then. 'Signora, have you any idea who gangs might have paid to do accidental killings?'

She shook her head. Suddenly she really did believe him. He had skirted around yesterday's shooting but the others, she was now certain that he had nothing to do with them.

There was silence, then Vincenzo said, 'Look, you give me one minute and I will put on clothes. You are hungry? You would like to eat?'

She glanced at her watch. It was mid-afternoon and she had had nothing since breakfast. 'Yes, I would.'

'Good. We go to dining room, we eat there or I can send for food? Whichever you like.'

She would have liked to stay here, in this room with this man forever, but commonsense prevailed and she said, 'Perhaps we should eat downstairs.'

'Then we will.' He gave her such a beatific smile that she knew that for the first time she was in love.

TWENTY-ONE

Alan arrived home to find Victor alone.

'Hello, where's Charity?' he asked, going to the fridge for a beer. He was aware that this little routine was becoming too much of a habit, but somehow the promise of a beer when he got home made more palatable the prospect of Charity's cooking.

'She's in London,' said Victor, pointing to the message on the table. 'She rang up just now to say that she has bumped into a friend and is going to stay up until tomorrow. She said that there are some frozen meals ready-made in the fridge for us.'

Alan looked surprised at the news of Charity's outing but, with a carefully disguised casualness, he said, 'Tell you what, shall we go out for a bite to eat?'

Victor readily agreed. He was still feeling exhilarated at the prospect of taking Pamela to the cinema, only this time it wouldn't be *Last Tango in Paris* or anything of that ilk. He was also relieved that Charity was not at home or he would have had to break to her the news that they were splitting up. The very words thrilled him. This was what other people did, have affairs, split up. It really made sense once you had got the hang of it.

Would Charity be upset? He really didn't know, having so far found no clue as to how to judge her reactions to anything, but buoyed up by the prospect of a new life he was prepared to face that hurdle when he came to it.

Alan and Victor went to the Canned Heat in the High Street, a rather obscure word play on the Cantonese cooking served in the restaurant. It meant crossing the road at the very junction at which Frenchie had met his end, and, unbeknown to the other, neither man relished the memory. A large placard with details of the accident was at each side of the crossing, with a request for anyone with any information to come forward.

It was quite early in the evening and the Canned Heat was empty. Victor and Alan sat at a table for two, even though the tables were quite small and they would have preferred to spread out. For a long time they perused the menu until at last their choices were made; the waiter took their order, bowed, and retreated to the back of the restaurant.

Alan was mulling something over in his mind. Among the personal effects of Fingers Kilbride had been a camera. Alan had copies of the photographs in his wallet and he wondered whether to show them to Victor and watch his reaction. In truth, they were not very good. Apart from some taken in what looked like a nightclub with some semi-naked girls partly obscured by the effects of a flashlight, the others had been taken outdoors at dusk. A few blurred pictures of flowers were accompanied by some shots of a pair of shoes and somebody sitting on a bench accompanied by a white dog. Unfortunately, the man's head had been cut off.

Alan wondered whether to spoil Victor's dinner or wait until afterwards. He decided to strike now.

'I got these today,' he started. 'They were with that chap who died the other day. I'm trying to work out where they were taken. Mind if I show them to you in case you have any ideas?'

Victor wiped his hands on his napkin to make sure that they were clean before accepting the pile with interest. He flicked quickly over the naked ladies, wondering if this might be a test and Alan was trying to discover what sort of man he was. Show too much interest and he might conclude that Victor was an unsuitable suitor for Charity – not that he intended to be her suitor for much longer. The next photos he came to were pretty vague – flowers, an expanse of grass, a wall – although the wall looked slightly familiar. He thought he recognised the quaint chalet at Rylstone and his hand faltered. The next picture was horribly familiar. There were his shoes, his work trousers, his clean shirt and his hand holding tightly on to Fluffy's lead. That was before Fluffy had jumped onto his knee and he had let down his guard, so that the poodle had broken free and chased that poor man already poisoned with the peanut butter sandwich. Fluffy had swung round as the photo was being taken so that his head was a blur and he appeared to be wearing several red collars. Victor's head was missing altogether. He had no idea what to say.

'Any ideas?' Alan was looking at him closely. He shook his head, guilt plastered across his face. Eventually he managed to blurt out, 'I-I-it l-l-looks a b-b-bit like me.'

'Yes, it does rather, that's what I thought.' After a pause, Alan asked, 'I don't suppose you were at Rylstone Gardens last Wednesday, were you?'

'Er – no, I don't think I was. At least, I did go there one day but I'm not sure when.'

'Ah well, it doesn't matter.' Alan took the photos back and put them away.

To change the subject, although not much, Victor asked, 'I don't suppose there is any news about when I can go home?'

'Not for a day or two I'm afraid.'

He wanted to ask about Fluffy but in the circumstances it seemed best not to mention the dog.

They ate their meal in near silence, Victor professing not to be very hungry and, when they arrived home, he claimed to be very tired and so he went to bed.

At the Royal Cascade, Charity was also in bed. The huge four-poster was the size of a tennis court and she felt as if she was literally floating – although whether from the second bottle of champagne she had imbibed or whether from the amazing attentions of Giuseppi, she wasn't sure. Giuseppi appeared to be asleep. She propped herself up on one elbow to study his face. He was just so handsome. In sleep there was an almost child-like quality about him, with his damp hair curling about his face like he was a dark angel. What would happen next she had no idea, and just at that moment she didn't much care. Vincenzo had murmured something about it being time to move on but he wasn't getting away that easily. Charity was prepared to move on too, and to go wherever he decided. Replete in every department, she gave a groan of pleasure but then fumbled under the sheet for just one more helping.

➤◄

Victor went into work the next morning, his euphoria of the day before rather dented by the sight of those photos. Was Alan on to him? Was he still a suspect in Frenchie's murder, and possibly that of Fingers and Mauler and Gruesome? The awful thing was, he couldn't talk to anyone about it. He wondered what Pamela would think if he said, 'Pamela, I think I should tell you that I may be accused of murder, not of one man but of four. What do you say to that?'

'Good morning Victor.' The object of his thoughts came into the office at that moment. She was wearing a dress he had never seen before, belted at the waist and with a button-through front that was unbuttoned rather further down than he would have expected. A flash of black lace revealed itself when she reached over to put her handbag under her desk.

'G-g-good morning P-Pamela.' To his chagrin, he blushed.

'How are you feeling?' she asked. 'Have you been able to go home yet?'

'N-no, not yet. I-I'm staying with a friend – a policeman I know.'

'Oh good. I – I was thinking, if you didn't have anywhere else to go, then mother and I would be delighted to put you up, just until you are able to go back to your house.'

'That's very kind of you Pamela.'

Pamela sat on the edge of her desk, something he had never noticed her do before. She lifted her skirt a little, and further black lace showed at the hem. He felt distinctly warm.

'I read in the paper,' she said, 'that you've got a little dog. Where is it now?'

'I'm afraid he's with the police. He might have bitten the man who tried to break into my house.'

'Oh, that's so unfair!' Her tender heart touched him.

'I expect I'll get him back in a day or two,' he said.

'I hope so. Did you say that he's a poodle?'

'Yes, a toy poodle.'

'How lovely, what is he called?'

'Er, Fluffy.'

She wriggled her shoulders. 'We've got a poodle too, a little girl, she's called Fifi. Isn't that amazing?'

Victor agreed that it was. Now in full flow, Pamela said, 'Mother has always said that Fifi ought to have puppies. It would be nice for her, wouldn't it?'

'Er...' Victor wasn't sure whether it would be nice or not. He suspected that Pamela was planning a marriage between her own dog and his. Immediately, he had that nasty feeling that things were moving too fast.

'They might not get on,' he said. 'These things take time. It would be a mistake to rush into something like that.'

'I'm sure you're right.

Good, he'd got that settled, then he looked at Pamela's little waist with her nice breasts hoisted into a bra and pointing in his direction and thought that perhaps it wouldn't be so bad after all.

TWENTY-TWO

The date for the Rodriguez brothers' appeal loomed, leaving Dodge feeling very apprehensive. If it were just a question of Randy coming home then everything would be wonderful, but at the thought of Reggie being around once more, that unwelcome edge of anxiety returned. This was one thing he hadn't missed while they had been away, that feeling of walking on eggshells, and he didn't want it back. Still, if they came back it would mean that he wouldn't have to think any more about Vincenzo Verdi or the Pretty Boys and how to deal with them. From then on it would be up to his brothers. Dodge made himself a coffee and ate a doughnut for breakfast. Since his Mum had died he had lived alone and he'd never really mastered the art of cooking. Making toast was just about his highest culinary achievement.

As the jam oozed from the wound made in the doughnut by his teeth, he thought that in one way it would have been nice to have sorted out the problems himself. It would have been great to dispose of Vincenzo or wipe out the Pretty Boys, but even if he still had the time, he had no idea how to go about it. Just stop worrying, that was the best thing.

On Friday, the day of the hearing, he went along to the office at Something for Everyone. Hopefully a decision would be reached that day, and either Reggie or Randy's barrister would phone up to tell him the good news. He should plan some sort of homecoming party, streamers and balloons, a huge sign saying 'Welcome Home Boys!' as if they had just come back from holiday.

He tried to tidy up some loose ends in the office but he couldn't concentrate. The day was dragging. He would have liked to go out but he had said he would be here, waiting for the news, so here he must stay. For lunch he sent out for a pizza and one of those little salads in a plastic tub. His mum had always been going on about eating fresh vegetables. He supposed that salad counted as vegetables, as well as carrots and peas.

He frittered the afternoon away and finally it was coming up to closing time and the workforce in the store were packing away, emptying their tills, talking about their plans for the weekend.

'You go on,' he said to the manager. 'I've still got a bit to do. I'll check everything before I go.'

He sensed the man's hesitation, reading in his actions that he wasn't sure that he could trust Dodge to lock up properly. The manager's thoughts annoyed him. 'You don't have to worry,' he said, 'I know perfectly well what I'm doing.'

'Of course. Good night, Mr Roger – and I hope there is some good news about Mr Reggie and Mr Randy.'

So it was common knowledge. Dodge hadn't said anything but clearly the news was out.

'Thanks,' he said, casually, speaking as if it was a foregone conclusion. Indeed, if the boys had fixed up some new alibis, bribed some new witnesses, then it would indeed be certain. He settled back to wait.

After a while, he found his way onto the shop floor. He hadn't meant to leave the office. He had told himself he would keep well away from the merchandise but the lure was too great. There was a lift so he took it up to the next floor, feeling strangely effervescent at being alone in the entire store. For ages he wandered among the displays, pretending to himself that he was merely checking the layout. After a while he sidled into ladies' fashions, suddenly wide-awake after the dullness of the day. The clothes here were of good quality, no market stall tat. In the eveningwear section he took a long sapphire satin gown off the stand and looked at the label. Size fourteen, just as he had guessed. The material felt delicious beneath his fingers. He held it up against himself, pressing it to him, twisting so that he could see the effect of the swirling skirt. Folding it over one arm, he went along to lingerie and picked out a strapless bra, some French knickers and a pair of silk stockings. He moved fast, like in one of those supermarket dashes where you could have everything you put into your trolley in five minutes. In the bridal department they had garters and he picked up two satiny, frivolous things with pink bows sewn onto them. The shoe department went up to size ten for women and he could just squeeze into that size. Hurrying along, he explored the shoe bar, ignoring the lace-ups and trainers, heading for the evening fashions. There was a pair in pearl satin, high heeled, strappy, a perfect contrast to the blue of the dress. Sweeping them up, he headed for the changing room.

For half an hour he flitted in and out, a quick trip to cosmetics, a sudden memory of seeing some new wigs, a vast array of jewellery, the most expensive perfume. Finally he allowed himself to turn round and face the mirror. There she was, a gorgeous, glamorous, elegant woman with long blonde hair and dazzling earrings, her nails painted, her lips shimmering and her eyelashes impossibly long and alluring. 'Hello,' he said to himself. 'You're beautiful.'

Barry was expecting the flight from Barcelona to arrive at five. He had decided to go to the airport himself and collect his brothers, taking a taxi. If he sent one of their own cars with a chauffeur he had no idea what the driver might tell them, fill their heads with rumours and misinformation. No, he had better go himself.

He was still smarting from the message Sonia had passed on, telling him not to do anything because when they got back, Harry and Gary would sort everything out. It was ridiculous. If he had more time he'd sort it all right, permanently, dispose of Vincenzo Verdi, put a rocket up the Blues Brothers, turn the tables and take over their operations – except that he found it hard enough to cope with their existing scams without adding more.

Something had happened to the weather. The taxi driver opened the partition that separated him from his passenger. He was listening to the traffic news on the radio. 'Sounds like there's a vast bank of fog heading across Europe,' he called through. 'They say that some flights are delayed.'

'Typical.' Barry thanked the driver and they commiserated about the unreliability of the weather.

When he arrived at the airport there was indeed bad news.

The girl at the desk had an expression that looked as if it might be painted on, sympathetic, understanding. 'I'm so sorry, Sir, but the flight from Barcelona hasn't even left yet. Weather conditions there are making things very difficult.'

When Barry groaned, she added, 'I would suggest that you go home and then phone later to see if there has been any change.'

'Does that mean they might not arrive tonight?' he asked, indignant in the face of having his plans disrupted.

'I'm afraid it might well be like that.'

There didn't seem to be any point in making a fuss. He might just as well go home.

He hailed another taxi but on the way back into town he decided to stop off and have a drink somewhere. He didn't relish the idea of hanging around for hours, so he headed for a bar and ordered himself a vodka martini. It was a drink you could rely on, sophisticated, favoured by a man of the world, out on the town, someone in control of his destiny.

Sitting on a bar stool, he pondered the crazy situation in which he found himself. A woman slid into the seat next to him and ordered a white wine. He glanced at her. She looked polished, glamorous. As he watched, she took out a compact and inspected her mouth – as if while she wasn't looking her lipstick might have suddenly gone mad and spread itself all over the place. He felt irritated, by women, by his brothers, by the weather, by everything. Picking up his drink, he moved to a seat in a corner, hopefully anonymous. That morning, Sonia had let slip that the Blues Brothers had an outfit at a department store called Something for Everyone. She was a proper mine of information was Sonia. She also told him that the Rodriguez brothers had appealed against their sentence and the case was being heard today. He pretended that he already knew but it was quite a shock. If they won the appeal then the case would be dismissed and they'd arrive home at the same time as his brothers. Then all hell might break loose. The thought jolted him into action.

Why didn't he go along now, to their office, see if he could make contact with the other brother, sound him out as to declaring some sort of truce. That would show Harry and Gary what he was made of. 'No need for you to have hurried back, boys. It's all sorted here.'

Buoyed up by the thought, he found another taxi and headed for Something for Everyone.

When he arrived, he was disappointed to find the store closed. He stood for a while looking in the window, where a beach scene was set up featuring an assortment of clothing, sports goods and suntan products all available inside the store. After a while, he glanced up and saw that lights were still shining on the floor above. Perhaps someone was still there after all. He went back to the main entrance looking for a bell and not finding one, but, to his surprise, when he pushed the door it opened. He stepped inside.

It indeed seemed to be empty – which was no real surprise as it was now way past closing time – and he wandered through the different sections, making his way towards the stairway. It was covered with heavy-duty carpet and he glided silently up to the next floor that advertised ladies' fashions, lingerie, and children's wear. A further set of stairs led to the top floor, electrical goods, bedding and furnishings.

'Hello?' he called out, but no one answered. He poked his head into ladies' fashions, wandered around a bit looking for the way through to menswear but not finding it. As he passed the changing rooms he thought he heard a sound. 'Hello?' he called out again but no one answered so, cautiously, he pulled back the curtain and looked inside.

A woman with long blonde hair was seated on a stool gazing into the mirror. Her face, reflected back to him, looked terrified. 'I'm sorry,' he started. 'I didn't think there was anyone here. I was looking for the owner.'

He backed up a few steps, afraid that she might start to scream. Her reflection in the mirror held his gaze, her eyes large, stricken.

'Really, it's alright. I won't hurt you.'

Barry had never been in this situation before. He thought that he should go but something made him ask, 'Do you happen to know where I can find Roger Rodriguez? I really would like to speak to him.'

The woman shook her head. Barry frowned. There was something not quite right about her. He noticed the shadow on her cheeks, the large, capable hands and the Adam's apple. Realisation dawned.

'Sorry,' he said again. 'Sorry if I'm interrupting something.'

To his shock, the woman/man started to cry, clasping his hand across his mouth to hold back some private horror. At heart, Barry was a kind soul. He went closer and held out his handkerchief. 'Hey, no need for that now.'

'What am I going to do?' the woman/man sobbed. 'This is it. When they find out…'

'When who finds out? Are you afraid I'm going to say something?' He bent closer, took the woman/man's arm, turned him gently towards him and bent closer to get his full attention.

'Honestly, I won't say anything.' By now his face was inches from the made-up face in the golden wig. Behind the grease and powder, someone very young with huge brown eyes was looking back at him, someone vulnerable and needing help. Barry put his arms around him. 'Come on now, don't get upset. We'll sort it out.'

Later, he couldn't believe what he did next. The generous boyish mouth, painted in a shade called Heavenly Pink, just cried out to be kissed. The lips beneath his were warm and yielding. The body beneath the turquoise gown so young and tender. Stripped of the bra, freed from the ridiculous French knickers, it was so beautiful that Barry could hardly breathe. As he held the young man's hand, the man in turn began to lead him from the changing room, across the store and up the stairs to soft furnishings. There, laid out like a superior boudoir, was a large, inviting display bed. Together they fell into it and into each other, loving, soothing, exploring, floating into a world neither had ever suspected existed.

Barry, cuddling his companion, kissed his damp hair and said, 'I'm Barry by the way.' Dodge, snuggling into the warm shoulder, replied, 'I'm Dodge.'

Arms around each other, the two fell asleep in the big bed, cushioned from the world, babes in the wood having only each other.

Eventually, some distant sound woke Dodge, that and the need to pee. It took several moments for him to realise where he was and slowly the entire evening flooded back to him. Panic, disbelief, exhilaration followed each other through his repertoire of feelings. He sat up so that he could look down on the man asleep beside him with, his soft brown hair and rather thin, fine features. Reaching out, he soothed a lock of hair away from his eyes and they flickered open, taking a moment to remember. Barry smiled.

'Hello.'

By way of response, Dodge kissed him. It seemed the most natural thing in the world. Reluctantly, he left the bed and went along to the toilets. When he got back, Barry was waiting for him and he slid beneath the sheets, into Barry's arms, melting into his body. 'You're amazing,' said Dodge,

'You're beautiful,' said Barry.

Inside the make-believe bedroom the light was a constant, soothing yellow designed to give an impression of peace and wellbeing. It gave no indication of the time. The first thing Dodge knew was the sound of voices somewhere in the store. He opened his eyes, frowned, blinked and then remembered.

'Omigod!' Like a greyhound released from the traps, he flew out of bed, hopping from one leg to the other and looking around.

He remembered that his clothes were downstairs in the ladies' changing room and, naked, he raced down the steps and retrieved them, racing back up again, by which time Barry was dressed and struggling to put on his shoes.

'What shall we do?' Barry glanced all around, looking for a way out. 'I'm done for if they find me. Is there a fire escape?'

Dodge nodded and together they set off along a corridor and down some functional stone steps until they came to an external door closed with a bar. Barry heaved the bar up, pushed the door open and they stepped out into the early morning light. They stumbled down the iron staircase and landed in the street.

'Let's get a taxi.' Barry took charge, dragging his lover around to the main street where the rush-hour journeys were in full swing. A moment later, he stopped and banged his forehead with the palm of his hand in a dramatic gesture. 'Omigod! I should have been at the airport. I'm supposed to be collecting my brothers.'

'Christ! I'm supposed to be waiting for news about *my* brothers!' They looked at each other. Barry frowned. 'You're not Roger Rodriguez?'

Dodge nodded. 'And you – you can't be Barry Hickman?'

'I am.'

The whole thing was too much for both of them. They stood staring at each other, shaking their heads. Finally Barry said, 'This is like Romeo and Juliet, you know? Two warring families and the lovers star-crossed.'

The image appealed to Dodge's romantic nature, and he said, 'This won't make any difference to us – will it?'

Barry shook his head. 'We won't let it,' he said. 'Now come on, let's find a taxi.'

In the cab, Barry took his hankie and wiped off as much of the make-up as he could from Dodge's face. He used spit, like Dodge's mum used to do when he had a sticky mouth. Dodge felt warm and looked after.

'Where are we going?' he asked.

'I've asked him to drop me off at our offices and then to take you on home. Is that alright?' Dodge nodded, trusting, wanting his new god to hold him tight and make everything alright.

'When will I see you?' he asked, suddenly fearful.

'Later today. Now give me your telephone number.' Seeing the anxiety in the younger man's face, Barry said, 'Look, if I don't speak to you before, I'll meet you in the El Sombrero cocktail bar at seven. I promise I'll be there.'

The taxi pulled into the kerb beside some shabby terrace and Barry prepared to get out. In spite of the fact that the taxi driver was looking too often into his rear view mirror, Barry gave Dodge a kiss, patting his arm.

'See you later, then, and take care.'

Dodge nodded, too filled with emotion to speak. As Barry stepped through the flaky wooden door, the driver asked Dodge, 'Where to, mate?' Dodge gave his home address and sat back, glowing.

TWENTY-THREE

Dodge was in big trouble when he arrived home. Instead of an empty house, he found Reggie and Randy there. Reggie was fuming.

'Where the hell have you been?'

Dodge didn't know what to say. His thoughts were still elsewhere, curled up with Barry, feeling for once like a millionaire. Everything else that cried out for his attention was the other side of the coin – worry, blame, humiliation.

'I – I'm afraid I got held up,' he started lamely.

'And what was so important that you had to do that rather than come and pick us up?' Reggie barked out.

'I was trying to sort things out, on the Pretty Boys' front.' He felt an inspired moment. Wasn't that what he had been doing, seeking some sort of truce with the Hickman brothers? Exactly how was something he would rather not explain.

Reggie was looking hard at him. 'You got make-up on your face?'

'No.' He felt his skin colouring beneath the remaining blusher.

Randy came to his rescue. 'You been out with some girl, Dodge? Good for you.'

Dodge remembered his painted nails and quickly pushed his hands into his pockets. He thought that there was some nail polish remover in the bathroom cabinet that had been used as a solvent for something or other. Thank God for that.

'I need the toilet,' he said, quickly making his escape.

Somehow he managed to get most of the polish off his nails, and he washed his face thoroughly. He still had no idea what he was going to say.

When he got downstairs, Reggie was on the phone. As Dodge came in, he put the receiver down. 'Were you the one to lock the store last night?'

Oh lord, here we go. Aloud he said, 'Yes.'

'Did you lock the front entrance?

'Of course I did.'

'Well, the manager has just been on to us. He's got the police there. Someone broke in during the night.'

'Did they take anything?' he was barely able to hear above his racing heart.

'Sounds more like vandals. Looks like some bastard actually slept in the bedroom display.'

'Really?'

'There is no sign of a break-in. Did you lock the door?'

'Of course I did,' he repeated. In an inspired moment, he added, 'Perhaps someone was already hiding in there when I locked up.'

'Didn't you check round?'

'I couldn't check every nook and cupboard in the entire building, could I?'

For once, Reggie seemed to accede and Dodge was glad of the breathing space. He could smell Barry's aftershave on his jacket and a wave of pleasure threatened to engulf him.

'Are you taking this seriously?' Reggie challenged him.

Randy said, 'I reckon our Dodge is in love. Met the girl of your dreams, have you?'

'Something like that.' He could not control the blush at the thought of the object of his dreams, or the anxiety about what would happen if ever his brothers found out.

Dodge felt guilty that he hadn't hung out the flags or made an effort to celebrate the boys' release. By way of compensation, he said, 'I'll take you out for a meal,' then, remembering his date with Barry, he added, 'Let's go out for lunch.'

'Why not tonight?'

That blush again. Randy was there before him. 'Dodge has got a date, haven't you? He doesn't want us along.'

Reggie eyed him shrewdly. 'I reckon we should inspect this girl. She must be something special to have captured Mr Fussy here.'

Dodge didn't know what to say. His life suddenly felt intolerably complicated. He needed to talk to Barry and find out what he was thinking. For a micro-second he wondered if he was making more of this than it was but in the same instant he knew that the feeling was mutual, that, like him, Barry had fallen instantly in love. One way or the other they had to get away.

Reggie was lining up some plan with Randy. He turned to Dodge. 'You know how to get in touch with Vincenzo, don't you?' Roger nodded, wondering what was coming next.

Reggie turned back to Randy and a low discussion continued. Dodge was only a couple of feet away but he felt excluded, the big boys making their own plans. Sitting back, Reggie said, 'What have you been arranging then? What's your big plan to sort out the Hickmans?'

'I – I thought about a meeting, try to iron things out.'

Reggie snorted. 'Yes, I bet they're only too willing to meet now that Randy and I are back on the scene, but that ain't good enough. They were only too keen to stab us in the back when they thought we were out of action. Now it's our turn.'

'What are you planning to do?'

'Fix up some sort of rendezvous and get Vincenzo to pop along and then pop them all off.' He sniggered at his joke.

Dodge felt dizzy. He had to stop this. He had to protect Barry at all costs. Reggie said, 'Give me the contact address and I'll set it up.'

'I'll do it.' Dodge waited for Reggie to override him but amazingly he shrugged and said, 'OK, time you showed us what you're made of.'

Oh help – where was this all going to end?

Harry was furious. As Barry walked into the boardroom he found both his brothers sitting at the table and Harry immediately launched into a tirade.

'And why the fuck didn't you send a car to pick us up?'

'I did. I went myself last night and the flight was delayed.'

'So where were you this morning? Where the fuck have you been?'

The door opened and Sonia slithered in, silent and malicious, hoping to enjoy the fun.

'What do *you* want?' Harry's tone was less than welcoming and Sonia looked affronted. Clearly she had been expecting a better reception from her lover. Barry felt better.

'I've been sorting something out,' he said, not sure what else he could add.

'Oh yes, and what's that then?' Harry squinted at him. His eyes looked bloodshot. Clearly he hadn't slept on the plane and his feathers were ruffled.

'I've been to see Roger Rodriguez.'

'That little poofter. What did you hope to get out of that?'

More than you can ever imagine, Barry thought. Aloud, he said, 'His brothers are due back at any moment. He would be prepared to negotiate some sort of settlement.'

'Oh he would, would he?' Harry's eyes narrowed. 'What sort of settlement?'

'I suggest we get together and thrash it all out,' Barry said.

'I suggest we get hold of Vincenzo and wipe them all out.' Harry sat back with a self-satisfied expression. 'Pop agrees. He says we've got to eliminate them, every last one – even your precious Roger.'

'He's not *my* Roger,' Barry started but his face flamed at the thought and he hoped that he was. He could still smell the perfume that Dodge had been wearing. *'What's that scent, Dodge?'*

'Parisian Ecstasy.' It was well named. They had made love then, with the perfume in his nostrils and his senses blown away by the joy of it all.

'Anyway,' Harry's voice cut into his reverie. 'Give me the contact details for Vincenzo and I'll set it up. Now, before they expect it.'

'I haven't got it here,' said Barry. 'Anyway, I can arrange it. Just tell me where and when and I'll get it organised.'

Reggie had a call from some crony of his and, to Dodge's relief, he arranged to meet him that evening. That left Randy, but his brother was much more understanding. 'You go on out and meet your girlfriend, Dodge. I know you don't want me hanging about. You go and enjoy yourself. We're just glad that you've found someone to take an interest in.' He paused. 'To be honest, we were beginning to wonder – well,' he sought around for the right words. 'We thought you might be, you know – batting for the other side.'

Inevitably Dodge blushed, but he managed to laugh it off.

'What's her name?' Randy asked.

'Barbara.'

'Has she got a friend? I could do with a bit of how's your father. Perhaps I'll go to one of the clubs and see what's on offer.'

Dodge didn't argue. There was a hollow under his ribs, wondering how long before his secret came out. He wanted to run away from it all, the gangs, the violence, Reggie, but he didn't know where they could go – it would have to be they – him and Barry. Please God let it happen!

As promised, Barry phoned in the late afternoon.

'You OK?' he asked.

'I'm missing you.'

'Me too. See you at the El Sombrero?'

'What time?'

'Eight?'

'I can't wait. And Bar – I love you.'

'Me too kid, me too.'

Dodge hadn't realised that the El Sombrero was a gay club and he was relieved that he hadn't mentioned where he was going to Randy. That would certainly have aroused his suspicions.

He saw Barry immediately, sitting at a table in an alcove. He wore dark pants and a turquoise shirt that even in the gloom emphasised the blue-green of his eyes. His face was thin, sensitive, and Roger yearned with love for this miracle who had so magically found his way into his life. Barry rose to his feet and came over and kissed him, making him feel wonderful. He couldn't imagine any other place where they might have embraced so openly and it gave him hope. Perhaps there would be a way round. Perhaps they could move to Amsterdam, or anywhere really that was out of reach of the four brothers who would make it their business to stamp out their love. Cynically, he thought that this was one thing in which the rival gangsters would be united. Who knows, perhaps they could settle their differences through their mutual hatred of his love for Barry Hickman.

For a while they compared notes, gently feeling their way around the central issue of what they should do next.

'My brothers are gunning for yours Dodge,' Barry confessed, taking his hand across the little table that was made from half a sherry cask. Castanets and sombreros hung on the walls, bunches of plastic oranges drooped from the rails and the whole place was lighted in such a way as to please the ecologists, using the lowest bulbs possible without actually resorting to darkness.

'My brothers want to set up some sort of ambush I think.' Dodge sighed, acknowledging what they were up against. For a while they were both silent, thinking through all the alternatives, then Barry leaned forward.

'Why don't we – you and I – set up a mutual meeting place. Harry wants to invite Vincenzo Verdi along to take you all out so we need to stop it.'

'Reggie has got the same idea.'

They stared at each other, a truth gradually dawning. 'Then why don't we set it up and pay off Verdi not to get involved?' Barry bristled with pleasure at the novelty of his plan.

'Will a hitman take a commission *not* to shoot anyone?'

'I don't see why not, it's easy money. All he's got to do is to come along and say that if they don't come to an agreement then he will finish off the lot of them on both sides. That's when we can step in and say that we arranged it and we want a settlement or else.'

'Or else what?'

Barry shrugged. 'Or else we'll go to the police?'

'And tell them what?' The idea was so fantastic that Dodge couldn't think beyond the ludicrousness of the Pretty Boys and the Blue Brothers asking the police to sort things out.

Barry shrugged. 'I don't know, nothing probably, but at least it should make them think.'

'What about us?'

'What about us?'

'When are we going to tell them – we are going to tell them, aren't we?'

'Of course we will. Perhaps we could blackmail them and say that unless they stop fighting we'll come out and then both sides will be embarrassed.'

'Are you ashamed of me Bar?'

'Of course I'm not ashamed. I don't know how it's happened, but I love you. This is our chance to get everything sorted.' He suddenly looked full of confidence. 'This is what we'll do...'

TWENTY-FOUR

At last the police gave Victor permission to go home. He felt guilty about being so pleased, because Charity was still away and in all conscience he shouldn't really leave Alan alone, but the lure of his own little house was too great.

Alan was clearly worried by Charity's sudden departure. Although she had phoned to say that she was staying overnight, she had failed to return the following day.

'I don't understand it,' Alan said for the hundredth time. 'She wouldn't just stay away without telling me. I'm sure that something has happened to her.'

Victor was equally sure that she was fine. She hadn't been able to hide the excitement in her voice and he was convinced that she was up to something.

He persuaded Alan to go to work because it was best to keep busy.

'I'm sure she is fine,' he reiterated, trying to reassure Alan yet again. From his experience, Charity was a girl who was more than capable of looking after herself.

'You don't think she's been kidnapped or anything?'

Victor shook his head, a definite no. 'I'm sure she hasn't. When she rang the other evening she sounded happy.' As an afterthought, he added, 'She even thought about what we were going to have for supper, remember?'

Alan nodded doubtfully. 'That's just like Charity, always thinking about others. I just wish I knew what this was all about.'

As Alan prepared to leave for work, Victor asked, 'What shall I do if she phones?' He had the day off so that he could go home and sort things out.

'Tell her to speak to me without fail. I shan't rest until I've heard that she is alright from her own lips.'

'I will.'

Victor washed up and dried the dishes, then spent some time ironing some shirts and tea towels and socks and underpants for Alan as a sort of thank you for putting him up. He put them into neat piles in the airing cupboard. Then, just as he was about to leave the house, the telephone rang. It was Charity.

'Charity, are you alright?' She didn't sound like a kidnap victim but you could never be sure.

'Of course I am alright, Victor. Is father there?' When he said that he wasn't, she continued, 'Then I want you to tell him that I am perfectly well but that something really important has come up.' She sounded positively bubbly but he tried to insist, 'Alan's worried about you. I really think you should speak to him yourself and reassure him that there is nothing wrong.'

'Surely you can do that? Tell him that I am going away for a few days but I will contact him as soon as I am settled. Tell him not to worry.'

'But Charity…'

'Oh, and tell him not to think about trying to trace me. I know what policemen are like. If he does that I will never forgive him.'

'Then why can't you…' he started but she cut across him.

'And another thing, I'm afraid I won't be seeing you any more, Victor. You have to understand that while you are very nice, I have met someone else. This, I'm certain, is the real thing.' She paused and her voice changed to one of caring concern. 'You won't do anything silly, will you? I know you will think that your heart is broken but one of these days you'll understand that I was right. I pride myself on having taught you a lot Victor and I'm sure that there will be someone out there who is really right for you, but that girl isn't me.'

'But Charity!' The line went dead and Victor was miffed that he didn't have the opportunity to say that it was he who was breaking off the relationship. He sat holding the phone and imagining all the things he might have said to her.

At that moment, Alan walked in, startling him.

'Just popped in to see if there was any news,' he said.

For some reason Victor felt guilty because it was he who had spoken to Charity, as if he had gone behind Alan's back, but there was nothing that he could do.

'You've just missed her,' he said. 'I asked her to phone you but she insisted that she is fine and that I should tell you not to worry – and not to try to trace her…' his voice trailed off and Alan leapt on the last remark.

'In that case I'm certain that she is in danger. That's her way of asking me to get help. There must have been someone there, holding a gun to her head, telling her what to say!'

'Honestly Alan, she sounded – well, happy. She – she said that she had met someone else and that she didn't want to see me any more. I think that you should wait for a day or two and I'm sure that she will turn up.'

Alan was a long way away, pursuing some fantasy of his own that involved rescuing his child from danger. Ignoring Victor's last remark, he said, 'I should have insisted that she didn't get involved with this case.'

'Which case?'

'You know very well which case, the gang warfare. I'm afraid one of them has got her and wants to hold her hostage until we meet their demands.'

'Has anyone made any demands?'

Alan looked annoyed that a little thing like that should get in the way of his righteous worry.

'Well,' Victor picked up his jacket. 'You could dial 1471; see if you can get the last number. That might tell you where she was phoning from.' But Charity had withheld the number. Clearly she was determined not to be found.

Alan went back to work and Victor shook the dust of Prince Consort Crescent from his feet. He was desperate to reach Princess Alice Cottage and shut the door, immerse himself in its cosy sanctuary. When he arrived, the blue and white and red and yellow tape had all gone. He looked closely but could see no traces of blood on the gravel. The memory of Groping

Joe, sprawled across the drive, sobered his mood and his fears returned with force. Was someone even now waiting in the bushes to take him out? They had got the wrong man when they shot Groping Joe but that wouldn't stop them from trying again. For a second, he wondered: what *was* Groping Joe doing in his garden, but he didn't want to pursue it. Quickly he inserted his key into the front door and went inside.

There was some post. He picked it up and took it through to the kitchen, wishing that he had stopped to buy some milk so that he could make tea. The first thing he saw was Fluffy's bed and a sudden yearning for the dog came over him. The kittens had been removed to a cat rescue centre for the moment. Victor wondered if they wouldn't be better off with someone else. After all, at any moment he might be wiped out by an armed killer and then they would be homeless again. Who knew, the nameless assassin might take his revenge on them too, on help-less animals who had nothing to do with anything. The thought upset him so much that he felt on the verge of tears.

Sitting at the table feeling thoroughly depressed, he riffled through the morning's post and his heart jolted not once, but twice. Amid the adverts for double glazing and thermal vests were one white and one brown envelope. With a groan, he tore them open. They both seemed remarkably similar.

The paper in the white envelope said: *Monday, 8.30, the old Congregational church. How much not to kill anyone?*

Deeply confused, he delved into the brown envelope. It said: *Next Monday, half past eight, the old empty church at Rowan Place. Name your price for skaring them without herting anyone.*

Really, this was too much. He still had the last cheque that he hadn't had the nerve to take to the bank. What was all this about? Killing, scaring, hurting, the thought of any such action terrified him. He pondered long and hard and then reached a decision. He would hand the letters over to Alan and hope for the best.

At that moment the phone rang, causing him to jolt so vio-lently that he nearly fell off the chair. Like a rabbit cornered by a stoat he stared at it, waiting for some pronouncement of doom. The answerphone cut in and a voice said, 'It's the police station here, Mr Green. Perhaps you would like to pick up your dog? We've finished with him now. He's at the kennels.'

He let the relief wash over him. Perhaps he should take the letters with him now and give them to Alan at the station, only it would call for a long, complicated explanation and even to his own mind it sounded so fanciful that he wondered if Alan would believe him. He decided that instead he would pop round later and see Alan at home, keep him company, cheer him up a bit. He felt angry with Charity for the pain she was causing her father and also the manner in which she had dismissed him as her lover. Clearly it had not occurred to her that he might have had second thoughts too. She was so full of herself that she couldn't even imagine that someone wouldn't want her. Righteously indignant, he went to the door and poked his nose outside, looking up and down the lane just in case, then he set out for the station.

On the way, he worried that Fluffy would have suffered further traumas and would now be even more neurotic than before. Remembering his guilt when the dog was 'arrested', he vowed to be more sympathetic from now on and nurse him back to full mental health.

At the station, he was shown round to the back. There was a yard with individual kennels where police dogs could spend their working hours when they weren't out catching crooks. A large black and tan Alsatian flew at the wire, barking a threat – or was it a greeting, Victor wasn't sure. He thought about poor little Fluffy, how frightened he was of other dogs and how he had trembled when he had been incarcerated at the Dogs' Home.

'Where is he?' he asked.

'In here.' The dog handler went to the cage at the end of the line and fiddled with the lock. Victor peered over his shoulder and saw a large sandy Alsatian sprawled out in the run. 'That's not my dog,' he started, but at that moment a white blob of fluff appeared briefly above the dog's shoulders.

'Our Bess has taken a proper shine to your pooch,' said the handler. 'Inseparable they are. She's going to miss him.'

He opened the gate, the bitch stood up and wagged her tail at him; Fluffy, emerging from behind, bared his teeth and made a run for the officer's legs. With great aptitude, the man grabbed Fluffy by the scruff of the neck and hauled him out. 'Vicious little – thing, isn't he?' he said through gritted teeth.

'He gets nervous,' Victor offered in Fluffy's defence, all his good intentions melting away at the sight of the squirming, snarling poodle.

The officer put Fluffy on the ground and when he saw Victor he squeaked and ran across, his tail trembling with emotion. Victor bent down and picked him up, enduring a prolonged face wash.

'Is – is anything going to happen – about the bites?' Victor asked.

'I shouldn't think so – not as long as he only bites criminals.' The man suddenly grinned and handed over Fluffy's lead.

'Take care then.' In view of the recent circumstances, the words took on a prophetic meaning.

—

Charity sat at the dressing table in the Royal Cascade suite and brushed her hair, thinking of those princesses in fairytales. She had certainly found her Prince Charming. At the moment he was slumped in the king-size bed, trying to replace the inordinate amount of energy he had expended at her behest.

Charity had never enjoyed herself so much. Vincenzo was the lover par excellence. When he wasn't making love to her he was attentive, ordering her dresses and jewellery and flowers by the bucket load. Somewhere, a member of the hotel staff was being kept busy just delivering his tributes. This was what she had been born for.

After two days they had talked about the future. 'Is time I leave this life behind,' Vincent announced. For an alarming second Charity wondered if he was about to suggest a suicide pact but he said, 'I am rich man, you know? I have many savings in Cayman Islands. Maybe I go there and live.'

I, he had said, not we. She hastily went to correct him. 'I have never been abroad,' she started.

'Then you come too.'

She smiled her relief, adding, 'I haven't even got a passport.'

'That is no worry. I get you one, today if necessary.'

She had always thought that you had to get your photo taken and collect a form from the Post Office and then persuade someone important like your MP or a Justice of the Peace to sign the form to say the photo looked like you. Clearly there were other ways of doing things.

After breakfast, Vincenzo took Charity to see somebody he knew. The man looked like a cross between a penniless refugee and an elderly professor of quantum physics. Vincenzo called him Rueben and explained that, 'My friend, she need papers, passport, visa.'

Rueben didn't say anything, just nodded and summoned Charity with a finger to go and stand in front of a white screen, where he proceeded to take her photograph. Afterwards, he and Vincent conversed in low voices and then Rueben went into another room. Her lover said, 'Now you will be Sophia Rosselini.'

'Why do I have to change my name?' she asked, alarmed at the prospect.

'Because maybe everyone looking for Charity Grimes. Maybe your Papa send out to airports to find you?'

She nodded, troubled by the thought of Alan's anxiety. She had come home to look after him and to make his single status bearable and now she had added to his stress, but the alternative was to go home. Looking at Vincenzo, oozing charisma, she knew that she could not take her eyes off him for a second.

'So, we are going to the Cayman Islands?' she asked.

'I think so. There we have good life. There you can be rich lady.'

It sounded appealing.

The passport turned out to be Italian, and although Charity complained that she couldn't speak the language and that was bound to arouse suspicion, Vincenzo assured her that all would be well.

'Never you worry, cara. Vincenzo and Sophia, we make a happy life.'

Charity/Sophia looked forward to it like a winner collecting her lottery money.

Alan decided to walk round to the chippy on the way home. Thinking of the times when he had longed to avoid Charity's cooking, he now felt that he was being punished for his disloyalty. If he was honest, he had wanted her to go, and now she had and he didn't know where. The pain was tangible. He had phoned his other daughter, Pru, wondering if Charity might have gone there, but when he asked Pru if she had been in touch with her sister lately, she said, 'Of course not. She never bothers to ring me and I'm far too busy to chase after her.' So much for sisterly devotion. He didn't say anything else because he didn't want Pru racing down to find out what was going on. In the meantime he continued to fret.

He ordered a take-away cod and chips and added lots of salt and vinegar as an act of rebellion. Charity did not allow salt in the house. He could hear her berating him. '*Your heart, father! Do you want to drop down dead before you reach your retirement?*'

As he stepped outside clutching his greasy parcel, he bumped into a lady walking past on her way to the Co-op.

'Whoops, sorry!' He reached out to steady her and realised that it was Edna Fairgrove.

'Edna, I...' He remembered that last evening he had gone round to explain about Charity being at home only to find Edna with another man, and a different pain claimed him. He had no right to feel affronted. Edna was a free agent. She could

invite home whomsoever she liked, but he had still felt insulted.
At the memory of her cooking, the prospect of cod and chips
suddenly lost its appeal.

'Alan?' Edna looked flushed. Perhaps she was embarrassed
and didn't want to have to speak to him.

'Just popping out for a fish supper,' he offered, stating the
obvious as the aroma of grease and vinegar encircled them.

'How's your daughter?' Her voice sounded brittle.

'She's —, well, actually, she's not here at the moment.' He
wondered for the thousandth time if she would ever come
back, wanting the reassurance that she was safe and at the same
time trying not to think of the gloomy prospect of having her
permanently with him.

'How are you?' he added. Then he brazenly asked, 'And how
is that man. Is he still coming round to your house?' Perhaps he
had already moved in, they might even be engaged.

'Oh, Harry.' She gave a shaky little laugh. 'He's my brother-
in-law. I feel I have to invite him over occasionally. My sister
died and I owe it to her to keep in touch – not that I have anything in common with him mind, but well, you know how it is.'

He did know how it was. He felt a glimmer of warmth in
his cold and anxious heart. Perhaps things weren't as bad as he
feared. Perhaps he'd get home and Charity would ring or even
turn up. Perhaps Edna…

'It's lovely to see you,' he started and she smiled.

'Just on the way to the Co-op.'

He wanted to say, 'Do you fancy popping in for a drink, or
perhaps a coffee?' but the smell of his supper made it impossible.

'Well, I suppose I had better get rid of this,' he glanced at his
greasy burden.

'Well, nice to see you Alan.'

'You too, Edna.'

He watched her walk away, afraid to say anything. Perhaps
one day…

TWENTY-FIVE

Alan had just opened his parcel of fish and chips when the doorbell rang. Cursing, he wrapped it up again and went to see who it was. For the merest second he thought that it might be Charity until he remembered that she had her own key, then he panicked in case it was one of his colleagues, sent round to break the news that her mangled corpse had been found on wasteground somewhere. He opened the door. It was Victor.

Alan struggled to hide his irritation. 'Victor? I thought you had gone back home.'

'I just came to see if you were alright,' he said, stepping over the threshold and wiping his feet on the doormat. He had the little poodle with him and Alan eyed it malevolently.

'I'm just having my tea,' Alan announced, returning to the parcel. Somewhat grudgingly, he asked, 'Have you eaten?'

'I'm fine thank you.' It was Victor's way of saying that he hadn't but Alan ignored him.

Victor sat at the other side of the table and Fluffy began to explore the room. For a terrible moment Victor thought that he was going to pee against one of the chair legs, but by calling his name, Victor distracted him and after that he seemed to forget about it.

'There's something very important I wanted to talk to you about,' Victor started.

Alan immediately looked on his guard. 'It's about Charity.' It was a statement rather than a question.

Victor shook his head. 'No, it's something else. I – I've been getting anonymous letters.'

'What sort of letters?' Alan was interested now. He tore off a piece of battered fish, popped it into his mouth and added a chip for good measure.

'Well, it started after my accident – with the man and the tree.'

Alan nodded, encouraging him to go on.

'Well, I got a letter telling me to go to Shanklin Chine and later on I got another one in different writing to go to Rylstone Gardens – and every time I went, no one turned up but there seemed to be some sort of an accident.' He placed the pile of letters on the table and Alan grabbed a tea towel and wiped his hands so as not to get grease on them.

'The last two,' Victor offered, 'arrived this morning. What do you think I should do?'

Alan looked at them all several times. He had no idea what might be going on but in view of the number of recent deaths he felt that it should be taken seriously. 'Have you got the envelopes?' he asked. He knew that in the CID they always asked for the envelopes and did some sort of test to establish where they had been bought and where posted. There might also be fingerprints.

Victor shook his head. 'To tell the truth they began to upset me so I threw them away – only I kept the letters just in case…' He wasn't sure in case of what.

This was a mystery. The last two letters from two different sources were asking Victor to go somewhere but not to do anything violent. He glanced across at Victor sitting upright with his knees close together. Unless he was totally mistaken, the most violent thing Victor might do would be to stamp on an ant.

'I think you should leave it to me,' Alan said. At the back of his mind he wondered whether he could unravel the mystery of what had been happening on his patch. He imagined rounding up both the Blues Brothers and the Pretty Boys and the Chief Constable sending round his commendation. He had learned only today that the notorious twins Reggie and Randy Rodriguez were back on the street. That could only mean trouble.

'I suggest you forget about it,' Alan continued. 'If you get any more letters just hand them to me and I'll sort it out.'

Victor was absurdly grateful. He felt that Alan was the perfect father figure, strong and knowledgeable, someone on whom he could rely.

Alan went to the fridge and brought out a couple of bottles of lager. 'One for you?'

Reluctantly, Victor nodded. He was not a lager fan. It was too gassy and you had to drink such a lot of it, not like a nice glass of red wine, or even better a small sherry.

Alan handed him the bottle without a glass and cautiously he sipped from the edge, wiping it carefully first.

'So Charity has dumped you?' Alan started.

Victor wanted to argue that it was he who had decided to end the affair but as this was Charity's father, he simply nodded.

'Upset, are you?'

He thought carefully before answering. 'Well, I am rather sad, but I can see that…' He could hardly say that he wanted his own ordered, cosy life back and not to be dominated by an opinionated woman who almost told him when to blow his nose.

'I met someone recently,' Alan volunteered. 'She's a nice woman. I think Charity thought it was disloyal to her mother's memory so I stopped seeing her but…' Again the unfinished statement. Sometimes it was best not to say exactly what you were thinking.

Alan had already emptied his bottle and went for two more. Victor eyed the second one with alarm. One he could just about force down but two!

'Tell me, Victor,' Alan said. 'What do you think has happened to my daughter?'

'I – I don't know but honestly Alan, she sounded really happy on the phone. I think she might not have wanted to speak to you because you might insist that she comes home – and perhaps at the moment she doesn't want to.'

Alan nodded, absorbing the wisdom of the remark. 'It wouldn't do any good me telling her what to do,' he offered, 'she can be a bossy little madam.'

You can say that again, thought Victor, but he remained silent.

Alan took a deep intake of breath. 'Do you know, Victor, when she first disappeared I wondered if you might have – done something to her.'

'Me?' The thought shocked him into wakefulness.

'Well, all those recent deaths. I wondered if Charity was on to you and you had to get rid of her.'

'Alan, I —,' He had no idea what to say.

Alan patted him paternally on the shoulder. 'I realise now of course that the idea was ludicrous, as if you…' Alan shook his head. 'Let's just say you couldn't knock the skin off a rice pudding, shall we?'

What was that supposed to mean? That he was a weakling? He didn't know whether to be offended or relieved that he was no longer a kidnap suspect.

'Anyway, as you assure me that you have spoken to her and that she is safe, I'll stop worrying – for the moment.' He gave a burp and leaned back in his chair. 'Well, I think I'm going to go to bed now, Victor.'

On the way over, Victor had wondered whether to ask if he could stay for the night. In view of recent events he was nervous about being on his own, but now he didn't feel that he could ask.

'I'd better be going then,' he said, standing up. In response, Fluffy dragged himself off one of Alan's armchairs, leaving a potent smell of dog in his wake. Victor thought that the odour probably came from his close association with the huge Alsatian.

Just as he was about to leave, Victor remembered that he hadn't asked Alan about the money. He realised that the cheques put a completely different complexion on the story he had told so far. Cautiously, he asked, 'Alan, what would you do if you were to receive some anonymous payments of money?'

Alan thought, his lips pushed into a sort of upside down U. 'That depends,' he said. 'If I didn't know where it came from I'd probably hang on and see if anyone asked for it back.'

'And if they didn't?'

'Well, I suppose you'd be within your rights to keep it.'

The next morning, Victor paid the third cheque into the bank.

—

Barry and Dodge sat in the El Sombrero holding hands under the table. This had become their place, the Barry Manilow song that blared out from an old-fashioned jukebox several times in an evening their tune. They were both silent, lost in their cosy little world of togetherness.

Barry remembered that at one time there had been some talk of the Pretty Boys taking over the El Sombrero. 'What would we want dealing with a load of poofs?' Harry had objected. 'It's a nice little earner,' Gary had suggested, but in the event it hadn't happened.

Barry thought that he would like to take it over himself and make it a happy place for gay couples to go, not a knocking shop but a sort of family place where partners and friends could relax and eat and drink without fear of trouble. He had enough money of his own so that he could afford to buy it. The idea appealed to him. For the moment, though, there were more immediate plans to make.

'Right,' said Barry. 'We're decided, are we? On Monday, when both our lots get together, we'll make the announcement?'

Dodge nodded. A nerve twitched in his cheek and Barry reached out to reassure him. 'Don't worry, I'll be there. When they see we both mean it they'll have to give in.'

Dodge nodded uncertainly. He could imagine Reggie's scathing laugh, feel humiliation being heaped upon him, upon them. He was going to have to be braver than he had ever been in his life but then his very life depended on coming out, telling the world that he and Barry were an item, bound together by ties of love to the grave.

'It's not as if we're doing anything illegal,' he said.

'No, we're not. All we have to do is make the boys accept it. Believe me, Dodge, it's going to be a piece of cake. I'll do the talking and you stand next to me and show that you agree.'

Dodge nodded again, trying to fight down the abject terror in his stomach. Only two more days to go and it would all be settled – one way or the other.

TWENTY-SIX

Victor invited Pamela to go to the cinema with him on Saturday evening. He had checked to see what was on and there was a special Musical season at the Regal. They were showing *The Sound of Music*. Victor had seen it before and as far as he could remember there was nothing untoward – certainly not on a par with *Last Tango in Paris*.

Pamela turned up wearing a very full floral skirt and white blouse with puffed sleeves. On her feet she had white sandals and ankle socks with lace around the tops. She reminded him of a little girl going to a birthday party, all marshmallow and sponge fingers.

They sat through the film without touching. During the film something strange happened to Victor. At a stroke he had gone off the idea of courting Pamela but he cautioned himself to see how it went, not to rush to end anything before it had begun. It was best just to see what turned up. With Charity things had happened too fast. Perhaps a more prolonged courtship was wise.

After the film, he walked Pamela home. He noticed that she was wearing cotton crocheted gloves. He hadn't seen a pair of those since the Christian Sisters' Union had taken away his mother's effects to raise money for the poor.

At her gate he wondered what was expected of him. Uncertainly, he said, 'Well thank you for coming, Pamela. Perhaps, tomorrow we might go for a walk with the dogs?' He quite liked the idea of taking Fluffy out with another poodle, someone of his own kind that he might relate to.

'Thank you Victor, that would be very nice, but I go to church in the morning and then cook mother her lunch.'

He declined the offer to join her at church and they arranged to meet at three.

Victor didn't think that Pamela would start to take off her
blouse and skirt there at the garden gate but he did risk giving
her a peck on the cheek. He felt her flinch. Her proximity
and the smell of Ashes of Roses made him risk a second kiss,
working his way round to her mouth. Her lips were clamped
in a tight line. He wondered what was expected of him so he
tentatively touched her breast just to see if she was expecting
something more. She jumped back as if he had stuck a pin into
her. 'Victor! Whatever do you think you are doing?'

'I'm sorry!' Clearly, judging all women by Charity was not a
good idea.

He backed away, trying to make it look as if the touch had
been accidental. Raising his hand in farewell, and with a quick
'see you tomorrow', he beat a retreat. As he walked home he
pondered on the mystery of life. There was no getting away
from it, Charity had awoken something in him, turned him
into a man with 'needs'. He guessed that it might be a very long
time indeed before those needs found an outlet with Pamela.

The next afternoon, wearing his *Safari Sun* chinos and *Cairo
Nights* shirt, he presented himself at Pamela's front door. That
morning Victor had given Fluffy a bath because he still had a
distinctive doggy odour that assailed his nostrils at every turn.
Shampooed, towelled dry, brushed out, Fluffy looked like a soft
toy version of Larry the Lamb. Together they walked across
town to the rendezvous.

Pamela's front door flew open almost before he rang the bell
and she scuttled out like someone in *The Great Escape*. 'Ssh!
Don't disturb mother.'

Pamela was dragging a rather rheumy eyed, brown version of
Fluffy behind her. At the sight of the bitch, Fluffy grew two inches
taller, his head erect, his tail trembling with emotion. Victor and
Pamela got into a bit of a tangle as they tried to negotiate the
front gate, Fluffy having woven his way around their legs prior to
introducing himself to Fifi, who snapped a warning at him.

Once they were sorted out, they set off along the road in the
direction of the seafront.

'Lovely day,' Victor offered.

'We had such a lovely sermon at church,' Pamela replied. 'You really should have come with me, Victor.' She began reciting the details of a convoluted story, the moral of which he never quite unravelled.

Victor liked to spend his Sunday mornings doing his house-work. To be honest, he didn't really like his routines interrupted and the idea of fitting in a couple of hours at church on top of everything else failed to appeal. However, he listened politely.

As they walked, Fifi was up ahead, glancing anxiously over her shoulders every now and then, while Fluffy trotted closely behind – perhaps too closely.

'I don't think Fifi likes to be sniffed,' Pamela offered, as Fluffy's pink nose came into contact with Fifi's rear end.

Fluffy, on the other hand, was enjoying himself enormously. They descended the steep slope to the Esplanade and Victor per-suaded Pamela that they should take the dogs onto the beach.

'I'm not sure that is a good idea. They'll get covered in sand. Besides, suppose they wander into the water and drown?'

The tide was a long way out, a large expanse of smooth, damp sand inviting them to leave their footprints in its virgin surface.

'Come along Pamela, let's take our shoes off and paddle, it will be fun.'

Regarding him as if he was suggesting the preliminary to skinny-dipping, reluctantly she began to remove her sandals and ankle socks, while Victor did likewise.

Stuffing his socks in his pockets, Victor let Fluffy off the lead and the dog gave a good impression of a greyhound, racing around in circles, scuffing up the sand and waiting for Fifi to join him. Clearly against her better judgement, Pamela released Fifi from captivity and the pair increased their athletic dashes. The call of black-headed gulls and the whoosh of the waves were drowned out by a duet of high-pitched barking.

Victor led the way along the beach, his feet up to the ankles in seawater. It felt exhilarating. 'What do you do for your holi-days, Pamela?' he asked, for something to say.

'I usually take mother to Eastbourne, although once we went to Worthing, but we like Eastbourne best.' As an afterthought, she asked, 'And what about you?'

Victor realised that he hadn't been on holiday for several years and even then it had been something similarly mundane, in his case a week in Bournemouth. In a wild moment, he said, 'I like to go mountaineering, or take in a few days in Paris.'

'Really?' Pamela risked a toe in the water, looking impressed.

'I sometimes take a winter skiing break,' he added, his tongue running away with him, 'and I once went hill walking at the base of the Himalayas.'

'Gosh!'

His heart beat faster, dreading the inquest that must follow, knowing that his inventiveness had now dried up. He had a terrible feeling that, against all the odds, Pamela might just turn out to be an expert in one of these activities and start bombarding him with technical terms he didn't understand.

Instead, she let out a sudden, ear-splitting scream. Victor leapt back, splashing his trousers with water. 'What is it? What's the matter?'

Pamela, speechless, was pointing across the sand. Victor followed the direction of her finger and there, at the edge where the waves broke onto the golden sand, was Fluffy, mounting Fifi with an ecstatic gleam in his eyes while the bitch braced herself for his attentions.

For a moment he thought that the scene was the canine equivalent of *From Here to Eternity*. He was enchanted by the pairing until Pamela cried, 'Victor, do something!'

There wasn't much that he could do. Even as they watched, Fluffy had worn himself out and now fell back to the ground, his little tail quivering with post-coital delight. Fifi looked like the dog that had got the cream.

Pamela began a hysterical weeping while Victor helplessly held out his hankie.

'Oh, oh, whatever is going to happen?'

Victor was lost for words. The worst that could happen would be that Fifi had puppies. Had Pamela not said that her mother thought it would be nice for Fifi to experience motherhood? He would have thought that these puppies would be highly suitable, being the product of two dogs of the same breed. He couldn't see what the problem was.

'Oh, oh, what will mother say?' Pamela was inconsolable. Victor took Fifi's lead from her and went to catch both dogs, now walking side by side, both with far-off expressions. In silence, Victor held out Fifi's lead and Pamela grabbed it as if her dog had just been rescued from kidnappers. She swept the poodle up into her arms, sand and all, kissing and comforting her for her worse than death experience.

'Perhaps we should go home?' Victor suggested.

As if she had been assaulted herself, Pamela forced her damp feet into her sandals and, with her nose pointing upwards towards the spire of St Saviour's Church, she hurried back to the Esplanade with Victor trailing confusedly behind. He had to hurry to keep up and by the time he reached her front gate Pamela was already through it.

'Pamela, I am so sorry,' he called out, but she simply poked her nose even higher in the air, opened the door and disappeared inside.

This was not the sort of afternoon he had envisaged.

><

On Sunday morning, Charity Grimes, aka Sophia Rosselini, along with her companion, now called Fabio Firenze, flew out of Heathrow Airport. Their flight was due to land at John F. Kennedy International Airport, where they would change planes for Georgetown in the Cayman Islands.

In her handbag Charity had two letters, one addressed to her father and the other to her solicitor. She had not mentioned either of them to Fabio/Giuseppi/Vincenzo.

Just before they landed at New York, she popped along to the plane's toilet and, while in the queue, struck up a conversation with a young American.

'You going to New York?' she enquired.

'I certainly am, Ma'am.' He turned his open, square-cut face to give her his full attention.

'I wonder whether I could ask you to do something for me?'

'Certainly, if I can.'

She produced the two letters. 'I didn't have time to post these before I left London and I am very anxious to send them – especially this, as it is to my father and he worries.'

'Of course.' He was nodding, already ahead of her.

'Would it be too much trouble to mail them for me from New York?'

'No trouble at all.'

She tried to give him a five-dollar bill for the postage but he refused to take it. He said, 'It will be my pleasure.'

Later, when they were on the plane to Georgetown, Charity said to Vincenzo, 'Just to make sure that everything is OK, I've posted a letter to father.'

'Why you do that for?' Vincenzo looked alarmed.

'Darling, my father will be worried. I didn't tell him where we were going, just not to be anxious.'

Doubtfully, he nodded.

Just as he was beginning to relax, she added, 'But I did also send a letter to my solicitor, to be opened if anything should happen to me.'

'But why?' He now looked seriously shaken.

'Just to be sure that nothing does happen to me.' She squeezed his arm, watching the emotions flicker across his face like a fast frame picture show.

'But what could happen to you?'

She shook her head and smiled. 'I'm just being silly.' To herself, she thought: A girl has to be careful. You are, after all, an assassin. To distract him, she nibbled the lobe of his ear and a familiar look of bliss appeared on his face so that she was reassured.

Sliding her hand under cover of the newspaper lying across his lap, she whispered, 'Nothing to worry about, darling. We are going to be very happy.'

TWENTY-SEVEN

Victor felt very awkward when he went into work on Monday morning. Pamela was already there and she ignored his tentative greeting. A chilly exclusion zone surrounded her and it was clear that anything he said would only make matters worse, so he decided to concentrate on his caseload. Deadlines were approaching for receiving completed tax returns and he had plenty to keep him busy.

Now that Charity had disappeared, he faced the problem of what to do with Fluffy when he was at work all day. As a temporary measure, he got up an hour earlier and took him for a very long walk then left the cat flap open so that the poodle could go into the garden whenever wanted to. He took the precaution of putting a padlock on the back gate so that no unsuspecting visitor could wander into the garden and be savaged.

He tried to work but the thought of the two messages about the meeting at the old Congregational church that evening would not go away. He was dying to know what might take place and wondered if he should not just happen to take Fluffy for his evening stroll past the building. He tried to imagine what Alan might be planning, some sort of stake out perhaps, with snipers strategically placed behind bushes, but perhaps this only happened in America.

About mid-morning a very pretty young woman came into the tax office with a query and it fell to Victor to advise her.

She said that she was an artist and while she knew that she could deduct money for the purchase of paint and canvas, she wondered about the rent she paid for her studio and the occasional fee she paid to models – 'and things like that.' Her magenta-coloured mouth formed a timid smile and Victor's heart felt distinctly rocky. She wore a top that looked rather like an action painting with vivid swirls of colour all over it. It reminded Victor of a spray of fuchsias. The girl pushed a very long strand of wavy burnished hair away from her forehead and said, 'I'm sorry to trouble you but I really am clueless about what I can claim as legitimate expenses.'

She smiled sweetly at him and to his horror he felt a very large erection asserting itself. He quickly crossed his legs and his voice gave an embarrassing squeak.

The young woman, whose name was Dolores, spread out her claim form on the desk and he had no choice but to lean over her shoulder. She wore some exotic, musky perfume, or it might have been her shampoo, but she smelt divine.

'For example, is it reasonable to claim for a taxi to transport my paintings to a gallery?' she asked.

Victor started to explain but he got terribly tongue-tied and his stutter forced him to a halt. Dolores waited patiently.

'S-s-s-so you s-s-s-see, th-this is a-a-a- v-v-valid cl-claim,' he eventually managed to say.

'Thank you so much, you've been brilliant.' Dolores smoothed her wonderful hair back behind her ears and Victor felt quite weak. He stared as she gathered her papers together before giving him a devastating smile. As she stuffed her paper-work into an old canvas shoulder bag, she said, 'I've got an exhibition at the Queen's Gallery next week.' She rummaged in the bag and withdrew a piece of paper. 'Here's an invitation to the preview. Please come, I'd love to have your opinion.'

Victor mumbled his thanks and placed the card in pride of place on his desk. For the rest of the day, the sight and the smell of Dolores kept him fully occupied.

><

Alan had spent the weekend wondering whether he should talk to his Inspector about Victor's mysterious notes. By themselves, they didn't really amount to much. At best they were probably some sort of practical joke that someone, or even some people, were playing on the young man. If Alan made a big to do about it then he would look a fool if nothing happened. At the same time, he had what he often thought of as a feeling in his water. It invariably turned out to be accurate and he certainly had a feeling that this rendezvous was significant. As a precaution, he explained the situation to Constable Isabelle Peters and asked her if she would like to come along with him, just to see if there was anything worth investigating.

'It's probably nothing,' he finished, 'but it's best to follow any leads. After all, you never know where it might – lead.' He gave a little laugh.

Isabelle laughed as well, a tinkly sound that was pleasing to the ear. She really was a very nice girl.

Alan decided that she should wait outside and as a precaution they would take radios along with them, just in case they needed to call for back up. That way Isabelle would be on hand to get help but at the same time she wouldn't be in any danger.

'Above all I don't want you to take any risks,' he assured her at the private briefing he arranged during their tea break. He felt quite paternal towards her. In fact, she had a lot of the qualities that he would have welcomed in a daughter. He was therefore quite unprepared when she said, 'I do think you're wonderful Alan. When this is sorted perhaps we could go for a drink?'

For the rest of the day he was all of a twitch.

Barry and Dodge spent Sunday night together at Barry's flat. It felt a bit risky in case Harry or Larry should happen to drop in, but, as Barry, said, 'By this time tomorrow everything will be out in the open so there is no point in waiting.'

'Do you think there will be any violence?' asked Dodge. 'I don't want to be the cause of a lot of fighting.'

'Listen, we've arranged this meeting and we're going to be in charge. We won't let it get out of hand. We'll just tell it like it is and persuade our families that the only sensible way forward is to work together. This – us, we'll be a sort of symbolic union bringing together our two families. Trust me.'

Dodge relaxed, reassured. 'Oh I do Bar, I really do.'

———

On Monday morning Harry called an emergency board meeting.

'Just to get our plans straight for this evening,' he started, 'I've put the word around. The lads will be there in force.'

'What lads?' Barry was shocked into interrupting his brother.

'The usual gang, Knuckles, Razor, the others. Meanwhile, we'd better get tooled up.'

'I thought this was just going to be us,' Barry felt distinctly faint.

Larry said, 'Shut up Bar, Harry knows what he's talking about.' He removed the back of the drinks cabinet cupboard and said, 'Don't fool about now, just get yourself a gun.'

Seeing no way out, Barry picked up a rifle. Looking down the black tunnel of the barrel, it was like looking along the road that led to hell.

———

There was a buzz of excitement at Something for Everyone as the word went round that the twins, Reggie and Randy, were in the building. They walked in together, causing both employees and shoppers to do a double take, for it was almost impossible to tell them apart. With an occasional nod of the head, they acknowledged their notoriety as they made their way up to the office.

Dodge was already there, looking nervous.

'Have you heard from Vinnie?' Reggie asked him.

'Vinnie?'

'Vincenzo. You were supposed to arrange for him to come and do a little job for us.'

'Oh, yes, I've been in touch with him.'

'Good.' The boys sat down. Reggie sent out for coffee and eclairs and, once they had been delivered, he said, 'Just to be sure, we'll take our own weapons.'

'Weapons?' Dodge swallowed hard.

'There you go again,' said Reggie, 'repeating everything I say. You're like a fucking echo.'

The echo felt sick.

As he sat trying to calm his breathing, Reggie placed an evil looking revolver in front of him. The firing end was pointing straight at him, as if without the aid of human hand it might just go off on its own.

'None of this overture nonsense,' Reggie said. 'The important thing is that we take them by surprise. Just you wait and see my boys, by this time tomorrow the entire manor will be ours.'

TWENTY-EIGHT

The old Congregational church had an air of dusty neglect, as if the congregation had gone home one Sunday evening and forgotten to return.

As arranged, Dodge and Barry met half an hour before the allotted time of the meeting. On the way to the rendezvous, Barry had stopped by the canal and thrown the rifle into the water. Breaking his journey, Dodge had stopped at the Chine and flung the pistol into the rushing stream.

As there was no one around, they embraced briefly and went in through the broken back door of the church.

'There's going to be trouble, Bar. My lot has got guns and they're bringing reinforcements.' Dodge tended to stutter when he was anxious and the words struggled over each other.

'Same here. What are we going to do?' Barry felt as if he had let a Rottweiler off the lead and it had just spotted a pit bull terrier. There was no calling the situation to heel.

By the time everyone arrived, it would be dusk and the electricity had been disconnected – but the church had high, leaded windows and Barry had thought to bring plenty of candles and torches. On the other hand, perhaps it might be better if the opposing sides couldn't actually see each other. That way it would be harder to start a fracas.

The pews were still there but stacked to one side. In the empty space in the middle the boys found an old table and some chairs, and placed two chairs behind the table and the rest in front for the Rodriguez and the Hickman brothers. Lesser mortals and late arrivals would have to squeeze into the pews wherever they could.

'What are we going to do if fighting breaks out?' Dodge was already panicking. With the best of intentions, they had set in motion a train of events over which they had no control.

'We'll just have to try and use persuasion,' Barry said. 'Show them by example that it is possible – indeed it's in all our best interests – to work together.'

Dodge nodded miserably, his stomach giving a good impression of a stormy sea.

Barry had a speech prepared. It was going to be hard to stand up to Harry and insist that he took the chair, but he would do it. Dodge was wondering how on earth he could pacify Reggie and make him at least listen before he started World War Three.

The first arrivals were quieter than expected, single individuals slipping in through the back door and taking up a position of their choice. Like guests at a wedding, they chose to sit on different sides, either the bride's or the groom's.

As Harry and Gary strolled in, Barry pointedly took a seat behind the table and said, 'Sit down, boys, we have something to tell you.' Harry looked surprised but did not argue. Gary, as usual, followed his lead.

Reggie was not so easily persuaded, trying to push Dodge out of the way, but Barry said, 'Please, Mr Rodriguez, first of all listen to what we have to say.' Grumbling, Reggie and Randy, the two peas in a poisonous pod, sat down next to each other and waited.

At exactly 8.30, Barry stood up and said, 'Gentlemen, we have called this meeting tonight so we can iron out our problems.' At this point he had to raise his voice, as Harry was muttering something about there being an easy way to do that.

Speaking louder, Barry said, 'There have been some deaths on both sides. We've all lost friends and I'm sure we don't want to lose any more. There are plenty of ways that we can work together. If we spend our time fighting each other then we will all be the losers.'

'Sounds like a fucking sermon,' Reggie announced to the world. As an aside to his brother, he asked, 'Where's Vincenzo?'

At this point, Dodge stood up. He was visibly shaking. 'I – I want you all to listen,' he stammered. 'Barry and me – we've become friends. We want us to be able to all work together.'

'What sort of friends?' Harry Hickman gave something resembling a snigger and Barry, stung by the tone, said, 'We love each other. Dodge and I are going to live together as family.' Appealing to the reluctant congregation, he said, 'That makes us all family…'

He didn't get any further before Harry leapt to his feet and produced a pistol from his pocket. 'What sort of arsehole talk is this?' he shouted, waving the weapon around.

'Harry, please!'

Seeing the weapon, Reggie was on his feet, his own revolver ready in his hand. 'Put that fucking weapon away. Threaten my brother and you'll be sorry.'

That was it. Like a stray spark in a firework factory, the church exploded with ricocheting bullets. Grabbing Dodge's hand, Barry made a dive for the empty pews, crawling between two rows and dragging his lover with him. They both crouched low, covering their ears against the intolerable noise.

At the back of the church, just inside the door, Alan had carefully let himself in ready to listen to whatever was being said and feeling like a lone lamb among a pack of wolves. He was hardly inside before all hell was unleashed, and, making a hasty dive for cover, he radioed through to Isabelle, who was lurking in the bushes outside.

'Send for the rapid response team, now!'

Slowly, Barry crawled his way along the length of the pews towards the door, Dodge close behind him.

'Now!' he whispered loudly and the two of them wriggled out and made a dash for the door.

'That's far enough!' They stumbled to a halt, finding their path blocked by Constable Peters, shining her torch directly at them. Their arms were still clasped around each other and they crouched like frightened children.

'Don't go in there!' Barry shouted at her. 'If you do you'll get hurt.' Inside the church it sounded like Guy Fawkes' night and he added, 'You'd better send for an ambulance, quick!'

Isabelle radioed the station. Caught off guard, the two escapees linked their arms through hers and said, 'Come on, let's take cover.'

'Let me go!' It took her a moment to realise that she was not being kidnapped but rescued.

Already the rapid response team was on its way and, crowded into a tiny doorway, they heard the increasing wail of sirens.

The scene that followed had all the ingredients of an extended version of *The Bill*. The sky outside was alive with flashes of blue, tyres screeched convincingly on the tarmac, men made huge by protective clothing scuttled like woodlice disturbed under a log. Somebody produced a loudhailer and in true cop fashion called out, 'We've got the place surrounded. Put your weapons down and come out with your arms above your head.'

'Look!' Isabelle produced her warrant card. 'Just let me out, I'm working.'

Their eyes large with surprise, Barry and Dodge stood back to let her past. 'You be careful!' Dodge called after her.

Outside the church there was silence, until at last the church door creaked open and a solitary figure walked out. 'Don't shoot!' he called out. 'It's me, Constable Grimes.'

'Alan!' From the shadows, Constable Peters ran towards him, showing a most unpolicewoman-like concern for his welfare. Inside the church it was what Barry thought of as deathly silent.

Victor had taken a nonchalant stroll past the Congregational church at precisely 8.15. As he drew near he saw several shadowy figures slipping round to the back with every appearance of being up to no good. As he wondered whether to stop and watch, he noticed another figure in the bushes. He quickly hurried on.

His walk took him to the end of the road then into the small public gardens. Just as he drew near to the church on his return journey – about fifteen minutes later – something resembling the soundtrack to a *Star Wars* movie began to play inside. At the first bang Fluffy gave a yelp and swung round, entangling his lead around Victor's ankles. Giving his own yelp, Victor toppled over, landing heavily on the pavement. With amazing strength, Fluffy began to gallop in the direction of home, dragging his owner along the ground. Just as Victor managed to untangle himself and climb shakily to his feet, the entire police presence of the county descended upon the road. Much as he would have liked to stay and watch these interesting proceedings, Victor had learnt that being in the neighbourhood of an 'incident' was tantamount to guilt. Rubbing his sore knees, he hobbled after Fluffy, who was giving a good impression of a greyhound. No doubt he would read all about it in the *Clarion* tomorrow.

—

'*Fraternal Fracas*,' announced the headlines of the early edition of the *Clarion*. A picture of two men carrying a stretcher with the subtitle '*Eight Dead in Mystery Mayhem*' completed the front page.

Victor turned to the inside to read the gory details. It seemed that the police had been tipped off by an 'unidentified source'. That's me, Victor thought with satisfaction. He wondered if there might be a reward for the capture – dead or alive – of so many miscreants. The *Clarion* went on to explain that the police had then attended an 'incident' at the old Congregational church, where a scene of carnage greeted them. Inside were eight bodies. They had all been shot. They were identified as Reginald and Randolph Rodriguez, twins who had recently been released from gaol on appeal; Harold and Garfield Hickman, well-known members of a gang known as the Pretty Boys; Nicos 'the Greek' Papadoulous; Gerald 'Knuckles' White; Eugene 'Razor' Wilkinson and Andy 'Sugar Boy' Sweetman. It was assumed that some sort of gang showdown had taken place. Two young men were seen leaving the scene but they had been picked up later and were helping the police with their enquiries. A man with a small white dog had been seen in the vicinity. He was not wanted in connection with the shooting although he was asked to come forward in case he had witnessed anything that might be useful to the police. The paper praised Constable Alan Grimes, shortly to retire from the force and familiar with many in the neighbourhood, who had risked his life by entering the church and was commended by the Chief Constable for his bravery.

Victor sighed and wondered whether to phone the station. Alan already knew that he had known about the time and place of the showdown. It wouldn't take him more than a second to recognise the description and conclude that yet again Victor had been lurking where he shouldn't be. He supposed that he should do his duty and come forward but there was really nothing that he could add. Perhaps he would just pop round and see Alan at home the next day and get his advice. On the other hand, perhaps he wouldn't.

Alan was on top form. Not only was he a hero but he had that morning received a letter from Charity from New York.

Dear Daddy, it started. *I know you must be worried about me and I am sorry not to have phoned you myself but to be honest, I just needed to get away and things are a bit complicated. Dad, I have fallen in love, really and truly in love, but my darling Vincenzo should not have been in England, which is why we had to leave without telling anyone. I am very happy. He has lots of money so there is no need to worry on that score. We just need some time to sort out the future. So, I will be in touch again and don't you worry. Lots of love, Charity.*

Reading the letter for the fourth time, Alan decided not to dwell on why 'Vincenzo' shouldn't be in the country and how he made his money. He knew that Charity didn't have a passport either and to get to New York she would need one. Still, his daughter was safe and that was all that mattered.

There was another reason for his high spirits. By the time they had finished at the police station the night before, it had been after 2 a.m. Seeing that technically neither he nor Isabelle were on duty and had been acting on their own initiative, once they had given their statements and helped with the general clearing up, they went home – together.

It wasn't what it seemed, for Isabelle was clearly in no state to go home on her own. It was the first time in her career that she had had to deal with mass murder.

'Oh Alan, I do feel rather shaky,' she confessed as they left the station.

'Shall I drive you home?' he offered.

'My landlady will be in bed. She won't be very pleased to be woken up at this time.'

He wondered why she didn't have her own key but didn't pursue it, instead saying, 'In that case, you had better come home with me.'

He meant it as a father to a daughter, an adult looking after someone not quite past childhood, only it hadn't exactly turned out as he had intended.

At Prince Consort Crescent, he made Isabelle a cup of Horlicks and a nice cosy bed on the put-u-up. 'You can have my bed if you'd rather,' he offered, but she wouldn't hear of it. He fetched her a clean towel, a new toothbrush from the bathroom cabinet and a pair of Charity's sensible pyjamas, placing them on the chair.

'You just go on up and wash or whatever and then try and get to sleep. I'll be just up the stairs.'

In spite of all the excitement, Alan actually fell asleep very quickly. He was feeling his age these days and the exertions of the evening had rather taken it out of him. When he awoke it took him a few moments to remember that a very beautiful young woman was asleep in his living room – only she wasn't in the living room but had mysteriously found her way into his bed.

'Isabelle?' He scrambled up then realised that he was wearing only his underpants, which he had kept on the night before in case he needed to get up in the night to go to the loo. He grabbed the duvet to cover himself, in the process unveiling Isabelle, who had stripped off the pyjamas at some point in the night and was deliriously naked.

'Oh, I'm so sorry!' He struggled to cover her up again whilst still trying to protect his own modesty.

'Alan, what are you panicking about? I got hot in the night that's all.' She made no attempt to hide away and he was mesmerised by her youth and desirability.

Stretching like a python about to coil itself around its prey, she said, 'I felt frightened in the night in case one of the gang had survived and came to get us so I came up and got in with you, only you didn't even wake up.' She giggled.

'Isabelle, I'm not sure…'

She laughed, a grown-up looking indulgently on a child. 'Oh Alan, you are wonderful; you are so old-fashioned. Honestly, it's no big deal if we sleep together. I know you're going to say that you are old enough to be my father and all that, but so what? I know that you are a widower. We are both free agents. Don't be such a stuffed shirt.'

And then it happened. Isabelle, wonderful, naked Isabelle, proceeded to give him what his colleagues referred to as a good seeing to. Afterwards he felt well and truly seen to!

—

Isabelle had to be at the station first so she left at 9.30, having had a good breakfast, because she declared that 'sex makes you hungry'. She also borrowed one of Charity's white shirts.

'I'll see you when you come on duty,' she called at the door and, after a second's thought, came back to kiss him.

'I, I don't think it would be wise to mention where you spent the night,' he started, but she gave her tinkly little laugh and said, 'Oh Alan, you are funny. I'm a big girl now. You don't have to worry. We're just colleagues, aren't we, and if being colleagues means that we also become – well, occasional lovers, then it's no big deal, honestly it isn't.'

As she walked down the drive, her hips gently swaying like a ship of the desert, he began to wonder if he had been killed the night before and was now in heaven.

An hour later he was at the supermarket. Clearly plenty of people had already heard the news and, feeling like a celebrity, he accepted the congratulations. Just as he got to the checkout another voice called out to him, 'Alan! Alan, congratulations.'

He swung round to find Edna Fairgrove pushing her way past several people to get to him. 'Oh, hello Edna.'

He thought how nice and wholesome she looked, mature and plump and – well, comforting. In spite of all the excitement before breakfast, he couldn't resist the thrill of desire that was already circulating like some greedy carnivore, gnawing at his insides and demanding satisfaction.

'Alan, I thought you were wonderful last night,' she started. 'Are you sure that you weren't hurt?'

'No, not even a scratch.' He gave a modest laugh, playing down his courage. 'All in the line of duty,' he added, playfully.

'Well, have you got time to pop back for a coffee?'

He glanced at his watch. He still had three hours before he was on duty. Something very reckless was going on in his mind.

'Well Edna, that would be very nice. To be honest, I rather fancy a stiff drink and a bit of a chat – I think I'm still in shock.'

To his surprise she bridled prettily, her cheeks flaring with a pink heat.

'Come along then, come and have a drink.' She didn't mention the chat but after last night he thought that even in daylight, something amazing might be on the cards.

As they made their way back to her house he thought, well, here's a turn up for the books. I seem to have the pick of a surrogate daughter looking for a sugar daddy and a foster mother wanting someone to cosset. Don't be greedy, he admonished himself, but then, after his heroism of last night, and just for today, why should he not have both?

TWENTY-NINE

Barry and Dodge were called in to identify the victims of last night's massacre. At the sight of his brothers, Dodge began to cry. Sometimes Reggie hadn't been very nice to him and sometimes Randy hadn't stood up for him the way he might have done, but they were still his flesh and blood. Apart from Dad in Spain, there was no one else now – except of course Barry. Barry was even now standing next to him and he moved closer to him for comfort.

'Can you tell us which one is which?' the officer asked. 'We're having trouble seeing any differences.'

'That's Randy.' Roger started to cry again and, in spite of the fact that other people were watching, Barry put his arms round him.

'There now, don't get upset. It wasn't your fault.'

They were questioned separately. Their fingerprints were taken and they were dusted for traces of residue from the cache of firearms that littered the church, but there was no evidence that either of them had used a gun.

'We wouldn't,' said Barry. 'We've been trying to stop the violence.'

In her statement, Constable Peters said that the two men had left the church before the shooting started and that they had both tried to protect her from any harm.

At last they were released with a warning not to leave town.

'Where will we find you?' asked Constable Peters.

They looked at each other. 'At my place,' said Barry, taking his partner's hand. 'That's where we'll be.'

At Barry's place, they made some sandwiches and curled up together on the sofa. Dodge did most of the talking, mostly about his brothers. It was clear that he was deeply grieved by

the outcome of their plan to bring peace to the neighbourhood.

'I loved them, you know.' he said for the hundredth time. 'I
know they did some bad things but…'

'You loved them, I know.' Barry was trying to think of the
wider implications, like what was going to happen to the two
empires run by the Pretty Boys and the Blues Brothers. For
himself he was not unduly concerned, for he had his own bank
account, all legitimately accounted for. As for all the other things,
the gambling joints and strip clubs, he didn't mind what happened to them. In fact, it would be such a relief not to have to
think about them and forever have his conscience troubling him.

'You can have all the assets,' he had said to the nice policeman
at the station. 'Take it. I don't want it. Give it to charity.'

All he wanted was the man curled up beside him sucking his
thumb in an endearing orphan of the storm way. 'Let's make
some plans,' he said, putting his arm around Dodge's shoulders.
'When this is all sorted we'll be free agents. Just think about it.'

'I think I'd like to go and see Dad,' Dodge said. 'He's bound
to be upset and I ought to tell him myself really.'

'A good idea.' Barry checked up and found that their fathers
were living within ten miles of each other on what was known
as the Costa del Crime. 'We'll do that, Dodge,' he reassured him,
'as soon as the police say we can leave.' He had no idea how
their respective fathers might react to the news that their only
remaining sons were now a couple, but for the moment it distracted Dodge from the present.

They would need to plan the funerals and Barry decided to
raise the subject now, get all the nasty things out of the way.

'About the funerals,' he started.

'We're Catholics,' Dodge replied.

'Are you? Do you go to church and confession and all that
stuff?' He wondered how that fitted in with murder and extor-
tion but remained silent.

Dodge gave a shaky laugh. 'No, of course we don't.' He
thought for a moment before adding, 'although I suppose now

I could confess and say that I wouldn't do anything bad any more, couldn't I?'

'You could, but wouldn't the Church frown on what we do together?' Barry asked.

Dodge looked disturbed. 'But it isn't bad, is it?'

'Of course it's not. Let's just forget about the Church, shall we? Now listen, what I was going to suggest is that we bury all four boys at the same time in the same cemetery, next to each other. That way it would be sort of symbolic and besides we could visit the graves at the same time.'

Dodge nodded, seeing the sense of the suggestion.

'Right then, I'll get that organised for when the time comes.' Seeing that Dodge was edging towards tears again, Barry added, 'Why don't you think of something nice to write on the gravestones.' Dodge gave a subdued nod.

Later, Barry asked him, 'What would you like to do, when all of this is over? We could do just about anything we want. No matter what happens to our enterprises, there's still plenty of money.'

Barry had already decided that when the dust had settled he'd like to buy the El Sombrero, or if that wasn't up for sale then to open his own club. Whenever he was feeling anxious he escaped into a daydream about what it would be like, planning every detail down to the tablecloths and the style of the sign outside the door. Yes, that would fulfil a dream.

'D'you know,' Dodge ventured, 'I'd really like to run a shop, one selling ladies' fashions like at Something for Everyone. I – I think I might have a bit of a flair for it.'

Remembering the first time they met, with Dodge a vision in sapphire, Barry had to agree.

'Or perhaps run a wedding shop? I could stock dresses and veils and all the accessories, things to decorate wedding cakes and garters and silver sandals.' As he talked he grew increasingly animated. Barry thought that there was a long way to go yet, an inquest, a trial, and a lot of loose ends to tie up, but one day in the not too distant future, they really would be free.

'I love you Dodge,' said Barry.

'I love you Bar,' said Dodge.

━●━

Now that Charity had censored his wardrobe, Victor was forced to buy some new clothes. He found himself looking to see what other men were wearing. His instinct was to take the lead from men of his father's age range rather than the young bloods about town, but then he began to realise that they were all dressing very much alike. When he went to look for the sort of things he had always favoured, they seemed to have disappeared from the shelves so he grew increasingly reliant on the wisdom of the shop assistants.

'Why don't you try this on?' they suggested or, 'If you would like my opinion…' Gradually he acquired a whole new range of trousers and shirts and jumpers, plus garments he'd never noticed before like fleeces and sweatshirts and gilets.

He sought advice in a rather up-market gentleman's outfitters about something suitable to wear to an art preview. The young man who served him and who might well have doubled for one of the Pre-Raphaelite boys, kitted him out in some very tight-fitting trousers, a purple shirt and a sparkly waistcoat.

'I can't possibly wear these,' Victor started, but the young Rosetti led him to the mirror. 'Just take a look, Sir. If you want my opinion…' Thus attired, Victor set off for the Queen's Gallery.

He had never been to an art preview before and had no idea what to expect. From the street he could hear the hum of voices and as he approached the door a positive crescendo of noise assailed him. Clutching his invitation he ventured inside.

The room was crowded with people but before he had taken two awkward steps, someone pushed a programme into his hand. On the front cover was a very swirly black and white drawing and the words 'Crossing the Bar'. On the back there was a photo of Dolores with details of her artistic career. Victor thought how sultry and exciting she looked. With slightly blurry eyes he began to read about her art schools, her exhibitions and prizes. Inside the programme was a list of the paintings on display, the medium in which they had been executed and their rather obscure titles. He stopped short as he saw the prices, for, with only one or two exceptions, they all ran into four or five figures. Clearly Dolores was an artist of note.

A waiter in a black bow tie came up to him, balancing a tray of what looked like champagne. 'If Sir would prefer something else?' he asked, but Victor was happy to grab the nearest glass.

Now he turned to look between the heads of the animated guests at the paintings on the walls. At first glance they were simply splashes of colour, what Mother would have referred to as daubs, but knowing that they must be good he tried to concentrate and see what they reminded him of. The first looked rather like his washing-up bowl when he had just washed the gravy saucepan in it. Another reminded him of the time he had had food poisoning. Try as he might he failed to identify anything concrete. He remembered those books he had had as a child, where you had to find tiny objects hidden in a drawing, perhaps a cat peering out of a tree or a teapot cleverly disguised as a pair of dungarees.

'I didn't think you'd come.' He swung round to find the star of the evening, Dolores, standing behind him. His face, of course, changed colour.

She smiled and took his arm, asking, 'Well, what do you think?'

'I – they're very nice.'

She laughed. 'Not quite your cup of tea?' Leading him over to a very large canvas she started to explain what it was all about. Victor hung on her every word, aware of the small hand tucked into the crook of his arm. He began to feel hot. 'So, that represents greed – can you find the avarice?' He looked closely and sure enough, the word *Avarice* was actually woven into the background greens and purples. So this *was* like those childhood books after all! There was more to this art than he'd imagined.

Dolores accosted a passing waiter and acquired two more glasses of champagne. 'What are those red spots for?' he asked, noticing the dots on some of the pictures.

'Those are sold.'

Ever the tax inspector, he did a quick sum and realised that already a small fortune had changed hands. He felt a growing respect for Dolores, apart from a growing sense of schoolboy adoration.

At that point someone came to take her away. 'It's Sir Charles Wetherby, Dee, he's interested in a commission, wants to talk to you.'

She gave Victor a regretful look. 'Take your time and promise you won't leave, will you? One or two of us are going out to eat afterwards. Say you'll come?'

He nodded, a puppy offered a Doggybic.

All in all, the evening was wonderful. The copious amounts of champagne that seemed to drift past and through Victor gave him a rare ability to hold court and say witty things. People actually laughed at some of his comments although later, in the cooler light of sobriety, he wondered if they might have been laughing at him.

But it didn't matter. Dolores had insisted that she should drop him off at home. He demurred but she said, 'You are very wise not to have brought your car. I hate drinking and driving.' She was being driven by someone she called her cousin, James, who also seemed to be a sort of minder. Victor wondered if he was also her lover. In his opinion, he didn't look up to much. Perhaps indeed they were just friends and cousins.

Sitting in the back of the roomy vehicle with Dolores next to him, it crossed his mind that he should take driving lessons and get himself a run-around. Another thought was beginning to bear fruit.

In spite of the investigation into the nefarious affairs of the Blues Brothers and the Pretty Boys, no hint had come to light about the money nestling in Victor's new bank account. Perhaps it would soon be safe to spend some of it?

At his side, Dolores tucked her arm through his again. It was a wonderful sensation. She gave a little sigh and said, 'Well, tonight was quite a success.'

Victor wanted to ask her how much money she had made but that would have been rude. Instead he said, 'Actually, I would like to buy one of your paintings.'

'Would you? Which one?' She sounded surprised.

'Well, I was going to ask your advice.' He couldn't quite visualise where it might fit into his home, where prints of puppies and kittens mainly ruled supreme.

Dolores gave a little giggle and said, 'Then you'd better pop along to the gallery, tomorrow?'

As he was about to say yes, thinking that he would take some flexi-time from work, she added, 'Better still, how about we do some bartering? I'll give you a painting in return for being a model?'

'Really?' He was too stunned to do more than gasp. Perhaps he had been too modest and that secretly he reminded people of Michelangelo's David? He felt his shoulders expanding and glanced at the car window to check his profile, but the image was too shadowy.

Dolores settled back in the seat, saying, 'Victor, you have a most interesting face and a – well, rather Aubrey Beardsley aura. I like that.'

'Really?' he said again. He had no idea who Aubrey Beardsley might be but perhaps he was another Greek God? Anyway, as long as he was someone who interested Dolores, he didn't care.

At his door they dropped him off and Dolores kissed him on both cheeks, saying, 'See you tomorrow.'

He let himself into the house, feeling light headed, light hearted. Inside it was blessedly peaceful until Fluffy came to yap a welcome.

Sitting down with his cocoa and the poodle on his lap, Victor thought that perhaps he should write Dolores a poem, show her his artistic side. For ages he let her name run over his tongue: *Dolores, Dolores...* but nothing else would come. It certainly didn't seem to rhyme with anything. Tentatively, he tried: *Dolores, Dolores, dark yet fair, What are you doing over there?* No. Perhaps he would save that for another time.

Finishing his cocoa, he gave a contended sigh and tipped Fluffy onto the carpet, where he immediately threatened to pee. 'Fluffy!' The dog seemed to shrug and made instead for his little bed by the radiator.

Victor thought that really, things couldn't be better. Tomorrow he would buy a painting and pose for the most beautiful girl in the world. Standing up he tried one or two poses, sticking out his chest, holding in his stomach and wondering how the rest of him would perform when he stood before her, with her studying him and transferring his image to canvas. Then he had a terrible thought – did she want him to pose naked? Perhaps he would be allowed to keep his pants on?

To calm himself, he thought, I must remember to tell her that I am a published poet. After all, that was his true nature and far more romantic than being a tax officer.

As he undressed, brushed his teeth and put on his pyjamas, he knew that he would sleep easily. Climbing into bed and cuddling up to his pillow, he thought: I've got enough money in the bank to do lots of things I've dreamed about, and a wonderful woman artist thinks I am a Greek God, or someone called Aubrey Beardsley. Who on earth could want for more?

THE END

Visit our website and discover thousands of other
History Press books.

www.thehistorypress.co.uk